Humphrey Lloyd

A Treatise on Magnetism

General and Terrestrial

Humphrey Lloyd

A Treatise on Magnetism
General and Terrestrial

ISBN/EAN: 9783742831057

Manufactured in Europe, USA, Canada, Australia, Japa

Cover: Foto ©Andreas Hilbeck / pixelio.de

Manufactured and distributed by brebook publishing software
(www.brebook.com)

Humphrey Lloyd

A Treatise on Magnetism

A TREATISE

ON

MAGNETISM,

GENERAL AND TERRESTRIAL.

BY

HUMPHREY LLOYD, D.D., D.C.L.;

PROVOST OF TRINITY COLLEGE, DUBLIN,

FORMERLY PROFESSOR OF NATURAL PHILOSOPHY IN THE UNIVERSITY.

LONDON:

LONGMANS, GREEN, AND CO.

1874.

DUBLIN:
PRINTED AT THE UNIVERSITY PRESS,
BY M. H. GILL.

PREFACE.

The present volume is a fragment of a work projected and partly completed many years ago, which was intended to embrace the various branches of physical science usually comprehended in the *Traités de Physique* of French writers. In the long interval which has elapsed since its commencement, the sciences of heat and electricity have been fully treated by English writers, their selection being in great measure due to their connexion with chemistry; while those of light, sound, and magnetism have not received the attention, here or elsewhere, which their intrinsic importance demands. The author has already endeavoured to supply in some degree this want, by the publication of a volume on the wave-theory of light; and he now seeks to satisfy it more fully by the production of a treatise introductory to the science of terrestrial magnetism.

The researches connected with this science may be classed under two heads—namely, first, the determination of the elements of the earth's magnetic force at several points of the earth's surface, and the laws of their changes of magnitude with change of place; and, secondly, the variations of the elements themselves at a given place dependent upon time.

The methods employed in recent years in the first inquiry owe their present perfection to the labours of Gauss and Weber, and those who have followed in their footsteps: they will be found explained in the sixth chapter of the present volume. In the scientific co-ordination of the results our sole guide is Gauss's beautiful memoir on "The General Theory of Terrestrial Magnetism."

The instrumental means employed in the determination of the variations of terrestrial magnetism, described in the present volume, are those of the Dublin Magnetical Observatory. They were devised by the author, when that Observatory was founded and placed under his superintendence by the governing body of Trinity College in 1838. They are based, in part, upon the principles of the Gottingen instruments, and are partly new in principle as well as in detail. These instruments were adopted at all the British Colonial observatories, as well as at most of the foreign magnetical observatories which took part in the magnetical co-operation inaugurated by the Royal Society in 1840; and they are thus invested with an historical interest which will justify the space given to their description and adjustments in the present volume. And it is to be observed, that the theoretical principles involved in their construction and use remain unaltered, however the instruments themselves may hereafter be modified in detail. It is hoped, therefore, that this portion of the present work may be found of service to those who shall hereafter be engaged in similar observations.

The account which the author has given of the principal results obtained in recent years in connexion with the variations of terrestrial magnetism, will, he trusts, serve the same purpose; while, at the same time, it presents the general scientific reader with a condensed summary of the leading facts of the science. As it would have been impossible to give in a moderate compass the numerical representation of the laws deduced at all the co-operating observatories, the course pursued has been to present the results obtained at a single station, at which all the general features of the phenomena belonging to the middle northern latitudes were fully developed, and to supplement the information by the results of observation at places widely removed from the former in geographical position, as well as in their relation to the sun's daily and yearly courses. The single station selected for this purpose is Dublin, partly because it fulfils the condition above described, and partly, also, because the reductions have been there made according to methods which appear to the author himself to be the most suitable.

The author has not entered upon the interesting speculation connected with the physical causes of the phenomena, further than to reprint a paper, published by himself many years ago, in which the agency of the sun and moon are shown not to be due to their direct operation as magnetic bodies. Notwithstanding the speculations of Lamont, Secchi, de la Rive, and others on this subject, the mode of agency of these bodies has not been established; and until this key be found, the subject must remain within the misty region of conjecture. The author will only here observe, that the electrical earth-currents, the existence of which is not confined (as was at first supposed) to days of abnormal change, must have their effect upon the magnetical variations recorded in our observatories, whether they be the sole or only a cooperating cause.

CONTENTS.

CHAPTER I.

GENERAL PHENOMENA.

CHAPTER II.

PROCESSES OF MAGNETIZATION. COERCITIVE FORCE. EFFECTS OF TEMPERATURE ON MAGNETS.

CHAPTER III.

MEASUREMENT OF FREE MAGNETISM IN MAGNETS. LAWS OF MAGNETIC DISTRIBUTION.

CHAPTER IV.

LAWS OF MAGNETIC ATTRACTION AND REPULSION.

CHAPTER V.

MAGNETISM OF ALL BODIES.

CHAPTER VI.

TERRESTRIAL MAGNETISM. DIRECTION AND INTENSITY OF THE EARTH'S MAGNETIC FORCE.

CHAPTER VII.

DIRECTION AND INTENSITY OF THE TERRESTRIAL MAGNETIC FORCE AT DIFFERENT POINTS OF THE GLOBE.

CHAPTER VIII.

MAGNETIC VARIATIONS. INSTRUMENTS AND METHODS OF OBSERVATION.

CHAPTER IX.

MAGNETIC VARIATIONS OF LONG PERIOD.

CHAPTER X.

ANNUAL INEQUALITY.

CHAPTER XI.

DIURNAL INEQUALITY.

CHAPTER XII.

LUNAR INEQUALITY.

CHAPTER XIII.

MAGNETIC DISTURBANCES.

APPENDIX.

LIST OF PLATES

MAGNETISM.

CHAPTER I.

GENERAL PHENOMENA.

(1) MAGNETISM is the property, commonly supposed to be peculiar to certain substances, of attracting iron. It was first observed in a certain ore of iron, thence called *magnetic iron ore*. This mineral—the loadstone of the ancients—is composed of the peroxide and the protoxide of iron, in combination with a small quantity of earthy substances. It is of a dark grey colour; and the fresh fracture possesses a metallic lustre. It is found in many parts of the globe, in connexion with other iron ores; but is particularly abundant in the iron mines of Sweden and Norway. When a piece of this substance is brought near to small fragments of iron, it attracts them; and this attraction is observed to be concentrated in certain points of the mass, thence called *poles*. Thus when a loadstone is brought close to a mass of iron filings, the latter are immediately attracted, and made to adhere; and the adhering particles are accumulated round certain parts of the surface of the mineral, leaving the remainder nearly free.

(2) Steel may be made to acquire artificially the properties which naturally belong to the loadstone. Thus, if a straight bar of steel be rubbed in the direction of its length

with one of the poles of the loadstone—care being taken to make it pass always in the same direction—the steel bar acquires the properties which were inherent in the loadstone: it becomes magnetic, and attracts iron in its vicinity. The same property may be communicated to the steel bar without the aid of the natural loadstone, by striking it on the end with a hammer, when held in a vertical position. The poles, or centres of attraction, of such a bar are situated close to its extremities. The middle of the bar is without action, and the section passing through it is called the *neutral section*.

Conversely, iron reacts upon and attracts the magnet with an equal force. This may be shown by holding a piece of iron near the pole of a magnet; if the latter be free to move, it will approach the former, until it finally adheres to it by one of its poles. When the two bodies—the magnet and the iron—are both free to move, they will approach one another until they meet, the spaces described by each being inversely as their masses. These effects take place without any diminution of action when any body, which is not itself magnetic, is interposed between the magnet and the iron.

Nickel and *cobalt* are acted on by the magnet, and react upon it, in the same manner as *iron*, although in a less degree, and are thence classed along with it as magnetic bodies. We shall hereafter see that this class of substances is unlimited.

(3) The poles of a loadstone, or of an artificial magnet, are endowed with *opposite* powers. To see this we have only to prepare two steel bars, by the methods explained, and to bring near to one another the two ends which were uppermost in the process of magnetization; these ends will be found to *repel* one another. The same effect will take place when the two ends which have been lowermost are brought near. But if the uppermost end of one be made to approach the lowermost end of the other, *attraction* will ensue. These

phenomena may be conveniently shown by attaching one of the magnets to a piece of cork, and allowing it to float on water; it will thus be free to move in every direction in the horizontal plane. The foregoing facts may be generally expressed by saying, that the *similar poles* of two magnets *repel* one another; *dissimilar poles attract.*

But further, the forces exerted by the two poles of the same magnet are *equal*, as well as opposite. This may be shown by bending the magnet, so as to bring the opposite poles nearly into contact. The action of the two poles upon a distant point will be found to neutralize one another.

No one can fail to be struck with the analogy of these phenomena to those of electricity. In magnetized, as well as in electrified bodies, there is a *duality* of force; and the two forces developed in the same body are *equal* and *opposite*. And in magnetized, as well as in electrified bodies, the parts which are in *similar* states *repel* one another, while those which are in *opposite* states *attract.*

(4) A magnetic bar, when free to move, and when uninfluenced by any other magnetic body in its vicinity, is found to take up a definite position with respect to the earth. Thus, if such a bar, *nos*, be suspended horizontally by a fine thread of silk attached to its centre *o*, it will turn, when left to itself, and finally settle in a position in which the line joining the two poles *ns* makes a certain angle with the meridian NS; and when disturbed from that position by any external force, it will return to it, after some oscillations on either side. The vertical plane passing through this line *ns* is called the *magnetic meridian;* and the angle, *Non*, which it makes with the terrestrial meridian, is called the *magnetic declination.* The end of the bar

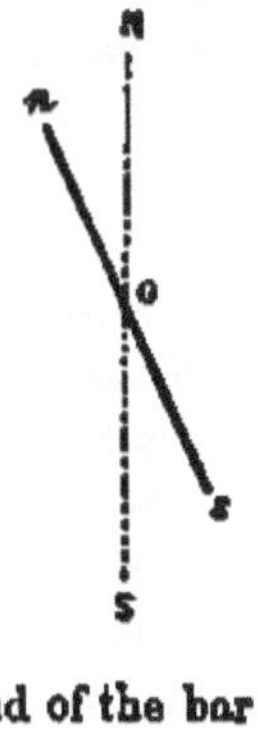

which was *lowermost* in the process of magnetization will point *northwards*, and is hence usually called the *north pole*; the opposite end, pointing southwards, is called the *south pole*.

This property of the magnetized bar is called its *polarity*; and it is reducible to the law of mutual action of magnets already stated, the earth (as we shall hereafter see) acting as a magnet—or rather as a collection of magnets—and exerting, at each point of its surface, a force having a definite magnitude and direction.

It is needless to dwell on the importance of this property to the mariner and to the engineer: the *compass* and its uses are well known. In its simplest form it is a light magnet, or *needle*, resting on a fine point by means of a conical cavity, or socket, at the middle, and rendered horizontal by suitably balancing the two arms.

With such a needle, inclosed in a flat case to protect it from the agitation of the air, and with a few bar magnets and pieces of soft iron, all the fundamental properties of magnets may be verified.

(5) A magnet has the power of communicating magnetism to iron at a distance, and without actual contact. Thus, if the north pole of a magnet be brought near to the end of a small bar of iron, that end becomes a south pole, while the remote end of the bar becomes a north pole. The opposite effect will take place when the south pole of the magnet is presented, the near end becoming a north pole, and the remote end a south pole. And, in general, the magnetism induced in the bar is such that a *contrary* pole is developed at the end *next* the inducing pole of the magnet, and a *similar* pole at the *remote* end. These facts may be shown by means of the compass needle. The end of the bar remote from the acting pole attracts one of the poles of the needle,

and repels the other, in a manner precisely similar to the acting pole itself. The magnetism developed in the end of the bar next to the acting pole is not so easily manifested; for the magnetic needle, placed near that end, will be acted on directly by the pole of the magnet itself, as well as by the induced pole of the iron bar, and the result will be complicated by the joint action.

The iron bar, thus rendered magnetic, exhibits all the other properties of a magnet. It attracts iron, the attractive force increasing from the centre to the two poles. If a sheet of paper, strewed with iron filings, be held close above the bar, the filings will collect over the two poles of the induced magnet, as in the case of the original magnet, the effect being only complicated by the action of the inducing pole.

When the pole of the inducing magnet is brought near to other portions of the iron bar, more complicated results follow. Thus, if the magnet be made to touch the middle of the bar (instead of the end), their longer sides being at right angles, an opposite pole will be developed by induction at the point of contact, and similar poles at the two ends. If a circular plate of iron be laid horizontally, and a bar magnet be allowed to rest upon it vertically at its centre, the plate will acquire by induction the *opposite* polarity to that of the acting pole at its *centre*, and a *similar* polarity at every point of its *circumference*.

The power of inducing magnetism in iron diminishes as the distance increases. When the inducing magnet is slowly removed, the forces exerted by the ends of the iron bar undergo a corresponding diminution; and they cease to exist altogether when the magnet is wholly withdrawn, and the bar returns to its natural or neutral state. Thus the magnetism induced in iron is *temporary* only.

(6) The iron bar, which has been rendered magnetic

by the inducing action of a magnet, *reacts* upon the magnet itself, and induces magnetism in it, which conspires with the magnetism already existing there, and therefore augments its amount. Thus a magnet, which induces magnetism in an iron bar in its vicinity, acquires, in virtue of that action, an augmentation of its own power. This is easily shown by holding a bar magnet in a vertical position, and observing the weight which it will support under the influence of an iron bar, and without it. Thus, let a small piece of iron be brought into contact with the lower end of the magnet, and by means of a scale attached to it, let weights be gradually added until the contact is broken, and the iron falls off. Let the same experiment be then repeated, with a bar of iron in contact with the magnet at its upper extremity; and it will be found that the weight supported is very much greater than that supported in the former case.

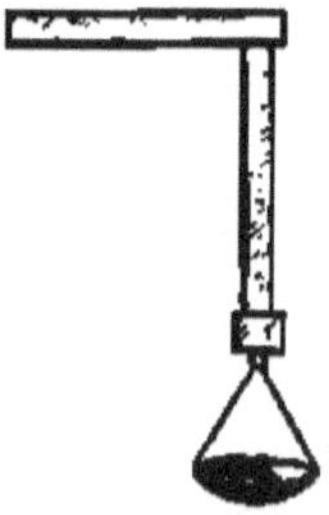

(7) The bar in which magnetism has been induced will act upon another bar, and render it also magnetic by induction; and this second bar may be made to induce magnetism in a third; and so on for several successions, the forces developed decreasing at each step. Thus, if a series of iron bars, m, m', m'', &c., be placed in the same right line, without contact, and the north pole of a magnet, N, be brought near the end s of the first, a south pole will be developed at s, and a north pole at n. This induced north pole will act in like manner on the second bar m', and will develop a south pole

at s' and a north pole at n'; and so on to the end of the series. The magnetism thus induced diminishes as the distance increases; and it ceases altogether when the inducing pole is wholly removed.

(8) If we repeat the original experiment with a bar of *steel*, in place of a bar of iron, the effect will be different in two respects. In the first place the amount of magnetism developed by the inducing force will be much less than in the former case; and, secondly, the magnetism induced is no longer temporary, but subsists in the bar when the inducing force is withdrawn. Accordingly, steel opposes a certain *resistance* to the inductive action, and it retains, with a proportional *tenacity*, the magnetism which has been once imparted. This power of resisting magnetization, or demagnetization, is denominated the *coercitive force*. The quality is imparted to iron by hardening, or by torsion; but the most effectual means of increasing it consist in the combination of certain foreign elements with the iron. Carbon, phosphorus, and sulphur combined with iron produce these effects. But when the proportion of these foreign elements exceeds a certain limit, they prevent altogether the magnetization of the bar by ordinary means.

The same resistance to the inductive separation of the magnetic fluids renders *time* necessary for the full development of the inductive action. When the pole of a magnet is brought near the end of a steel bar, the latter does not acquire instantaneously its full power. The end of the bar next the pole of the magnet acquires a contrary polarity from the commencement of the action; but the remote end does not acquire at once a similar polarity. It is found, in fact, that the polarity of the same kind as the acting pole is propagated *in time* from the near end of the bar to the remote end. It sometimes happens, when the steel bar is of great length, that the polarity of the same kind as the acting pole does not reach the extremity of the bar, in which case it is usually followed by a contrary polarity of weaker intensity, and so on for some alternations. The bar has then what are denominated *consecutive poles.*

(9) The foregoing facts enable us to account for the *attraction* of iron by the magnet, and to reduce the phenomenon to the general principle of the attraction of opposite, and the repulsion of similar poles.

When the pole of a magnet is brought near to a mass of iron, the immediate effect, we have seen, is to render the latter a magnet by induction, an *opposite* magnetism being developed in the part of the mass which is *nearest* to the acting pole, and a *similar* magnetism in the part which is most *remote.* Now, as opposite poles attract one another, while similar poles repel, attraction will ensue between the acting pole and the nearer parts of the iron mass, and repulsion between the same pole and the remoter parts; and the former of these forces will preponderate, being exerted at a shorter distance. It follows from this that *attraction* must always result, whichever pole of the magnet be presented to the iron.

Since the magnetism which has been induced in a piece of iron imparts a similar condition to a second piece in its vicinity, and that to a third, and so on, it follows that attraction must ensue between these several pieces, although with diminished energy, as they are more distant from the acting pole; and the first will support a second, the second a third, and so on, if only the weights of the successive pieces be proportioned to the diminished forces.

(10) The inductive action, here explained, enables us to account for many phenomena, which at first sight seem at

variance with the general laws of magnetic forces. When the similar poles of two magnets are brought near, they repel one another; while the dissimilar poles in the same circumstances attract. Now the forces emanating from the two poles of the same magnet are equal; and accordingly the repulsion of the similar poles of the two magnets should be equal to the attraction of the dissimilar poles at the same distance. This, however, is observed not to be the case, the latter force being always greater than the former. This difference is explained by the effect of induction. When the *dissimilar poles* of the two magnets are presented to one another, each pole induces the opposite magnetism in the near part of the other magnet; and the magnetism so induced is *added* to that which it already possesses, and the two polar forces become *stronger* than they were when the magnets were apart. On the other hand, when the *similar poles* of two magnets are presented to one another, the magnetism induced in each by the presence of the other is *opposite* to that which it already possesses, and the resulting polar forces are *weakened*. Hence the attraction of the dissimilar poles always exceeds the repulsion of the similar poles at the same distance.

It may even happen, by the effect of induction, that the repulsion of the similar poles is converted into attraction. Thus when the similar poles of two magnets, which are very unequal in size and power, are brought near, the opposite polarity induced in the near end of the smaller, by the action of the pole of the larger, will, at a certain distance, just balance the similar polarity which it possesses; while, within that distance, the induced polarity will exceed the other, and the resulting action will become attractive. Accordingly, when the pole of a strong magnet is presented to the similar pole of a weak one, at a considerable distance, repulsion will take place. As the interval between the poles is lessened, the polar force of the weaker magnet is gradually diminished; and at a certain distance there is *no action*. Within that distance, the polar force *changes sign*, and the repulsion is converted into attraction.

Thus it is that two magnets of unequal strength always adhere, when brought into contact by their similar poles.

(11) When two or more pieces of iron are acted on simultaneously by the pole of a magnet, the effect of induction may under certain circumstances cause them to *repel one another*. This effect is strikingly shown in the following experiment of Cavallo. Two short pieces of iron wire, of the same dimensions, are suspended vertically, side by side, by two equal threads attached to their upper extremities. When the pole of a strong magnet is brought into the same vertical line below the wires, they will be observed to diverge from one another by the effect of their mutual repulsion, as in the first figure of the annexed diagram. This phenomenon is readily explained. For whatever be the nature of the acting pole, it will induce *similar polarities* in the *adjacent* ends of the two bars; and these ends will consequently repel one another. This divergence will increase, as the distance of the acting pole diminishes, up to a certain limit, when the direct action of the pole on the lower extremities of the two bars begins to exceed the force with which they repel one another, and they will assume the position indicated in the second figure, the upper extremities being still maintained apart by their mutual repulsion.

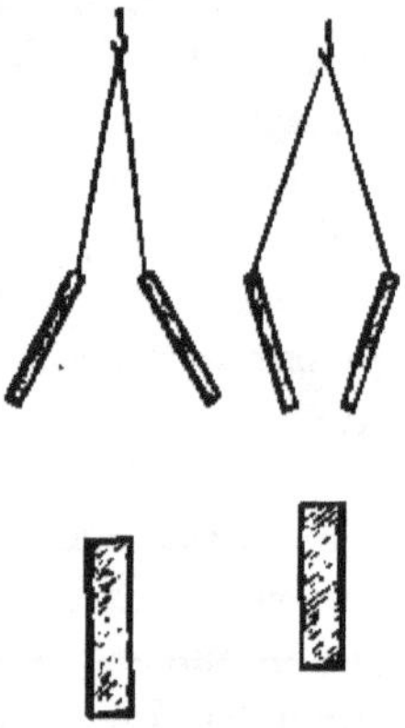

The mutual repulsion which is observed to take place

among the filaments of iron filings which adhere to a magnet by their ends is easily seen to be a case of the same kind.

(12) When two magnets act simultaneously upon the same iron bar, the effect produced will depend upon their relative positions. When the two magnets are in the same

right line, with their opposite poles facing one another, and when the iron bar is in the same right line between them, the inducing actions of the two magnets will conspire, and the induced magnetism will much exceed that produced by either bar acting singly. It will even surpass the *sum* of their separate actions. For the magnetism induced by either pole in the remote extremity of the bar, will act by induction upon the other pole, and augment its free magnetism; and this again will react on the bar, and increase the induced effect. The maximum of induced effect will take place when the two opposite poles are in contact with the opposite ends of the bar.

When the *similar* poles of two magnets are brought near the two ends of the same bar, the effect will be to induce an opposite polarity at the two ends, and a similar polarity at the middle of the bar. The distribution of free magnetism in the bar will, in fact, correspond with that in *two* permanent magnets in the same right line, having their similar poles in contact.

(13) The phenomena of magnetic induction go far to complete the analogy which we have already noticed between magnetized and electrified bodies. When an electrified body is presented to a conductor of an oblong form in its natural or neutral state, the two electricities of the latter are sepa-

rated, and are accumulated upon the opposite faces of the body. The end next the inducing body becomes charged with the *opposite* electricity; while the remote end is charged with electricity of the *same* kind as that of the acting body. These facts resemble closely those above described, in which the two magnetic powers which reside in soft iron, and which neutralize one another in its natural state, are separated by the inducing action of a magnetic pole. There is, however, a fundamental difference between the two classes of phenomena, which we now proceed to notice.

When a conductor of an oblong form, which has been rendered electric by induction, is divided in the middle, the two electricities which had been accumulated at the two ends are wholly separated, and can no longer return and recombine by their mutual attraction when the inducing body is withdrawn. In this manner we obtain bodies charged with a single species of electricity. In like manner, electricity may be *withdrawn* from the body in which it is developed, and *transferred* to another; and either body may thus be rendered electrical in excess or defect. The properties of a magnet, whether induced or permanent, are in this respect wholly different. When a magnet is broken in the midst, the two halves no longer exhibit, as before, the separate polarities. Each of them becomes a distinct magnet with *two poles*, the end next the fracture having the opposite polarity to that of the outer end of the same half. Similar results will follow when the magnet is subdivided into several parts: each part will become a distinct magnet, possessed of two poles.

(14) These curious facts can only be explained by the supposition that the two forces, which are separated by magnetization, are confined within the limits of each molecule, and do not pass from one molecule to another, much less

pass (as electricity does) without the limits of the entire mass.

In accordance with this, magnetic bodies are supposed by Coulomb to be charged with two fluids, endued with opposite qualities, the molecules of each of which repel one another, while they attract those of the other fluid. These two fluids have been called the *Austral* and the *Boreal* fluids. Every magnetic body, and every molecule of the same, is supposed to possess equal quantities of the two magnetic fluids, which cannot pass from one molecule to another. In the natural state of the body these two fluids are *uniformly diffused;* and as they exist in equal quantities at each point, they neutralize one another's effects. The process of magnetization consists in the separation of these fluids in each molecule, the separation being effected in such a manner that the same fluid is accumulated on the same sides of all the molecules. The body, so modified, is no longer neutral, but exhibits (as we shall hereafter show) powers of attraction and repulsion, increasing from the centre to the two poles. This theory is analogous to that of the two fluids in electricity—the difference being, that the separation of the magnetic fluids is limited by the bounds of each element, while the two electrical fluids may be separated to the utmost limits to which the conducting mass extends.

The transfer of the two fluids, within the limits of each molecule, is resisted by a force whose magnitude is different in different substances. This coercitive force, as it is called, operates both to prevent the *separation* of the two fluids under the inducing action, and their *reunion* when that action ceases; and thus is equally opposed to magnetization and to demagnetization. This force is analogous to the resistance which imperfect conductors interpose to the passage of the electric fluid.

CHAPTER II.

PROCESSES OF MAGNETIZATION. COERCITIVE FORCE. EFFECTS OF TEMPERATURE ON MAGNETS.

(15) When the pole of a magnet is brought near the extremity of an unmagnetized bar of steel, the latter is (we have seen) rendered magnetic by induction; and the magnetism so imparted is retained after the inducing cause is removed, and the steel bar becomes permanently magnetic. Most of the methods of magnetization which have been devised derive their efficacy from this principle. In applying it, we have to consider, in the first place, in what manner the inducing action may be most effectively applied; and, secondly, the conditions under which the property so imparted is best retained.

The inducing action may be derived from the earth itself, or from a magnet, whether natural or artificial. The earth, it has been already stated, operates as a magnet, and at each point of its surface the magnetic force emanating from it has a fixed direction and intensity. Now the effect of inducing action is much increased by mechanical concussion, or any other cause which imparts molecular vibration to the bar while under the action of the inducing force. Hence, to magnetize a steel bar, we have only to hold it in the direction of the earth's magnetic force, and to strike it on the end, while so held, with a hammer. The bar will be found to acquire by this simple process a considerable amount of magnetism. As the direction of the earth's magnetic force, in the higher latitudes, is not far from the vertical, the effect produced will be nearly the same, if the bar be held vertically.

This effect may be considerably augmented by allowing the lower end of the steel bar to rest on the upper end of a long iron bar—such, for example, as a common poker—also held vertically. The reason of this is evident. The iron bar becomes temporarily magnetic under the inducing action of the earth's magnetic force, and its magnetism conspires with that of the earth in its effect upon the steel bar. Dr. Scoresby succeeded, by these means, in imparting a considerable degree of permanent magnetism to bars of steel. The method is chiefly useful as the first step in the process of magnetization, when artificial magnets are not to be had; and the magnets so formed may be used, in combination, to magnetize others.

(16) The magnetizing power of an artificial magnet of moderate size may be made to exceed considerably that of the earth, its proximity to the bar acted on more than compensating for its smaller inherent force. In applying it, the magnet may be made to act upon the bar when they are both at rest, as in the preceding experiment. But the efficacy of the inducing action is much increased by bringing the magnet in contact successively with different parts of the bar in the following manner.

The steel bar to be magnetized, *ns*, is placed horizontally on a table, and one of the poles of the magnetizing bar, NS, held vertically, is brought into contact with it at one of its extremities The magnetizing bar is then to be drawn, parallel to itself, along the surface of the steel bar to the other end; after which it is to be lifted, and replaced in its first position, and the operation repeated. After ten or twelve such rubbings, the steel

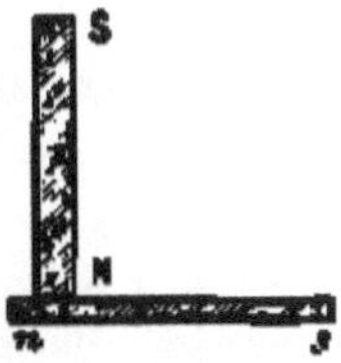

bar is to be inverted, and the same process repeated upon its other face, taking care that the same pole of the acting magnet is employed, and that it is always moved in the same direction.

This process is called the method of *single touch.* Its efficacy depends upon the fact that each molecule of a magnetized bar is a separate magnet, having its poles similarly directed to those of the entire bar. Now, when, for example, the north pole of a magnet rests upon any point of a steel bar, a *southern* polarity will be induced at the end of each molecule nearest to the acting pole, and a *northern* polarity at the remote end; and the two portions of the bar will have *opposite* polarities on the two sides of the point of contact. But, as the acting pole is moved, it *reverses the poles* of the molecules on the side towards which it is moving; and when it has passed over the whole length of the bar, it leaves the poles of all *similarly placed,* the north poles being all turned towards the end at which the movement began, and the south poles towards that at which it terminates.

This process will answer sufficiently well when the needle to be magnetized is of small dimensions. It cannot impart to large bars all the magnetism of which they are capable; and it has the inconvenience of generating *consecutive poles,* when the bar to be magnetized is long, unless much care be taken in giving an equable motion to the moving magnet.

(17) The first improvement in the process of magnetization was made by Dr. Knight, in the year 1745. In Dr. Knight's method *two* magnetizing bars are employed instead of one; and each of them is moved over *one-half* of the bar, commencing at the middle. The two magnets *ns*, *n's'*, are joined end to end, with their dissimilar poles in contact, and are laid flat

upon the bar to be magnetized, the point of junction being

directly over its middle point. The bars are then to be separated, and drawn slowly and regularly in opposite directions along the two halves of the magnetized bar, until they parted from it at its two extremities; after which they are to be removed to some distance, rejoined, and the operation repeated. When one side of the bar has been thus rubbed a sufficient number of times, the bar is to be inverted, and the same process repeated on the other side. It is evident that the two magnets *conspire* in their inducing effect upon all the molecules of the bar situated *between* them—i. e., ultimately, upon all. On the other hand, their inducing effects are *opposed* in those portions of the bar which are exterior to both, where the induced magnetism is opposite to that ultimately acquired. For both reasons, the combined effect of the two magnets greatly exceeds that of either alone.

(18) The efficacy of this process is greatly increased by combining with it the inducing action of two *fixed* magnets, whose poles are in contact with the bar to be magnetized at its two ends. Two strong bar magnets are to be placed in the same right line, with their dissimilar poles facing each other, and at a distance somewhat less than the length of the bar to be magnetized. The latter is then to be laid upon them, so as to overlap them equally, and is fixed so as not to shift its place during the process of magnetization. Another pair of magnets are then employed, as in Dr. Knight's process, to rub the two halves of the bar, care being taken that the pole in contact with each half is of the same name with the fixed pole at its extremity; and the process is to be repeated, as before, on the other face of the bar. This and other modifications of Dr. Knight's method, based upon the same principle, are due to M. Duhamel. The efficacy of this method may be further augmented by employing, in the rubbing process, piles of magnets bound together, with their

similar poles conterminous. Such compound magnets can be made much more powerful than single bars of the same dimensions; for the separate magnets composing them can readily be magnetized to saturation before they are combined.

In Duhamel's method, the moving bars are inclined to the bar to be magnetized at an angle of about 45°, in opposite directions instead of being laid flat upon it as in Knight's process. It is now ascertained that a smaller inclination is more advantageous.*

(19) In the method of *double touch* the opposite poles of the moving magnets are attached together, with an interval of about a quarter of an inch between them, and are moved *together* over the bar to be magnetized, in *both* directions. In order to avoid an inequality of strength in the two halves of the bar, it is proper to commence the operation by placing the acting poles in contact with the middle of the bar, and after moving them forwards and backwards the same number of times over each half, to terminate the operation at the same point, and then to remove them in a direction at right angles to the bar. The efficacy of this process is easily understood. The two poles conspire in their inducing action upon the points of the bar situated between them, while their effects upon the other points of the bar are opposed. But, on account of the proximity of the acting poles, the sum of the conspiring effects is much greater than in the process of single touch, while the difference of the opposing effects upon the external points of the bar is less. The

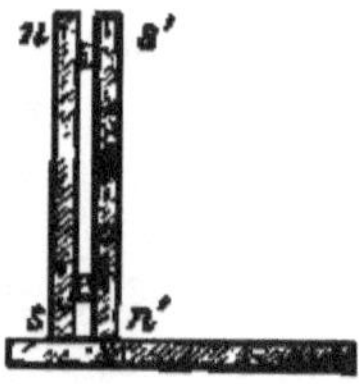

direct effect of induction consequently exceeds the inverse

* According to Captain Kater, the maximum effect is produced when the inclination of the magnetizing bars is reduced to two or three degrees.

effect by a greater amount than in that process, and therefore the induced magnetism is greater.

The same method may be employed to magnetize several bars at the same time. For this purpose the bars are arranged in a straight line, and the inducing magnets are moved forwards and backwards over the entire series, commencing and ending the operation at the middle point. The magnetism acquired by the several bars in this process diminishes from the middle to the two extremities. This inequality is remedied by transposing the bars, and repeating the operation until they all acquire the utmost amount of magnetism which they are capable of retaining.

This method is the invention of Mr. Mitchell, of Cambridge, and was published in 1750. It was subsequently improved by Æpinus, by combining with it the inducing action of two fixed magnets after the method of Duhamel. It is better adapted to the magnetization of large bars than the methods previously described; but it has the disadvantage that the magnetism imparted is less regularly distributed, and that consecutive poles are often formed. Hence the methods of Knight and Duhamel are generally preferred in the manufacture of compass needles, and their power may always be augmented by employing compound magnets both for the fixed and the moveable parts of the magnetizing apparatus.

The degree of magnetism which can be communicated to a given bar of steel has a fixed limit, which is attained when the resultant of all the forces, exerted upon any molecule by all the others, is in equilibrio with the coercitive force. This limit is the maximum degree of magnetism which the bar can retain, and is called the state of *saturation*.

(20) The comparative efficacy of the several methods of magnetization has been carefully studied by Coulomb, the

magnetic moments of the bars magnetized by the different processes being compared by observing the number of oscillations performed by them in a given time, when vibrating freely under the action of the earth's magnetic force. Coulomb found that steel wires of small diameter may be magnetized to saturation by any of the ordinary processes. For thin plates of steel of greater width, the methods of Duhamel and Æpinus were found to be the most efficacious; the advantage being greater as the steel is harder, and the plates thicker. For plates whose thickness is less than one-twelfth of an inch the two methods were found to be nearly equal in efficacy; but the process of Æpinus had the advantage when the thickness surpassed that limit. The relative advantages of the different methods of magnetization, as also the influence of *surface* and of *form* upon the magnetic moments, have been subsequently investigated by Captain Kater.

(21) It is frequently desirable to bring the two poles of a magnet into action at the same time—as, e. g., when the magnet is employed in lifting considerable weights. For this purpose it is bent into the *horse-shoe* form, so that the two poles may be simultaneously applied to the same bar. Horse-shoe magnets are often made of several bars, magnetized separately, and then riveted together with their poles of the same name side by side, when great magnetic power is needed. Such magnets, whose poles are close together, may be conveniently substituted for the pair of magnets in the method of magnetization by double touch.

(22) Every process of magnetization is reducible to magnetic induction. When the pole of a magnet is brought near the end of an iron bar, we have seen that an opposite polarity is developed at the near end of the bar, and a simi-

lar polarity at the remote end. We have likewise seen that the effect is due to the separation of the two magnetisms in each molecule of the body, the separation taking place in the line of the acting force; and that there is no transfer of these magnetisms from molecule to molecule, much less from one body to another. All bodies in which the two magnetisms are capable of separation, under the action of an inducing force, are said to be *magnetic*. Now this separation is more or less resisted in different bodies; and the power which is thus called into play is denominated the *coercitive force*. The same power resists the recombination of the two magnetisms, when they have been once separated; and thus the power of *retaining* magnetism is proportional to the difficulty of *inducing* it. Thus, *hard steel* retains the greater part of the magnetism which has been induced in it, and is thus rendered permanently magnetic; while *soft iron* parts with its magnetism readily, the two magnetisms which were separated by the inducing action recombining by their mutual attraction when that action is withdrawn. This difference of bodies, in relation to the coercitive force, is analogous to the difference which exists in different bodies as conductors of electricity.

(23) The circumstances upon which the coercitive force chiefly depends are *hardness*, and the presence of *foreign ingredients* in the iron.* Steel owes its coercitive force to the carbon which it contains; and it has been found that similar properties are imparted to iron by the combination with it of phosphorus, sulphur, and arsenic in small quantities. When these foreign elements are combined with the iron in large proportions, they resist altogether the development of mag-

* A change in the molecular arrangement of the body is found likewise to affect its coercitive force. Thus iron is rendered capable of retaining magnetism by *twisting* it.

netism by any ordinary means. It is stated by Dr. Matthew Young that the magnetism of iron is wholly destroyed by the admixture of antimony, even in a very minute proportion; and nickel is deprived of its magnetic quality by the addition of arsenic.

The following are the capacities for inductive action possessed by the different varieties of iron and steel, as measured by Mr. Barlow :—

Malleable iron,	100
Soft cast steel,	74
Soft blistered steel,	67
Soft shear steel,	66
Hard shear steel,	59
Hard blistered steel,	53
Hard cast steel,	40
Cast iron,	48

(24) The capability of induction, and the correlative power of retaining the induced magnetism, are both greatly affected by any mechanical or other force which excites a vibratory motion in the particles of the iron. Thus we have seen that when a bar of iron is held in a vertical position, the induced magnetism which it receives from the inducing action of the earth is greatly increased by striking it on the end with a hammer. The same effect is produced by transmitting a powerful electrical discharge through the bar held as before, the effect of the passage of electricity being to excite molecular vibration. The magnetism which is found to be imparted to upright iron rods which have been struck by lightning is explained by the same cause.

On the other hand, the magnetism of a steel bar is weakened, or even wholly destroyed by the same means, the vibratory motion which is imparted to the molecules of the body favouring the recombination of the separated magnetisms, and therefore the return of the body to the neutral state. It is thus that the power of a magnet is seriously lessened, or altogether destroyed, by a fall from a height upon a hard pavement.

(25) Heat is also found to weaken the coercitive force of iron, and therefore to facilitate its magnetization and demagnetization. When a bar of iron is heated, and exposed to the inductive action of a strong magnet, the magnetism developed is augmented. This effect increases up to a *dull-red* heat, at which it is a *maximum*. At a *bright-red* heat the capability of induction ceases altogether. *Cast iron* and *steel* present the same results. The maximum force imparted to soft iron has been found by M. Ed. Becquerel to be 1 04, that imparted at the ordinary temperature of the air being unity; and it is a remarkable circumstance that the maximum force induced in *cast iron*, and in *steel*, is precisely the same as that of *soft iron*, although at ordinary temperatures their induced magnetisms are very different. It appears from these facts that the coercitive force of these bodies vanishes altogether at a *dull-red* heat.

If the iron be perfectly soft, and perfectly pure, the bar will return to its neutral state when the inducing force is withdrawn. If, on the other hand, hard steel be subjected to the same process, it will retain a great part of the magnetism which it thus acquires. This furnishes a very efficacious and simple method of magnetization. To practise it most effectually the bar to be magnetized should be placed between the opposite poles of two powerful magnets, and raised to a high temperature by spirit lamps placed beneath. The bar should then be suddenly cooled, before the magnets are withdrawn, by means of cold water.

(26) A steel bar which is already magnetic undergoes a

loss of magnetism by an increase of temperature. This loss increases with the temperature, and at a *bright-red* heat the magnetism of the bar is wholly destroyed.

But here a fact is observed, which has no analogue in the laws which we have been hitherto considering. When the heat applied to a steel magnet is moderate—when, e. g., it does not exceed that of boiling water—part of the magnetism which had disappeared on the increase of temperature reappears when the original temperature is restored. It follows from this that heat produces two effects, which (in the present state of our knowledge) must be considered as distinct. Like the mechanical action before considered, it permanently *destroys* a portion of the existing magnetism by enabling the two magnetisms which had been separated in each molecule to recombine. And on the other hand, it *renders latent*, or neutralizes, another portion of the same magnetism, which portion reappears again when the temperature is reduced to its original state.

This two-fold operation of heat, although fully recognised as a fact, has not been sufficiently considered in reference to the cause. There seems reason to believe that the two effects, so dissimilar in their conditions, are in fact referrible to distinct causes; and that while the permanent loss of magnetism is a *dynamical effect* due to the *molecular movement* in which heat is known to consist, the recoverable portion is probably to be ascribed to the *dilatation* of the body, and to the diminution of the reciprocal action of the magnetic elements consequent upon their increased distance.

(27) The changes of the magnetic moment of a bar with variations of temperature have been carefully studied, chiefly on account of their complication with the phenomena of terrestrial magnetism. The first careful experiments on the subject are those of Mr. Christie. Mr. Christie found that the temperature to which a magnet could be raised without any

sensible permanent loss of magnetism was about 100° Fahr. The diminution of the magnetic moment corresponding to a given increase of temperature was observed not to be constant, being more considerable at the higher temperatures. On lowering the temperature, on the other hand, the magnetism was found to increase. By wrapping a magnet in lint moistened with sulphuret of carbon, and inclosing it in the receiver of an air pump along with a vessel containing sulphuric acid, Mr. Christie succeeded in reducing the temperature below zero of Fahrenheit, and the magnetism was found to increase continually. It decreased again when the temperature was restored by readmitting the air.

The effects of temperature upon the amount and distribution of magnetism in steel magnets have since been studied by Hansteen, Kupffer, Lamont, and others. The most accurate mode of observing them is to deflect a freely suspended horizontal needle by the magnet to be examined, taking care that the two magnets shall be always at right angles, and to observe the deflection produced when the deflecting magnet is at different temperatures. For this purpose the magnet is to be inclosed in a vessel containing water, the temperature of which can be readily altered by mixing. The force exerted by the deflecting on the suspended magnet is $mm'U$, in which m and m' are the magnetic moments of the two magnets, and U a function of the distance between them. This is equilibrated by the force exerted by the Earth upon the supended magnet, or by $m'X \sin u$, in which X is the horizontal component of the earth's force, and u the deflection of the magnet from the magnetic meridian. Hence

$$mU = X \sin u.$$

Differentiating this with respect to m and u, and dividing by the equation itself, we have

$$\frac{\Delta m}{m} = \text{cotan}\, u \,.\, \Delta u.$$

Hence, by observing the angles of deflection at different temperatures of the deflecting magnet, we can determine the relative changes of the magnetic moment.

(28) The value of $\frac{\Delta m}{m}$, corresponding to a given increase of temperature, is found to be different for different magnets, and appears to depend chiefly on the temper of the steel. In highly hardened steel magnets, such as those employed as dipping needles, the value of $\frac{\Delta m}{m}$ corresponding to an increase of 1° Fahr. is usually about .00015; in the larger magnetic bars, which are not capable of such thorough hardening, the corresponding quantity is often double of this, or even greater. But (as has been already stated) it is not the same, even for the same magnet, at different parts of the thermometric scale. For temperatures below 100° Fahr. it is found that the value of $\frac{\Delta m}{m}$ may be represented by the formula

$$\frac{\Delta m}{m} = -\alpha t + \beta t^2;$$

in which t denotes the excess of the observed above the standard temperature, and α and β two constants peculiar to each magnet.

(29) We have seen that magnets undergo a loss of power by any action which favours the recombination of the separated magnetisms. Such effects, we have seen, are produced by mechanical concussion, or by augmentation of temperature; and accordingly in order to preserve the force of magnets, they must be guarded from the operation of such causes. There is no difficulty in this protection, so far as relates to the effects of temperature; as a magnet of hard steel will

suffer little permanent change by any variation of temperature within the ordinary atmospheric range, and the exposure to artificial heat is easily guarded against. It is not so easy to protect magnets—especially such as are carried from place to place for the purposes of observation—from mechanical vibration. An accidental fall, especially upon a hard surface, will certainly impair the force of a magnet, and a like effect will be produced by rubbing or grinding. The concussions incident to transport are best guarded against by inclosing the magnet in a case with an elastic lining.

Another cause of the deterioration of magnets is the inducing action of other magnets, or that of the Earth itself. When the similar poles of two magnets are brought near, or are made to touch, they will both undergo a loss of force by magnetic induction, the force of the weaker being most impaired. A similar effect will take place when a magnet rests for any considerable time with its poles in a contrary direction to that in which they would be placed by the directive action of the Earth.

(30) The most effectual mode of guarding a magnet from the deteriorating effects above described is to connect its poles by a piece of soft iron. Such an auxiliary is called an *armature*. We have seen that when one extremity of a bar of soft iron is brought near the pole of a magnet, magnetism will be developed in it by induction, which will react upon the magnet itself, and augment its force. The effect increases as the distance diminishes, and is greatest when the bar is in contact with the pole of the magnet. This enables us to understand the action of the armature of a magnet, and its effect in preserving its force. It is obvious from the preceding that two separate pieces of soft iron, the extremities of which are in contact with the two poles, will operate as an armature, and resist the tendency of the two magnetisms

to recombine. But, from what has been stated in (12), it will readily appear that a much greater effect will be attained by means of a single piece of soft iron, so shaped that the two ends may be in contact with the two poles of the magnet; for the magnetism induced in such a bar is much greater than the sum of the effects produced by the two poles acting separately, and consequently its reaction on the magnet itself more considerable.

An armature, such as we have described, is easily applied to a magnet of the horse-shoe form; and its efficacy is shown by the load which the magnet is thus rendered capable of sustaining, and which considerably exceeds the sum of the weights carried by the two poles acting separately. The armature which is applied to the native loadstone is constructed on similar principles.

When two bar magnets are placed near one another, they may be still more effectually protected. We have only to place them in a case, parallel to one another and at a short distance, with their dissimilar poles conterminous. These poles are then to be united by short pieces of soft iron.

CHAPTER III.

MEASUREMENT OF FREE MAGNETISM IN MAGNETS. LAWS OF MAGNETIC DISTRIBUTION.

(31) EVERY magnet on the earth's surface is acted upon by the magnetic force of the terrestrial globe, which tends to place it in a certain definite position, the amount of the directive action depending upon the magnetic force of the Earth, and upon that of the magnet acted on. This principle furnishes, as we shall presently see, a simple mean of measuring the magnetic forces of magnets. In order to understand this it will be necessary to consider briefly the laws of the directive action.

The magnetic force of the Earth, at a given place and epoch, is very nearly constant, both in magnitude and direction. In the northern hemisphere it *attracts* the *north* pole of the magnet, and *repels* the *south* pole; and as these two *contrary* forces are also *equal*, they constitute what is termed in Mechanics *a couple*, and tend to produce rotation only. Thus, the magnet, if free to move in all directions, will take up a position in which its magnetic axis (or the line joining the two poles) is in the direction of the acting force. Usually, however, the magnet is constrained by the nature of its support to move in a certain plane; and we have to consider in these circumstances the force by which it is solicited, and the position which it tends to assume.

(32) For our present purposes it will be sufficient to con-

sider the case in which the magnet is constrained to move in a *horizontal* plane. When the magnet is supported at its centre by a thread attached to a fixed point, or by a pivot, and when the vertical component of the earth's magnetic force is balanced, by slightly loading one arm of the needle, the magnet will be effectively influenced only by the *horizontal component* of the same force. If a line be drawn through the centre of the needle in the direction of the earth's magnetic force, the projection of this line upon the horizontal plane in which the needle moves, NoS, will be the direction of the effective force, and its magnitude will be equal to that of the whole force, multiplied by the cosine of the angle contained between the two directions. Let this horizontal component be denoted by X; and let μ be the quantity of free magnetism which we shall suppose to be concentrated in each pole of the magnet. Then the north pole of the magnet, n, is *attracted* by the force

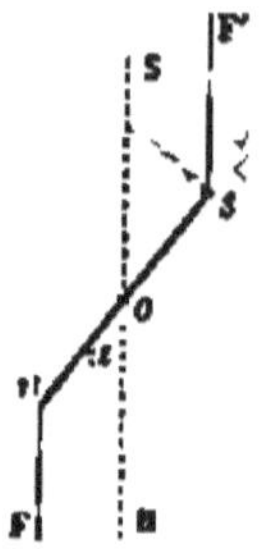

$$\mu X,$$

and the south pole, s, is *repelled* with an equal and parallel force; and the two forces conspire to make the magnet revolve round its centre, until it takes up a position in which its axis coincides with the direction of the acting force, NS. That there is no force tending to produce *translation* of the magnet in space is shown by the fact that when the magnet is supported by a thread attached to a fixed point, the thread remains vertical.

Now let the magnetic axis of the magnet form any angle, $Non = a$, with the magnetic meridian; and let the horizontal component of the earth's magnetic force be resolved into two, in the direction of the axis of the magnet, ns, and the direction perpendicular to it. The two former forces, applied to the two poles, are equal and opposite, and therefore balance one another. The two latter conspire to turn the magnet round its point of suspension, and to bring its axis into the magnetic meridian NS. The magnitude of each of these forces is $\mu X \sin a$; and the moment of each to turn the magnet is $\mu X \sin a \times \frac{1}{2}l$, l being the length of the magnet. Hence the total moment of the directive force is

$$\mu X l \sin a.$$

The constant co-efficient in this expression, μl, is denominated the *magnetic moment* of the magnet.

(33) It appears from the preceding that the magnet when disturbed from its position of rest, is urged to return to it with a force proportional to the sine of the angle of deflection. This law has been verified experimentally by Coulomb in the following manner. The magnet being introduced into the balance of torsion, the torsion head was adjusted so that the magnetic axis was in the magnetic meridian. This being done, the arm of the torsion circle was turned through any angle, θ; and the magnet was deflected from the magnetic meridian. If a denote, as before, the angle of deflection, the actual angle of torsion will be $\theta - a$. Hence, if k denote the co-efficient of torsion, the force of torsion is $k(\theta - a)$; and, as this force is in equilibrio with the magnetic directive force,

$$\mu l X \sin a = k(\theta - a).$$

Accordingly, for the same magnet and the same thread $\frac{\theta - a}{\sin a}$ is constant, whatever be the magnitude of the angles θ and a. This was found to be the case on trial.

(34) Coulomb applied this principle to the measurement of the magnetic moments of different bars in the following manner. The bars being introduced in succession into the balance of torsion, the arm of the torsion circle was turned until

they were all deflected through a given angle, α; and the corresponding angle, θ, was observed. It follows from the preceding formula that the magnetic moments, μl, are in this case proportional to the angles of torsion, $\theta - \alpha$. In this way Coulomb was enabled to determine the influence of dimension, and of form, upon the strength of magnets, when magnetized to saturation; and he was led to the following conclusions:—

1. In cylindrical magnets of the *same diameter*, and formed from the same steel, the magnetic moments are *proportional to the lengths*. The same proportionality was found to subsist in flat rectangular needles, of the same breadth and thickness.

This law does not hold in magnets whose length is less than one inch.

2. In cylindrical magnets of *similar* dimensions, formed by uniting several magnetized wires into one, the magnetic moments are as the *cubes of the lengths*.

3. Of two needles formed from the same plate of steel, and of the same weight, one of which had the form of a rectangle, and the other that of a lozenge, or oblique parallelogram the diagonal of which coincided with the magnetic axis, the magnetic moment of the second was found to exceed that of the first by about one-eighth part.

(35) Having studied the total moments of free magnetism in different bars, the next step was to determine experimentally the law according to which free magnetism is distributed in them. For this purpose also Coulomb made use of the balance of torsion. A magnetic needle was suspended in the apparatus, as before, and a wooden rule was fixed vertically, in the plane of the magnetic meridian passing through its centre, so that the needle should just touch the rule when the torsion of the suspending wire was re-

moved. A magnetic wire, about 27 inches long, was placed vertically in contact with the rule on the opposite side, the similar halves of the two magnets being in juxtaposition; and the wire was made to slide in a groove cut in the wood, so that it might always be at the same distance from the pole of the suspended needle. In these circumstances the suspended magnet was repelled by the fixed one. The torsion head was then turned, so as to bring the needle back to its primitive position, at a fixed distance from the acting magnet. The angle of torsion requisite to produce this effect was read off on the torsion circle: it measures the repulsive force exerted by the magnet upon the suspended needle. This observation was repeated with different points of the magnetic wire on a level with the suspended needle, and thus the relative amounts of free magnetism contained in them were determined.

(36) Coulomb also measured the amount of free magnetism at the several points of a long magnet by observing the time of vibration of a short and massive needle, under the combined action of the magnet and of the Earth. The magnet was placed vertically, in the plane of the magnetic meridian passing through the centre of the suspended magnet, and at an invariable distance from it. In this method of observation the forces emanating from other parts of the magnet conspire with that which is in the same horizontal plane with the suspended needle, in its action upon it. These forces, however, are exerted more obliquely, the more remote they are from that part; and it may be fairly assumed that the effective force emanates from a portion of the magnet of moderate length, extending equally above and below the plane containing the suspended needle. Now the free magnetism of any two sections of the magnet, equally distant from this plane above and below, in the one case ex-

ceeds, and in the other falls short of, the free magnetism of the section under examination, and by an amount nearly equal in the two cases,* their distances from that plane being small. Accordingly, the mean of their actions will be, very nearly, the same as that of the section in the horizontal plane containing the moveable needle.

If, in any plane passing through the axis of the magnet, *ns*, perpendiculars, *aa'*, *bb'*, be raised, proportional to the intensities of the forces emanating from the corresponding points, the extremities of these ordinates will form a curve, which may be called the *curve of intensities*. This curve consists of two branches, which, when the magnet has been regularly magnetized, are similar to one another. At the middle

of the bar, *o*, and for a considerable distance on either side of that point,† the curve of intensities coincides nearly with the axis of abscissæ, the intensities of free magnetism at these points being insensible. The curve rises rapidly on opposite sides, as the point approaches either extremity of the magnet; and at the extremities themselves the ordinate is a maximum. If the centre of gravity of each of the surfaces comprised between the curve, the axis of abscissæ, and the extreme ordinates be found, the perpendiculars from these points upon the axis of the magnet will meet the latter in the two poles. It is easily seen, from the form of the curves, that these points are not far removed from the two extremities of the magnet.

* It is obvious that this would be *strictly* true if the curve of intensities were a right line.

† The intensity is nearly evanescent at four and a half or five inches from the ends, in all magnets whose length exceeds the double of that quantity.

M. Biot has found that the curve of intensities is analytically expressed by the formula

$$y = A(\mu^x - \mu^{l-x}),$$

in which l is the length of the magnet, x the distance of any point from one of its extremities, and y the intensity of free magnetism at that point. The quantities, A and μ, are constants, which are different for each magnet. The constant, μ, is always less than unity; and its value approaches to $\frac{1}{2}$ when the length of the magnet is considerable. Hence, when the magnet is a long one, the intensity at any point, not far from one extremity, will be nearly represented by the formula

$$y = A\mu^x,$$

the term μ^{l-x} being nearly insensible.

(37) One of the most remarkable of the conclusions obtained by Coulomb was the perfect identity of the curve of intensities in magnetized wires of the same diameter, whose length exceeded eight or nine inches, the curves differing only in the interval which separated the two branches, and throughout which the intensity was evanescent. In such magnets, consequently, the poles are at the same distance from the extremities of the magnets, and are endued with equal forces. It follows from this that the magnetic moments of such magnets are *q. p.* proportional to their lengths, as has been otherwise directly shown. In cylindrical needles of different diameters, the distances of the poles from the extremities of the needles are proportional to the diameters themselves.

In very short needles, the distance of each pole from the extremity of the needle is, very nearly, one-sixth of the length of the needle. In fact, the curve of intensities may in that case be regarded as a *right line;* and consequently the centre of gravity of each of the triangles which it forms with the axis of the magnet is situated at the distance from the vertex of the triangle equal to two-thirds of its altitude.

(38) It remains to inquire in what manner the distribution of free magnetism, whose empirical laws we have been considering, can be explained upon the hypothesis already advanced.

We have said that, according to this hypothesis, every molecule of a magnetic body is supposed to possess equal quantities of the two magnetic fluids, which are separated in the process of magnetization, that separation being limited by the dimensions of the molecule itself. In the case of a single molecule, in which the two fluids have been thus separated, the fluids tend to recombine by their mutual attraction, and this tendency is resisted by the coercitive force which maintains them separate. The mutual attraction of the two fluids is therefore balanced by the coercitive force.

Let us next suppose *two* magnetic molecules, m_1 and m_2, in which the *austral* fluids, a_1 and a_2, have been, in the process of magnetization, brought to the corresponding ends of the two molecules on one side, and the *boreal* fluids, b_1 and b_2, to the corresponding ends on the other.

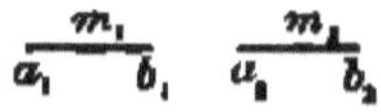

There will then arise *two repulsive forces*, viz., between a_1 and a_2, and between b_1 and b_2, one of which co-operates with the attractive force between the two elements of the *same* molecule to cause their recombination, while the other opposes it. These forces are exerted between equal masses, and at equal distances; and therefore neutralize one another. Similarly, of the *two attractive forces*—between a_1 and b_2, and between a_2 and b_1—the former tends to produce a recombination of the elements of the same molecule, and the latter to resist it; but these forces are no longer equal, the force between the near elements of the two molecules, a_2 and b_1, exceeding that which subsists between the remote elements, a, and b_2. Accordingly, the force which resists the recombination of the two fluids exceeds that which favours it; and the effect of the second molecule upon the first is to *augment the separation* of the two elements, or to increase the magnetism developed in it.

(39) Now let us consider the mutual action of any row of molecules

$$m, \ m_1, \ m_2, \ldots m_{n-2}, \ m_{n-1}, \ m_n,$$

in each of which the magnetic elements are separated, and in the same direction in all. The extreme molecule, m, will be

acted on by all the others, although with decreasing intensity as they increase in distance, and these actions will concur in resisting the recombination of the two elements, a and b, whose separation will thus be augmented. The second molecule, m_1, will be in like manner acted on by all the others; and this action will be more powerful than that exerted on m. For the action between m and m_1 exceeds that between m and m_n, being exerted at a shorter distance; and all the other actions are the same in the two cases. In like manner, the third molecule, m_2, is acted on more powerfully by the others than the second; and so on, the actions increasing up to the middle of the series. It follows from this, that the masses of the two elements separated in each molecule by the action of the rest, and therefore the amount of magnetism which it acquires, will increase from the end to the middle of the magnet; and the quantities of the two fluids which are separated in the same molecule being equal, it follows that $a_1 > b$, $a_2 > b_1$, $a_3 > b_2$, &c., up to the middle of the magnet, after which the order of magnitudes is reversed. Now the *free magnetism* at any point of the magnet is the difference of the masses of the opposite elements, which are accumulated at the two sides of the interval of two adjacent molecules, or $a_1 - b$, $a_2 - b_1$, $a_3 - b_2$, &c., and these differences are *positive* in one-half of the bar, and *negative* in the other half: in other words, the *free austral fluid* preponderates in one half of the bar, and the *free boreal fluid* in the other half. The former half therefore attracts the boreal magnetism of an external point, and repels the austral; while the latter attracts the austral, and repels the boreal. The poles of the magnet are the points of application of the resultant forces emanating from the two halves of the bar. They are sometimes distinguished by the species of free magnetism which preponderates in the corresponding halves, the pole which turns to the *north* being denominated the *austral pole*, and the pole which turns to the *south*, the *boreal pole*.

When the resultant of all the forces, exerted on any molecule by the rest, is equal to the coercitive force, the magnet is magnetized to *saturation*.

(40) When a magnet is broken in the middle, the poles of the molecules which were next the surface of separation, and which (wholly or nearly) counteracted one another, now operate with their entire force. But the masses of the two fluids which were separated in the molecules of each half will no longer be the same as before, the assisting action of the molecules of the other half being suppressed. Thus a new distribution will take place in these molecules, the molecules nearer to the point of fracture losing more magnetism than those more remote, until finally, the magnetism developed will become equal in the two extreme molecules, and will increase from thence to the central one. The free magnetism, on the other hand, will increase from the centre to the two ends; and each half becomes a magnet similar to the whole, but of weaker intensity.

CHAPTER IV.

LAWS OF MAGNETIC ATTRACTION AND REPULSION.

(41) Before we can determine the forces of attraction or repulsion exerted by two magnets on one another, it is necessary to know the law according to which the mutual action of any two *magnetic elements* varies, as their distance is changed. This law, which may be regarded as the fundamental principle of magnetic science, was experimentally investigated by Coulomb, and was proved to be the same as the law of gravity, the force varying inversely as the square of the distance. The force is *repulsive* between two magnetic elements of the *same* kind, and *attractive* between two elements of *opposite* kinds.

Coulomb made use of two different experimental methods in this investigation. In the first of these he employed the balance of torsion. A magnetic needle, 650 millimetres long, and three millimetres in diameter, was placed in the stirrup attached to the suspension wire; and the whole apparatus was turned, so that the line joining the divisions 0° and 180° of the divided circle coincided with the magnetic meridian. The moveable arm of the torsion circle was then turned, until the magnet pointed to the zero of the scale; in which case the suspension wire is without torsion. These adjustments having been completed, a magnet of the same dimensions as the suspended one was introduced into the box in a vertical position, through an aperture in the top immediately above one of the poles of the suspended magnet; and this magnet was lowered until its acting pole, which was of the same name as the near pole of the suspended magnet, was in the same horizontal plane with it. The suspended magnet was immediately repelled, and deflected from the magnetic meridian; and its new position of equilibrium is that in which the directive force of the Earth, added to the force of torsion, is equal to the repulsive force exerted between the two similar poles. By turning the torsion circle through any arc, the moveable pole may be made to approach the fixed pole, and thus a new relation between the acting forces is obtained at a new distance.

Let θ denote the angle through which the arm of the torsion circle is turned, and a the deflection of the suspended needle from the magnetic meridian. The angle of torsion is $\theta + a$; and the force of torsion brought into play is $k(\theta + a)$, k being a constant quantity. Also, the moment of the force exerted by the Earth upon the needle is

$$mX \sin a,$$

X being the horizontal component of the Earth's magnetic force, and m the magnetic moment of the suspended needle. Hence, when there is equilibrium, the repulsive force exerted by the pole of the fixed magnet upon that of the moveable one is

$$f = k(\theta + a) + mX \sin a.$$

When the angles of deflection are small, as is ordinarily the case, we may substitute a for $\sin a$. Hence, if we make

$$mX = pk,$$

the foregoing expression becomes

$$f = k[\theta + (p + 1) a].$$

(42) The repulsive forces, corresponding to different angles of torsion and deflection, being calculated by this formula, it only remained to compare them with the corresponding dis-

tances of the acting poles. These distances are the chords of the angles of deflection, and are proportional to the angles of deflection themselves, when these are not considerable. Now, the observations of Coulomb showed that

$$[\theta + (p + 1)\, a] \times a^2 = const.$$

whatever be θ and a; and, consequently, that the repulsive forces were inversely as the squares of the distances.

The observations are made in the following manner :

The value of the constant, p, is experimentally determined by turning the arm of the torsion circle through any given angle, and observing the corresponding deflection of the suspended needle from the magnetic meridian before the fixed magnet has been introduced: p is the ratio of the corresponding angles of torsion and deflection. Thus, the upper extremity of the wire being turned through two circumferences, or 720°, the needle was deflected through 20°. Hence the angle of torsion is 700°; and $p = \frac{700}{20} = 35$.

The fixed magnet being now introduced, the following results were obtained:—

$\theta = 0$	$a = 24°$	$f = k \times 864$
3×360	17	$k \times 1692$
8×360	12	$k \times 3312$

The numbers in the third column are the values of the repulsive forces, corresponding to the distances 24, 17, and 12, as calculated by the formula of the preceding article. It will be seen that they are, very nearly, inversely as the squares of the latter numbers.

(43) The law of magnetic attraction and repulsion may also be established by suspending a short and massive magnet horizontally by a fine thread of silk, and making it oscillate under the combined action of the Earth and of a fixed magnet. The fixed magnet should be one of considerable length,

so that the action of the remote pole may not sensibly affect the suspended magnet. It is to be placed vertically, in the plane of the magnetic meridian passing through the centre of the suspended magnet, one of its poles being in the same horizontal plane with the latter. The variation of distance of the moving pole being small, relatively to the whole distance from the pole of the fixed magnet, the direction and intensity of the force exerted by the latter may be regarded as constant. Hence, denoting this force, as before, by f, the resulting moment will be

$$m(X+f)\sin a,$$

X denoting the magnetic force of the Earth.

When the deflection, a, is small, the angle itself may be substituted for its sine. Accordingly, the vibration of the moving magnet is governed by the law of the pendulum; and the time of vibration is given by the formula

$$T = \pi\sqrt{\frac{K}{m(X+f)}};$$

in which K is the moment of inertia of the moving magnet. Hence we have

$$m(X+f) = \pi^2\frac{K}{T^2};$$

and, for the same magnet,

$$X+f \propto n^2,$$

n being the number of vibrations performed in any given time. Let n_0 be the number of vibrations performed in the same time under the influence of the *Earth alone:* then we have $\frac{X+f}{X} = \frac{n^2}{n_0^2}$; and

$$f = X\left(\frac{n^2}{n_0^2} - 1\right).$$

Now, let f and f' be the forces exerted at any two distances, and let n and n' be the corresponding numbers of vibrations performed in a given time at each: then

$$\frac{f}{f'} = \frac{n^2 - n_0^2}{n'^2 - n_0^2}.$$

The ratio, thus calculated, is found to correspond with that of the squares of the distances, inversely.

(44) The law of the force exerted by a *single pole* being thus known, we may proceed to determine the direction and intensity of the force exerted by a magnet upon a magnetic element.

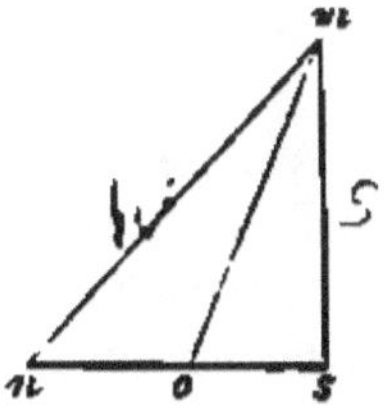

Let ns be a magnet; m the magnetic element acted on; and mo the line connecting it with the middle point of the magnet. When the distance of the point acted on is considerable, in comparison with the length of the magnet, the forces exerted by the latter on the former may be reduced to two, one attractive and the other repulsive, emanating respectively from the two poles. Let the distances mn and ms, be denoted by r and s. Then the forces exerted by the poles n and s are

$$\frac{\mu\mu'}{r^2}, \quad \frac{\mu\mu'}{s^2};$$

μ being the quantity of free magnetism contained in each of the poles, and μ' that of the magnetic element. If μ' be *austral*, the former of these will be *repulsive*, and the latter *attractive*. Now let each of these forces be resolved into two, in the directions mo and ns respectively. Then if the lines mo and no be denoted respectively by a and l, the former components are $\frac{\mu\mu' a}{r^3}$ and $\frac{\mu\mu' a}{s^3}$; and the latter are $\frac{\mu\mu' l}{r^3}$ and $\frac{\mu\mu' l}{s^3}$. Hence, denoting the total forces in the directions *mo* and *ns* by P and Q, respectively, we have

$$P = \mu\mu' a\left(\frac{1}{s^3} - \frac{1}{r^3}\right);$$

$$Q = \mu\mu' l\left(\frac{1}{s^3} + \frac{1}{r^3}\right).$$

Accordingly, the force exerted in the line connecting the point acted on with the centre of the magnet is much smaller than the force exerted in the direction of the axis of the magnet itself; and consequently the direction of the resultant action must always approximate to parallelism with the latter direction.

We can now deduce the direction and intensity of the resultant force.

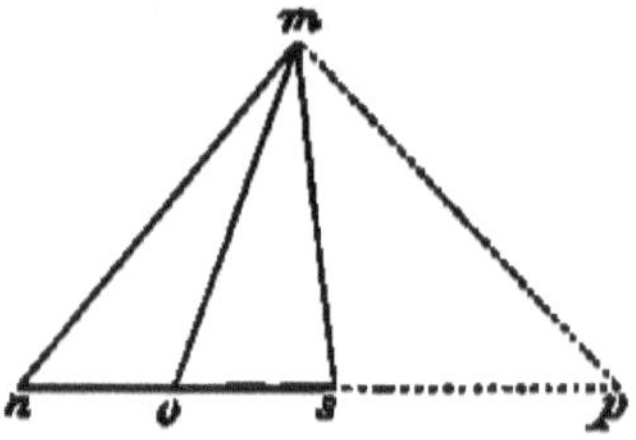

Let the line *mp* be drawn in the direction of this resultant, to meet the line *ns* produced in *p*. Then the sides of the triangle *mop* are proportional to the forces in their directions; consequently

$$mo : op :: P : Q :: a(r^3 - s^3) : l(r^3 + s^3);$$

and therefore

$$op = l \cdot \frac{r^3 + s^3}{r^3 - s^3}.$$

(45) When the distance of the point acted on is considerable, in comparison with the length of the magnet, the

preceding results admit of a remarkable simplification. If we denote the angle *mop* by ϕ, we have

$$r^2 = a^2 + l^2 + 2al \cos\phi, \quad s^2 = a^2 + l^2 - 2al \cos\phi.$$

Hence, expanding, and neglecting the powers of $\frac{l}{a}$ above the first,

$$r^{-3} = a^{-3}\left(1 - 3\frac{l}{a}\cos\phi\right), \quad s^{-3} = a^{-3}\left(1 + 3\frac{l}{a}\cos\phi\right).$$

Wherefore

$$s^{-3} + r^{-3} = 2a^{-3}, \quad s^{-3} - r^{-3} = 2a^{-3} \times 3\frac{l}{a}\cos\phi.$$

Substituting in the expressions for P and Q, and making, for abridgment, $2\mu l = m$; we have

$$P = \frac{m\mu'}{a^3} . 3 \cos\phi, \quad Q = \frac{m\mu'}{a^3}.$$

Accordingly,

$$P = Q \times 3 \cos\phi.$$

Now, let the angle *omp*, which the direction of the resultant makes with the joining line, be denoted by ϕ'. Then $\frac{P}{Q} = \frac{\sin mpo}{\sin omp} = \frac{\sin(\phi + \phi')}{\sin\phi'}$. And substituting for $\frac{P}{Q}$ its value just obtained, we have $\sin(\phi + \phi') = 3 \cos\phi \sin\phi'$; whence, finally,

$$\tan\phi' = \tfrac{1}{2} \tan\phi.$$

When the point acted on is in the line of prolongation of the axis of the magnet, or $\phi = 0$, we have also $\phi' = 0$, and the resultant force is exerted in the same line.

The direction of the resultant is the same, when the magnetic element is in the line perpendicular to the magnet erected at its middle point. For, in this case, $\phi = 90°$, and therefore also $\phi' = 90°$; i. e., the force is exerted in a direction perpendicular to the joining line, or parallel to the magnet.

(46) The magnitude of the resultant force is given by the formula,

$$R^2 = P^2 + Q^2 - 2PQ \cos \phi.$$

Whence, substituting for P and Q their values above obtained, we have

$$R = \frac{m\mu'}{a^3} \sqrt{1 + 3 \cos^2 \phi}.$$

Accordingly, when the point m is on the prolongation of the axis of the magnet, or $\phi = 0$, we have

$$R = \frac{2m\mu'}{a^3}.$$

On the other hand, when that point is situated in the perpendicular to the magnet raised at its middle point, $\phi = 90°$, and

$$R = \frac{m\mu'}{a^3}.$$

Hence the force exerted in the former case is double of that exerted in the latter, the distances being equal.

(47) We can now determine the force exerted by one magnet on another, the length of each being supposed small in comparison with the distance between them.

In this case the force exerted is *directive* only. For the distance being considerable, in comparison with the lengths of the two magnets, the force exerted by one of them upon the two poles of the other may be regarded as *equal* and *parallel*. And as these forces are also exerted in *opposite* directions, they have no single resultant; and can produce rotation only.

Let ns and $n's'$ be the two magnets, and let their axes form the angles ϕ and ϕ' with the line joining their centres. Then the moments of the forces P and Q exerted by the magnet ns upon the magnet $n's'$, will be obtained by multiplying them by the sines of the angles which they form, respectively, with the axis of the second magnet, and by the length of the latter. Accordingly, the total moment of the force exerted by ns on $n's'$ is

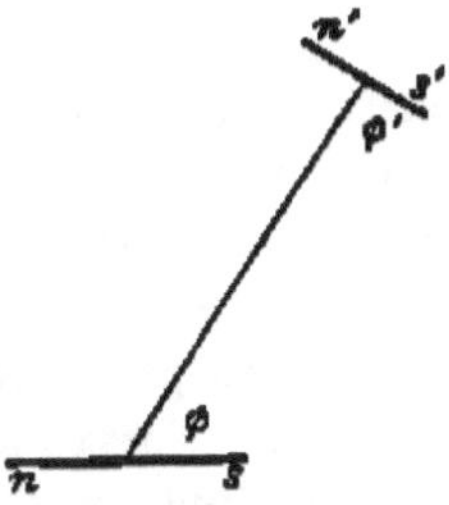

$$2l'\{P \sin \phi' - Q \sin (\phi + \phi')\};$$

l' denoting half the length of the magnet acted on. Wherefore substituting for P and Q their values already obtained (45), and making $2\mu l' = m'$, the moment is

$$\tfrac{1}{2}\frac{mm'}{a^3}\left\{\sin (\phi + \phi') - 3 \sin (\phi - \phi')\right\};$$

in which m and m' are the magnetic moments of the two magnets, and a the distance of their centres.

When the axes of the two magnets are at right angles—as is the case with two of the principal magnets in a magnetic observatory—we have $\phi + \phi' = 90°$; and the general expression of the moment is reduced to

$$\tfrac{1}{2}\frac{mm'}{a^3}(1 - 3 \cos 2\phi).$$

This will vanish, when

$$\cos 2\phi = \tfrac{1}{3}.$$

Accordingly the direction of the second magnet will be unaffected by the first, when the joining line makes the angle 35° 16′ with the axis of the first magnet.

(48) If in any plane passing through the axis of a fixed

magnet, a series of consecutive points be taken, constituting a curve so conditioned that the tangent at each point shall be in the direction of the force exerted by the magnet at that point, the curve so formed is called a *magnetic curve*. An infinite number of such curves surround the magnet, as represented in the annexed figure; and they all pass through the two poles. These curves may be easily displayed to the eye, by strewing iron filings on a sheet of paper placed above the magnet, and communicating to them a slight agitation, by tapping gently on the paper. For the filings, being rendered polar by induction, will arrange themselves in the direction of the resultant forces at each point.

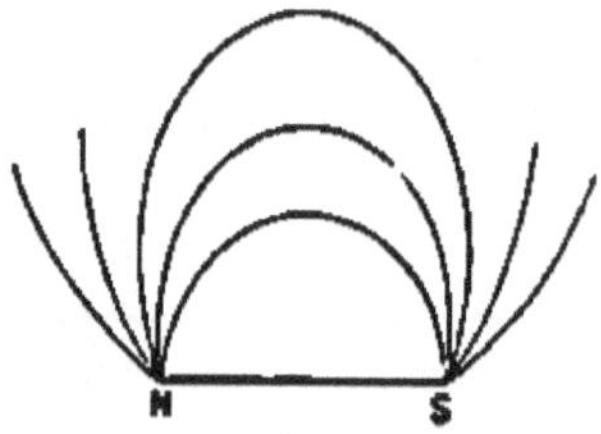

(49) If vectors be drawn from any point of a magnetic curve to the two poles, the difference of the cosines of the angles which these lines form with the axis of the magnet, measured on the same side, is constant.

Let NS be the magnet, o and o' any two indefinitely near points of the magnetic curve. Then the line oo' being in the direction of the magnetic force, the sines of the angles, Noo', Soo', which it makes with the two vectors, are inversely as the forces emanating from the corresponding poles, and therefore directly as the squares of the corresponding distances; i. e.,

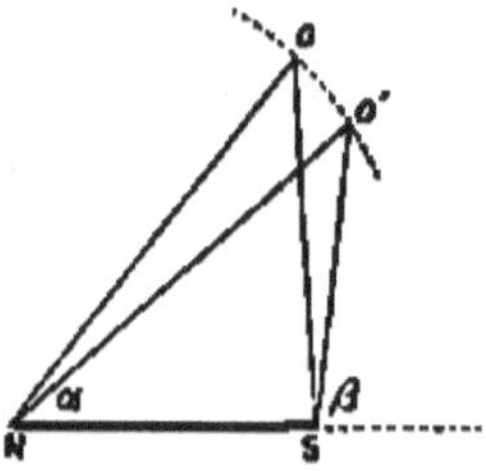

$$\frac{\sin Noo'}{r^2} = \frac{\sin Soo'}{s^2}$$

Denoting the angles which the two vectors form with the axis of the magnet by a and β, we have

$$\sin \text{N}oo' = r\frac{da}{ds}, \quad \sin \text{S}oo' = s\frac{d\beta}{ds};$$

and, substituting in the preceding equation,

$$\frac{da}{r} = \frac{d\beta}{s}.$$

Multiplying by $r \sin a = s \sin \beta$, we have $\sin a da = \sin \beta d\beta$; whence

$$\cos a = \cos \beta + const.$$

(50) The foregoing property suggests the following mode of constructing the magnetic curve.

Let two rulers of equal length, Nn and Ss, revolve round their extreme points, N and S, as centres, in such a manner that their other extremities are always situated in a right line perpendicular to NS; then the successive positions of their points of intersection, o, will describe a magnetic curve. For Np is the cosine of the angle oNp, to the radius Nn; and Sp is in like manner the cosine of the angle oSp to the equal radius Ss; and their difference, NS, is constant. Dr. Roget has devised a system of rulers which fulfil the foregoing conditions, and therefore construct the curve mechanically.

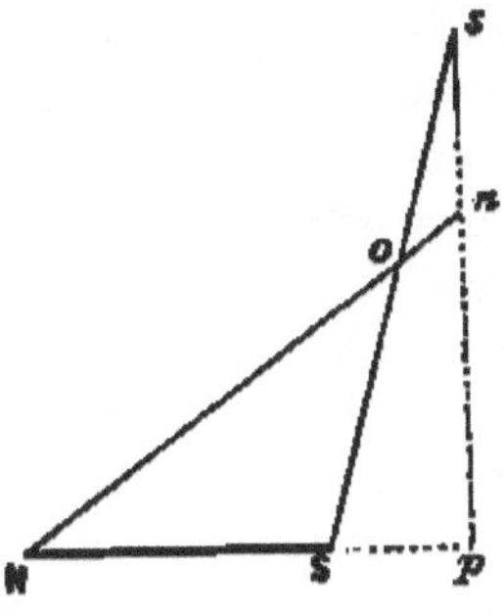

If two *similar* poles act together, they will give rise to a series of magnetic curves analogous to the preceding; the fundamental property of which is that the *sum* of the cosines of the angles made by the vectors from any point to the two poles, measured on the same side, is constant. This case may be realized by placing two equal magnets parallel to one another, with their poles in the same direction. For points near either pair of poles, the action of the remote poles may be neglected.

(51) The laws of the distribution of free magnetism in a magnetic body, under the influence of any external inducing forces, have been studied by Poisson. We have seen that every element of a magnetic body contains equal quantities of the two magnetic fluids, the particles of each of which *attract* those of the other, while they *repel* those of the same kind. In the natural or neutral state of the body, the two fluids are uniformly diffused throughout the element, and consequently they neutralize one another's effects upon an external point. Under the action of inducing forces, however, the two fluids are separated, the fluid of the same kind as the acting pole being repelled to the remote surface of the element, and that of the opposite kind attracted to the near surface; and, as the result of this separation, the mass acquires *polarity*, one or more portions of it attracting the particles of the austral fluid, and repelling those of the boreal, while other portions have the opposite qualities. The problem is thus reduced to determine the direction in which the two fluids are separated in each element, and the force which that element exerts upon any point in virtue of the separation.

But the separation of the two fluids in each element, under the influence of inducing action, and their reunion when the inducing action is withdrawn, are both resisted by the *coercitive force*, whose magnitude is different in different bodies. M. Poisson has confined his investigation to bodies in which this force is supposed to be nothing; and he has deduced the equations which express the laws of distribution of the magnetic fluids in such bodies, and the relation of the forces exerted by them upon any point. It is not possible to solve these equations except in some of the simpler cases. But M. Poisson has shown that the resultant of all the actions of the magnetic elements of the entire body is equivalent to the action of a thin stratum of each of the two fluids covering the entire body, the two fluids being equal in quantity, and their total action upon any interior point being nothing.

When the magnetic body has the form of the *ellipsoid*, and when it is exposed to the action of a *single inducing force*, having a determinate magnitude and direction, the problem admits of a complete solution. The solution of course comprehends the case of the sphere; and its results are found to accord with those empirically deduced by Professor Barlow for a body of that form, the force being proportional to the cube of the diameter of the sphere directly, and inversely as the cube of the distance of the point acted on. The case of the ellipsoid virtually includes that of a cylindrical bar, whose diameter is very small in comparison with its length, and also that of a circular plate of uniform thickness—such bodies being nearly identical with ellipsoids of revolution, whose axes of revolution are very great, or very small, in comparison with their other dimensions.

CHAPTER V.

MAGNETISM OF ALL BODIES.

(52) It has been already stated that iron, nickel, and cobalt, are capable of being attracted by the poles of a magnet. It was natural to inquire whether this capacity was peculiar to these bodies, or whether, on the other hand, it was a property of all bodies.

This inquiry was undertaken by Coulomb at the commencement of the present century. The substances which were the subjects of experiment were formed into small needles, about one-third of an inch in length, and were suspended by a fibre of silk between the opposite poles of two strong magnets. All the substances so tried were found to be attracted by the poles of the magnets. The needles took the direction of the line joining the two poles; and when disturbed from that position, they oscillated round it, the time of oscillation being in many cases much shorter than when the magnets were removed. Needles thus formed of gold, silver, copper, lead, tin, glass, wood, bone, and other organic substances, presented the same result. Later researches have shown that many of these substances are *repelled* by the poles of a magnet, and that when placed between the opposite poles of two magnets, they take up a position at *right angles* to the line joining the poles. Accordingly, if the results obtained by Coulomb are to be relied upon, they are probably to be accounted for—in some cases at least—by the presence of ferruginous particles in the substances examined. This was the conclusion of Coulomb himself; and he showed that a portion of iron, the $\frac{1}{130000}$th part of the mass, is sufficient to impart a sensible magnetism to metals, which exhibit no sign of magnetism when in a state of purity.

M. Ed. Becquerel resumed the inquiry begun by Coulomb, and sought to determine the specific magnetism of various substances, whether it be inherent, or due to the presence of ferruginous particles. His mode of experimenting consisted in forming the substances into short needles, of the same length and diameter, and observing their times of vibration when suspended between the opposite poles of two magnets. Various crystallized minerals, and vegetable substances, were thus examined; and it was found that the time of oscillation of all was affected by the presence of the magnets, although in different degrees. M. Becquerel ascribed this action to the presence of iron; and he concluded that the only substances which were magnetic *per se* were iron, nickel, and cobalt.

(53) The great discovery of the magnetism of all bodies was made by Faraday, in the year 1845. Employing a method of research not unlike that of Coulomb, Faraday has shown that *all bodies*, whether solid, liquid, or gaseous, are acted on by the poles of a magnet, and are consequently *magnetic*, some of them being *attracted* by the magnet, while others are *repelled*.

In reference to these properties, therefore, all natural substances are divisible into two classes. Those which are *attracted* by the poles of a magnet are called by Faraday *paramagnetic*; and their magnetic properties are similar to those which had been already recognised in iron, nickel, and cobalt. Substances which are *repelled* by the poles of a magnet are denominated *diamagnetic*; and they constitute a much more numerous class than the former. As iron is the type of paramagnetic substances, so bismuth may be taken as that of the diamagnetic, inasmuch as it possesses the property of diamagnetism in the highest degree.*

(54) In these researches Faraday made use of the electro-magnet, on account of its great power. It has been constructed by M. Rumkorff in the following form, with a special view to such experiments. Two cylinders of soft iron are surrounded each with a long coil of copper wire, and are fixed with their axes in the same right line. When the current from a battery is transmitted through the coils, the iron cylinders become powerful magnets. By means of a commutator introduced into the circuit, the circuit may be closed or interrupted, and the direction of the current changed at pleasure; and thus the magnetism of the two poles may be inverted or destroyed. In order to vary at pleasure the interval of the acting poles, these cylinders are attached at their remote extremities to two upright pieces of soft iron, which slide in a horizontal groove formed in a support of the same metal. A horizontal rule, attached to this support, enables the observer to adjust the interval of the acting poles. The apparatus is provided with pieces of soft iron of various forms, which can be screwed on the acting ends of the two bars, so as to vary the extent and form of the polar surfaces. When it is required that the magnetic forces shall act with nearly equal intensity throughout a considerable space, we employ circular discs of large diameter as armatures, the *magnetic field*, as it is called, being in such

* This property of bismuth was noticed in the last century. In 1774, Brugmanns observed that a bar of bismuth *repelled* the magnetic needle; and the same property was noticed in antimony, as well as in bismuth, by M. Lebaillif, in 1828. Indications of an analogous property were also noticed in unmetallic substances, such as wood, gum-lac, &c., by M. Becquerel. These bodies seemed to be acted on by the poles of a magnet, some of them assuming a transversal position between the two opposite poles.

circumstances considerable. On the other hand, when we desire to concentrate the forces emanating from the two poles, we employ as armatures cones with rounded extremities.

The polar surfaces being concentrated by the means last described, the substance to be examined is formed into a light needle, and suspended horizontally by a fibre of silk without torsion, so that its centre shall be at the middle point of the line connecting the two poles. When the circuit is completed, the cylinders of soft iron become magnetic ; the suspended needle is deflected, and takes up a definite position under the action of the inducing forces. This position coincides with the line connecting the two poles, when the needle is attracted, i.e., when the substance of which it is composed is paramagnetic. On the other hand, the position of equilibrium is at right angles to the line connecting the poles when the needle is repelled, or the substance of which it is composed *diamagnetic*. The former position is denominated *axial ;* the latter *equatorial.*

If the needle be disturbed from its position of equilibrium, whether it be axial or equatorial, it will always return to that position, which is accordingly one of stable equilibrium.

(55) By the means above described Faraday ascertained that all solid bodies examined were magnetic. Some of them are attracted by the poles of the magnet, and assume the axial position between the two poles ; others, forming a much more numerous class, are repelled, and assume the equatorial position. The following is the order of the principal metals belonging to the two classes, each substance being more powerfully magnetic than those which succeed it in the list :—

Paramagnetic Metals.	*Diamagnetic Metals.*
Iron.	Bismuth.
Nickel.	Antimony.
Cobalt.	Zinc.
Manganese.	Tin.
Chrome.	Cadmium.
Cerium.	Sodium.
Titanium.	Mercury.
Palladium.	Lead.
Platina.	Silver.
Osmium.	Copper.
	Gold.
	Arsenic.
	Uranium.*
	Rhodium.
	Iridium.
	Tungsten.

(56) The position of equilibrium of the needle between the opposite poles of two magnets is, however, not the fundamental fact by which the two classes of magnetic bodies are to be discriminated. The axial direction is in general the result of *attraction*, exerted by the pole of the magnet upon the paramagnetic body; and the equatorial direction of *repulsion*. Oersted and others have shown, however, that these results are not invariable; and that the *same body* may at one time assume the axial, and at another the equatorial direction, according to its position in the magnetic field and other circumstances. The two classes of magnetic bodies are therefore to be distinguished, not by the directions which they assume, which is a complex result, but by their tendency *to* or *from* the centre of force; *paramagnetic* bodies

* According to the more recent observations of M. Verdet, uranium is paramagnetic.

being urged towards those points in which the intensity of the magnetic action is *greatest*, and *diamagnetic* bodies towards those points in which the intensity is *least*.

(57) But even attraction and repulsion themselves are not ultimate facts. We have already seen that when a piece of soft iron is brought into the vicinity of a magnetic pole, the attraction which ensues is a consequence of a *polar change* induced in the iron by the acting pole, a pole of the *opposite* kind to that of the acting body being engendered in the *near* portion of the mass, and a pole of the *same* kind in the *remote* portion. Hence, as similar poles repel one another, while contrary poles attract, attraction will ensue between the inducing pole and the near portion of the iron, and repulsion between the same and the remote portion, and the resulting action will be the difference of these opposing forces. It is evident that it must be attractive, the attraction being exerted at the shorter distance. The same explanation of course applies to the attraction of all paramagnetic bodies.

We are led by analogy to infer that the repulsion exerted by a magnetic pole upon a diamagnetic body is, in like manner, to be explained by a polar change induced in the body by the acting force. But the polarity induced in this case is necessarily different from the former. As the repulsive force predominates, we must assume that a *similar* pole is induced in the *near* portion of the diamagnetic, and a *contrary* pole in the *remote* portion. This view, however, has not been admitted without much discussion. Professor Weber has adduced the following experiment in confirmation of it. A coil was fixed to the polar surface of an electro-magnet, the axis of the coil being in the prolongation of the axis of the magnet; and the ends of the coil were connected with the poles of a delicate galvanometer. When a cylinder of bismuth was introduced into the coil, it was rendered magnetic by the induction of the electro-magnet; and at the same moment an induced current was transmitted through the coil, which deflected the needle of the galvanometer. An opposite current was induced in the coil when the bismuth cylinder was removed. M. Weber found that these currents were the *opposite* of those which would be produced by a cylinder of soft iron under the same circumstances; and he concluded therefore that the bismuth cylinder had been rendered *polar* by the inducing action of the electro-magnet, the polarity being the *inverse* of that engendered in soft iron.

(58) This view of the phenomenon has now been completely established by the experiments of Professor Tyndall. The apparatus employed by Professor Tyndall was one devised by Professor Weber. The substance to be examined was formed into a cylinder, and was acted on by the induction of a coil through which a voltaic current was transmitted; and the polarity of the end of the bar was examined by allowing it to act upon a compound magnetic needle, which was rendered *astatic*, or indifferent to the action of the Earth. In order to increase the effect, two cylinders and two helices were employed; and the corresponding poles were made to conspire in deflecting the needle. By an ingenious mechanical arrangement, either pair of poles could be brought rapidly into action upon the needle; and the direction of the deflection was read off by means of a telescope, and a mirror attached to the needle, which reflected the divisions of a distant scale. Professor Tyndall experimented by these means on a great variety of substances, both paramagnetic and diamagnetic; and he ascertained that the latter were *polarized*, as well as the former, under the inducing action of an electric current; but that the positions of the poles induced in paramagnetic and in diamagnetic bodies, by the action of the same current, were *contrary*.

We may conclude therefore—

1. That all bodies are *polarized* under the action of a magnetic force.

2. That in soft iron, and other *paramagnetic* bodies, the pole induced in the side next the inducing pole is of a *contrary* kind; and that, consequently, the body is *attracted*.

3. That in bismuth, and other *diamagnetic* bodies, the pole induced on the near side is of the *same* nature as the inducing pole; and that, therefore, the body is *repelled*.

(59) Fluids, whether liquid or gaseous, are acted on by magnetic forces just as solids, some of them being paramagnetic, and attracted to the centre of force, while others are diamagnetic, and are repelled.

The magnetic properties of *liquids* were discovered by Faraday by means similar to those applied to solid bodies. The liquid to be examined was inclosed in a thin tube of glass, and suspended by a silk thread between the opposite poles of a strong electro-magnet. Some liquids were thus found to take the axial position, and are consequently paramagnetic; while others rested only in the equatorial position, and are therefore diamagnetic. When these liquids are inclosed in thin spheres of glass, and are exposed to the action of a single pole, those of the former class are attracted, and those of the latter repelled.

The same method was also applied by Faraday to the investigation of the magnetic properties of *gases*. The gases examined were inclosed in thin spheres of glass, and these spheres were attached to the extremities of a horizontal lever supported by a fibre of silk; by these means the slightest action exerted upon them by the acting magnetic pole could be rendered sensible. Oxygen was thus found to be strongly paramagnetic; carbonic acid gas, olefiant gas, and cyanogen are diamagnetic. Hydrogen and nitrogen are very feebly acted on. Atmospheric air itself is paramagnetic; but it probably owes this property to the oxygen which it contains, its other principal constituent being nearly neutral.

M. E. Becquerel has measured the magnetism developed in various gases, and under different circumstances, and has concluded from his experiments that in the same gas, and under the inducing action of the same pole, the magnetism developed is proportional to the density.

(60) Since the fluids by which bodies are encompassed are acted on by the magnetic force, as well as the bodies immersed in them, it follows that the attraction and repulsion which are exerted on the latter are *apparent* only, and equal to the excess of the action exerted on the immersed body, and on an equal volume of the fluid which it displaces. For when the immersed body is removed, the portion of the fluid which occupies its place—being at rest relatively to the remainder—is acted on by the pressure of the surrounding fluid with a force *equal* and *opposite* to that by which it is urged by the magnetic pole; and it is evident that the body, which occupies the same place, must undergo an equal negative action. The case, in fact, is analogous to that of heavy bodies immersed in fluids, and acted on by gravity; in which case we know that the resultant action is the excess of the weight of the body over that of the displaced fluid.

It follows from these considerations that the *same* body may be either *attracted* or *repelled* by the same magnetic pole, according to the nature of the fluid in which it is immersed. This fact was discovered by Faraday at an early period of his investigations. A dilute solution of protosulphate of iron was inclosed in a thin tube of glass, and suspended horizontally between the poles of an electro-magnet. The liquid being paramagnetic, the tube immediately assumed the axial position. The same thing occurred when the tube was immersed in water instead of air; and the resulting action was even stronger. When, however, the tube was immersed in a solution of the protosulphate, of the same strength as that contained in the tube itself, it was found to be *indifferent* to the action of the magnetic pole, and to rest in any position in which it was placed. And when the surrounding solution was more concentrated, the liquid contained in the tube was *repelled*, and the tube rested in the *equatorial* position.

(61) In order to understand clearly these various effects, let μf denote the force exerted by the magnetic pole upon any body immersed in a fluid, and $\mu' f$ that exerted by the same pole upon the fluid displaced. These forces are in contrary directions, and are applied to the same points of the immersed body; consequently the resultant force exerted upon the latter is

$$(\mu - \mu')f.$$

Hence, when the body immersed, and the encompassing fluid, are both paramagnetic, μ and μ' are both positive; and accordingly the resultant action will be positive or negative, and the body will be *attracted* or *repelled*, according as μ is *greater* or *less* than μ'. When μ' is equal to μ, the resultant vanishes, and the body is indifferent to the action of the magnetic force, or neutral.

When the body, and the fluid in which it is immersed, are both *diamagnetic*, μ and μ' are both negative; the formula becomes

$$-(\mu - \mu')f;$$

and the body will be *repelled* or *attracted*, according as μ is greater or less than μ'.

When the body immersed is paramagnetic, and the fluid diamagnetic, μ' is negative, and the formula becomes

$$(\mu + \mu')f.$$

Thus the resultant action is always attractive, and more energetic than if the body were *in vacuo*. When, on the other hand, the body is diamagnetic, and the fluid paramagnetic, μ is negative, and the formula becomes

$$-(\mu + \mu')f.$$

The resultant action is therefore always repulsive, and more energetic than that exerted upon the body alone.

(62). The specific magnetic powers of different substances were compared by M. E. Becquerel by means of the balance of torsion. When the bodies to be tried were solid, they were formed into needles of the same form and dimensions, and were suspended between the poles of a strong electro-magnet, by means of a fine silver wire. The forces of attraction or repulsion exerted upon them were then measured by the angles of torsion, which it was necessary to communicate to the wire in order to maintain the needles at a constant angular distance from the line connecting the acting poles. The magnetic forces thus measured are the magnetic powers *in air*—i. e. the differences of the absolute powers of the bodies experimented on, and that of the air by which they were encompassed. M. Becquerel concluded from his experiments that soft iron, nickel, and cobalt had all the same specific magnetism. The specific magnetism of manganese was found to be such as would result from the presence of the $\frac{1}{1000}$th part of its weight of iron: that of gold is equivalent to a mixture of the $\frac{1}{113000}$ part of iron.

The magnetic powers of liquids were found by measuring the resultant action exerted by the magnetic pole upon the same solid when immersed in different liquids.

The force of the solid in air being known, the powers of the liquids are readily calculated from the formula

$$(\mu - \mu')f = p(\theta - a);$$

θ being the angle of torsion which produces a given deflection, a; and p a constant depending on the distance and upon the suspension wire. The quantity, f, is proportional to the square of the intensity of the current which traverses the coils. The same method is applicable to the gases.

(63) The following table is extracted from the results obtained by Faraday in the same line of research. The numbers given are the magnetic powers of the substances *reduced to a vacuum*, and under equal volumes. The positive sign denotes that the force exerted is attractive, or the body paramagnetic; the negative sign indicates that the force is repulsive, or the body diamagnetic.

Oxygen . .	+ 17.5	Absolute alcohol	− 78 7
Atmospheric air .	+ 3.4	Camphor .	− 82.6
Azote . .	+ 0.3	Olive oil .	− 85.6
Carbonic acid gas	0.0	Wax . .	− 86.7
Hydrogen . .	− 0.1	Nitric acid .	− 88.0
Cyanogen . .	− 0.9	Water .	− 96.6
Glass . . .	− 18.2	Sulphuric acid	− 104.5
Zinc . . .	− 74.6	Sulphur .	− 118.0
Ether . .	− 75.3	Bismuth	− 1967.6

(64) It remains to describe the effect of the physical conditions of the body upon its magnetism.

The dependence of the magnetic power of a body upon its state of condensation has been carefully studied by Professor Tyndall and M. Knoblauch. It has been shown by these experimentalists that when a body is compressed in any direction, it is more powerfully acted on by a magnetic force in that direction than in others; and, consequently, that when placed between the opposite poles of an electro-magnet, the axis of pressure will assume the axial or the equatorial direction, according as the substance is paramagnetic or diamagnetic.

Thus, if carbonate of iron, in the state of powder, be formed into a paste with water, in which gum has been dissolved, and be then compressed by a strong pressure into a thin disc, this disc, when suspended vertically between the poles of an electro-magnet, will rest with the *line of pressure* in the axial direction, and therefore with its *plane* in the equatorial direction. Thus the body appears to comport itself as a diamagnetic. On the other hand, if the disc be formed in the same manner of bismuth in a state of powder, and be similarly suspended, it will rest with the line of pressure in the equatorial direction, and therefore with its plane in the axial direction, as if the mass were attracted instead of being repelled.

If either of these discs be suspended *horizontally* between the poles of the magnet, it will rest indifferently in any position, the line of greatest condensation being vertical, and therefore passing through the point of suspension.

If a cube of solid bismuth be suspended between the poles of an electro-magnet, it will rest indifferently in any position. But if a compressing force be applied to two of its opposite faces, which hang vertically, it will turn until the line of greatest pressure is equatorial.

If a rectangular prism be formed of a number of equal rectangular metallic plates, placed side by side in the direction of the breadth of the prism, and be suspended between the poles of an electro-magnet, the axis of the prism will take the axial or the equatorial position, according as the metal is paramagnetic or diamagnetic; for the line of greatest condensation is parallel to the surface of the plates, and therefore to the axis of the prism. But if the plates be laid side by side in the direction of the length of the prism, the axis of the prism will take the equatorial position when the metal is paramagnetic, and the axial position when it is diamagnetic. Thus the position of equilibrium depends upon the direction of the planes of the plates, and not upon that of the axis of form of the entire mass.

These results fully account for the facts observed by Faraday and Plucker, when a crystal is suspended between the poles of a magnet. The molecules of a crystal are more condensed in directions parallel to the planes of cleavage than in the direction perpendicular to them. Hence if a crystal be suspended between the poles of a magnet, so that the line perpendicular to any set of these surfaces shall be horizontal, this line will take the *equatorial* position when the crystal is *paramagnetic*, and the *axial* position when it is *diamagnetic*. Thus the position of equilibrium of a crystal in the magnetic field is governed by the direction of the planes of cleavage, and not by that of the axis of form; and it consequently assumes a position different from that of an amorphous mass of the same material.

(65) We have already seen that iron is attracted less powerfully by a magnet when its temperature is raised beyond a certain limit, and that at a bright-red heat it loses nearly all its magnetic power. The same phenomenon is exhibited by nickel and cobalt, although the temperatures at which they cease to be magnetic are different. Analogous effects have been observed in diamagnetic bodies. Thus the repulsion of bismuth by the pole of a magnet is considerably weakened as the temperature of the metal approaches its point of fusion.

Different substances are, however, affected in very different degrees by the same change of temperature. Thus mercury is found to undergo no perceptible alteration in its capability of magnetic induction between the temperatures of 0° and 300° cent.; and sulphur is not sensibly affected in this respect, even at the temperature of fusion.

Faraday has shown that the gases are subject to similar laws; and that the magnetism of oxygen and of atmospheric air is sensibly diminished by augmentation of temperature. According to M. E. Becquerel, the diminution of the magnetic powers of the gases, produced by increase of temperature, is solely due to their diminished density.

(66) Let us now briefly consider the bearing of these results upon magnetic theory.

The phenomena of magnetic induction compel us to admit that the separation of the two magnetic fluids, under the action of an inducing force, is limited to the molecules of the body;* and we must suppose that the intervals of these molecules are either absolutely void, or are filled with some substance of a different nature, which is impervious to the magnetic fluids. The magnitude of these intervals is of the same order as that of the molecules themselves; but the proportion of these magnitudes is probably different in different bodies. The ratio of the sum of the volumes of the magnetic molecules to the entire volume may be termed the *magnetic density* of the body. Its magnitude will vary, even in the same body, with temperature and other physical conditions; and it is upon it that the capacity of the body for magnetism appears to depend.

This view is confirmed in a remarkable manner by the other properties of the magnetic metals. Iron and nickel

* It is not necessary to assume that the elements by which the movements of the magnetic fluids are circumscribed are the molecules of the body itself, although this is the most natural assumption. All that it is requisite to suppose is that their dimensions are extremely small.

are, as we know, the most powerfully magnetic of all known substances. But, when we compare the specific gravities of the metals with their atomic weights, we find that these very metals are those in which the space occupied by the molecules bears the greatest ratio to the entire volume, i. e., in which the magnetic density is greatest. We are therefore justified in concluding that the capacity for magnetism in these, and therefore probably in other metals, is due to the proximity of the molecules.

These views are strikingly confirmed by the effects of compression, and of temperature, which we have just been considering. We have seen that the capacity for magnetism in the same body is augmented by mechanical compression, and is even made to differ in different directions, according to the mode in which the compressing force is applied. When the density of the body is, by nature, different in different directions—as in crystals—its magnetic capacity is likewise different. The same view is likewise confirmed by the changes of the magnetic capacity produced by changes of temperature.

Quantum placet
at (as much as it pleases)

CHAPTER VI.

TERRESTRIAL MAGNETISM. DIRECTION AND INTENSITY OF THE EARTH'S MAGNETIC FORCE.

(67) When a magnet is supported by a thread passing through its centre of gravity, its magnetic axis assumes a definite direction, which is that of the Earth's magnetic force at the place and time of observation. If now the magnet be removed to any near point, whether on the Earth's surface, or above or below it, the new position of its axis is *q. p.* parallel to the former. We conclude, therefore, that for all near points the directions of the Earth's magnetic force are sensibly parallel. Consequently, in its action upon the bodies at its surface the Earth's magnetism, like gravity, constitutes a system of parallel forces; and we may apply the theory of such forces to determine their resultant.

(68) But magnetic bodies differ from other heavy bodies in an important particular, and the actions to which they are subjected have a corresponding difference. In the language of Æpinus, which we may use for convenience, they are charged with *two* fluids, one of which is *attracted*, and the other *repelled*, by the same magnetic pole; and these two fluids are *equal in quantity*. In the natural, or *neutral* state of these bodies, the two fluids are combined; the attraction and repulsion therefore balance one another, and there is no resultant action. The act of magnetization consists in the separation of the two fluids in each molecule of the body;

and this result, we have seen, is equivalent to a separation of the free magnetism in the entire mass, one portion of which becomes charged with one kind of free magnetism, and another with the opposite. In this condition the force exerted by the earth on the magnetic body is *directive* only, and has no tendency to produce translation in space. For, since the forces exerted by the Earth on the free magnetism of the several portions of the body constitute a system of *parallel* forces, their resultant must be equal to their algebraic sum. And as the two *opposite* magnetisms are *equal* in quantity, this sum is nothing, or the forces have *no single resultant*.

(60) In order to understand this inference more clearly, let μ denote the quantity of free magnetism in the unit of mass, at any point of the body. Then μdm will be the quantity contained in the element of the mass, dm; and the force by which this is solicited is $R\mu dm$, R denoting the magnetic force of the Earth. These elementary forces being all parallel, their resultant is equal to their sum, or to $\int(R\mu dm)$. But, as we have already seen, the force R may be regarded as constant for all near points; so that this resultant is

$$R\int(\mu dm).$$

Now the quantities of the opposite kinds of free magnetism in the entire body are equal; and consequently

$$\int(\mu dm) = 0.$$

Hence the resultant of the forces exerted by the earth upon the several parts of the body is nothing; and these forces can impress upon the magnetized body *no motion of translation in space*.

The preceding consequence may be easily verified experimentally. If a magnetic needle be supported by a thread attached to its middle point, and be rendered horizontal by the addition of a small weight to one of its arms, the suspending thread will be found to preserve always the vertical position. The horizontal component of the Earth's force, therefore, has no tendency to produce a movement of translation in the needle. The same thing may be shown to be true of the vertical component, by weighing the needle in a delicate balance, before and after magnetization; for the action on the arms of the balance will be found to be the same in the two cases.

(70) The effect of the Earth's magnetic force is to cause the needle to rotate, until it takes up a position in which its axis is parallel to the direction of the acting force.

In order to estimate this effect, let μdm denote, as before, the quantity of free magnetism at any point of the needle, and r the distance of that point from the centre. Then the moment of the force exerted by the Earth upon the element dm of the mass, is $R \sin \omega \; r \mu dm$, ω being the angle formed by the axis of the needle with the direction of the force; and, since R and ω are constant throughout the whole length of the needle, the total moment is

$$R \sin \omega \int (\mu r dm).$$

The factor, $\int (\mu r dm)$, in this expression, is denominated the *magnetic moment* of the needle. It is evidently not evanescent; for r changes sign at the same time as μ, and the action upon the two halves of the bar *conspire* to turn it. Let this magnetic moment be denoted by M, or

$$\int (\mu r dm) = M;$$

then the moment of the Earth's force to produce rotation in the needle is

$$MR \sin \omega;$$

and it vanishes only when $\omega = o$, *i. e.*, when the axis of the needle is in the direction of the force.

(71) It follows from the preceding, that the direction of the Earth's magnetic force may be experimentally determined, by supporting a magnetic needle by its centre of gravity, in such a manner that it shall be free to move round that point in every direction. For the action of gravity being thus counteracted, the axis of the needle will rest in the direction of the Earth's magnetic force. In the same hemisphere, the same extremity of the needle always *dips* below the horizontal plane passing through the point of support. The end of the needle which is lowermost in the northern hemisphere is commonly called the north pole; and that which is lowermost in the southern hemisphere the south pole.

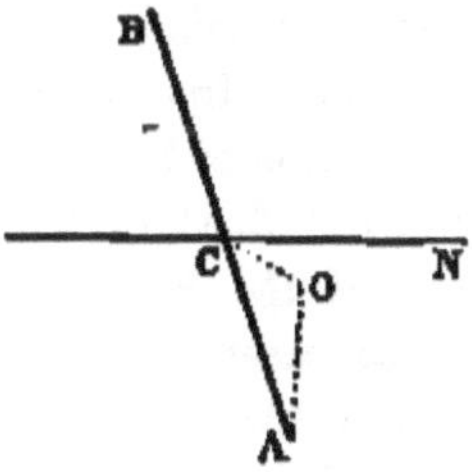

Let ACB represent the needle so balanced, A the north pole, and B the south. From the point A let fall the perpendicular AO on the horizontal plane passing through the centre of gravity of the needle, and draw CO. Then the direction of the needle in space will be known, when we know the angle, ACO, which its axis makes with the horizontal plane passing through C, and the angle, OCN, which its projection on that plane makes with the meridian. The latter angle is denominated the *declination*, and the former the *inclination* of the needle; the plane, ACO, is called the *magnetic meridian*. The terrestial magnetic force is completely determined, when these two angles, and the intensity of the force itself, are known.

We shall treat of the means of observing each of these in the following sections.

I. *Magnetic Declination.*

(72) The instruments contrived for the measurement of the magnetic declination are very various. We shall describe the principal, beginning with the simplest.

The Azimuth Compass is a horizontal magnet supported on a pivot, and carrying a circular card which is graduated on its edge. It is contained in a cylindrical box of brass, covered at the top with a plate of glass to protect it from the agitation of the air. The *sights* are a hair, or fine wire, and a slit in a piece of brass through which it is viewed. The wire occupies the middle of a rectangular frame of brass, which is attached to the exterior rim of the box in a direction parallel to the axis of the cylinder. The brass plate with the slit is similarly fixed on the opposite side of the box. The object whose azimuth is sought is viewed through the slit, and the instrument is turned in the horizontal plane until the object is bisected by the vertical wire. The division on the card, which is immediately below the slit, indicates (in degrees and parts of a degree) the azimuth of the object measured from the magnetic meridian.

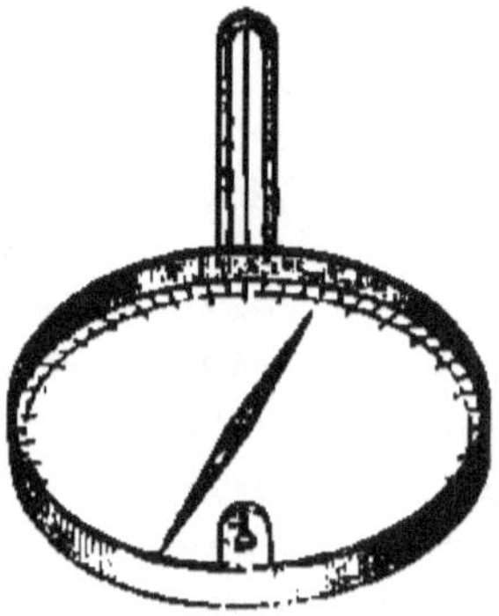

(73) In Kater's azimuth compass, the middle is 5 inches in length; and it carries a circular plate of talc, to the circumference of which is attached a card ring, divided to half degrees. Within the box is fixed a small plate of ivory, which projects over the margin of the divided ring; and a black line, engraved on this plate in the plane of the sights

serves to determine the coinciding division. The rectangular sight frame is moveable on a hinge, so as to be inclined to the top of the box at any angle, or to be folded down upon it when the instrument is not in use. This frame contains a sliding piece, in which is a segment of a glass cylinder, whose focal length is 5 inches.

The portion of the apparatus last described is used in observing the azimuth of the Sun. The frame being turned towards the Sun, and inclined to the top of the box at an angle equal to the complement of its altitude, a well-defined linear image of it will be thrown upon the ivory plate. The instrument is then to be turned in the horizontal plane, until this image coincides with the zero line on the plate. The division of the card which corresponds with the zero line gives the azimuth of the sun measured from the magnetic meridian. For the purpose of observing this coincidence, and reading the coinciding division, the instrument is furnished with a diagonal eye-piece attached to the plate which carries the eye-slit, and immediately below the latter. The magnetic azimuth of the sun being thus observed, its true azimuth is to be computed from the time, or from the observed altitude; and the difference of the two azimuths is the angle contained between the planes of the two meridians, or the magnetic declination.

(74) Dollond's variation transit is an altitude and azimuth instrument furnished with a magnetic needle; the needle being contained in a box which is attached to the plate of the horizontal circle. For the purpose of observing its position, the telescope of the instrument is converted into a microscope, by means of a small additional lens of short focus, fixed in a cap which fits upon the frame of the object-glass.

The cap must be so adjusted that the vertical plane containing the line of collimation of the telescope shall be unaltered by the additional lens. For this purpose it is divided into twelve equal parts, which are made to coincide successively with a fixed line on the frame of the object-glass; and the magnet being fixed, the vertical wire in the focus of the telescope is made to coincide with a fixed mark near one end in each case. Let a_0, a_1, a_2 --- a_{11}, denote the readings of the horizontal circle; it will be found that the difference of the readings corresponding to opposite points of the circumference of the cap, $a_6 - a_0$, $a_7 - a_1$, $a_5 - a_{11}$, &c., is a maximum at a certain point, and evanescent (or nearly so) in a position at right angles to the former. In this latter position the line of collimation of the telescope is in the same vertical plane, with and without the additional lens; and it is therefore the position to be employed in all future observations.

The mode of using this instrument is obvious. The additional lens being in its place, the vertical wire in the focus of the telescope is to be brought to coincide successively with two fixed marks near the two ends of the needle. The mean of the two readings of the horizontal circle is then the reading corresponding to the axis of form of the magnet; and, when corrected for the deviation of that axis from the magnetic axis, it is the reading corresponding to the magnetic meridian. The cap being now removed, the telescope is to be directed to the sun, or some other celestial object; and the horizontal and vertical circles read. The difference of the readings of the horizontal circle in the two cases is the *azimuth* of the sun at the time of observation, measured from the *magnetic meridian*. The azimuth of the sun, measured from the astronomical meridian, is deduced from its observed altitude, and the difference of the two azimuths is the angle between the two meridians, or the magnetic declination.

The deviation of the axis of form from the magnetic axis is found by inverting the needle, and noting the angles read off on the horizontal circle, when the wire in the focus of the telescope is made to coincide with its extremities in the two positions. As the magnetic axis will rest in the magnetic meridian, the axis of form will deviate from it in opposite directions in the two cases, and by an amount equal to the angle between the two axes; consequently the difference of the two readings is double of the deviation sought. This angle being once accurately determined, its amount may be applied as a correction to the observed reading of the ends of the needle, the needle being thenceforward used in one position only.

(75) The magnetic theodolite is a more perfect intrument. The following is a brief description of its essential parts:—

A divided circle, similar to that of a theodolite, is supported horizontally on a tripod base, with levelling screws. The upper plate of the circle has a projecting arm, carrying a pair of adjustable Y supports for the reading telescope, at a distance of 6 inches from the centre. The telescope rests in these supports on a transit axis,* which is rendered hori-

* This instrument has been modified so as to observe the celestial object *by reflexion*, the necessary adjustments being tranferred to the small mirror used for that purpose. A light gun-metal frame is attached to the uppper plate of the theodolite. Near one end of this frame are two Y supports, placed longitudinally, to receive the observing telescope; and near the other are two similar supports, placed transversely, to receive the cylindrical axle to which the mirror is attached. The magnetometer box is placed between, over the centre of the divided circle. The telescope, accordingly, remains *horizontal*, and is always in adjustment for the observation of the collimator magnet; and the image of the celestial object is brought to the cross of wires in its focus, by turning the apparatus in azimuth, and at the same time, causing the mirror to revolve. The axle is furnished with a slow motion for the purpose.

There are three adjustments required:—

1. The axle to which the mirror is attached must be horizontal when the instrument is levelled. This is tested by a small riding level. It may be effected permanently, with sufficient exactness, by filing one of the Y's.

2. The *mirror* must be parallel to the axis of the cylindrical axle to which it

zontal by means of a riding level. The magnet is a hollow cylinder, having an achromatic lens at one end, and a glass scale in its focus at the other. It is suspended by a silk fibre, and is inclosed in a small rectangular box of copper, which is made to fit on the upper plate of the circle. The suspension thread is contained in a tube, screwed into an aperture in the top of the box. The tube is furnished with a graduated cap at top, and a sliding pin to which the suspension thread is attached.

The point of the divided scale corresponding to the magnetic axis is found by clamping the horizontal circle, and observing the points of the scale which coincide with the fixed wire of the telescope, when the magnet is in its usual position, and when it is inverted in its support. The mean of these is the point corresponding to the magnetic axis; and it is with this point that the wire in the telescope is to be made to coincide in the observation of the declination.

(76) We must now consider the mode in which the position of the magnet is affected by the torsion of the suspension thread.

Let u denote the angle which the magnetic axis of the magnet makes with the magnetic meridian, and v that which it contains with the plane of detorsion. The moment of the force of torsion is $H v$, H being a constant coefficient. This

---

is attached. This is tested by reversing the axle in its Y's, and by noting the reflected division of a scale cut by the wire in the focus of the telescope, before and after reversal. The adjustment is effected by means of three screws at the back of the mirror.

3. The line of collimation of the telescope must be perpendicular to the axis. This may be tested by observing a well-defined distant object in the horizon, first by reflexion, and afterwards directly; the deviation of the line of collimation from the normal to the mirror is half the supplement of the angle through which the telescope is moved. The adjustment may be most readily made by moving the wire plate in the focus of the telescope.

is resisted by the earth's magnetic force, the moment of which is $mX \sin u$, or mXu, *q. p.*, the angle u being small; and therefore the equation of equilibrium is

$$Hv = m Xu.$$

Hence if w denote the angle contained between the plane of detorsion and the magnetic meridian,

$$w = v + u = \left(\frac{mX}{H} + 1\right)u.$$

The value of the coefficient, $\frac{mX}{H} + 1$, is determined experimentally, by observing the readings of the scale attached to the magnet, corresponding to two positions of the arm of the torsion circle connected with the upper extremity of the suspension thread. Let w_1 and w_2 denote the values of w in the two positions; u_1 and u_2 the corresponding values of u; then denoting the coefficient for abridgment by p,

$$w_1 = pu_1, \quad w_2 = pu_2.$$

Whence, subtracting and dividing,

$$p = \frac{w_1 - w_2}{u_1 - u_2};$$

in which $w_1 - w_2$ is the angle contained between the two positions of the arm of the torsion circle, and is therefore known; and $u_1 - u_2$ is the difference of the observed scale-readings converted into angular value.

The value of $u_1 - u_2$, in this expression, must be corrected for the actual changes of declination which take place in the interval of the two readings; or else the observations must be instituted in such a manner as to eliminate, of themselves, these changes. The former course is that recommended by Gauss, and usually followed, the actual changes of declination being determined by simultaneous observations with an auxiliary apparatus. But in this, and in all similar cases in which the interval of the observations is small, the effect of such changes may be eliminated with more certainty by repeating the readings alternately in an opposite order for a few successions. Thus the errors arising from a want of exact correspondence either in the movements, or in the times of observing the two instruments, are avoided.

(77) In order to determine the deviation of the plane of detorsion, w, the coefficient p must be altered, so as to change the value of u while that of w is unchanged. The usual course adopted for this purpose is to diminish the magnetic moment, m, by substituting a weaker magnet. The value of the altered coefficient is to be determined experimentally in the manner already described: let it be denoted by p', and let u' be the new angle which the magnetic axis forms with the magnetic meridian. Then if the magnetic axis of the second bar be made to occupy the same position, with respect to the stirrup and suspension thread, as that of the first,

$$w = p'u' = pu.$$

But, if a and a' denote the angles which the magnetic axes of the two magnets form with the line of collimation of the observing telescope, supposed fixed,

$$u' - u = a' - a;$$

and eliminating u' between this and the preceding equation, the error in the position of the magnet is

$$u = \frac{p'(a' - a)}{p - p'}.$$

Finally the error of the plane of detorsion is

$$w = \frac{pp'(a' - a)}{p - p'}.$$

The torsion cap is to be turned, through this angle, in the opposite direction.

The process which has been here described is a troublesome one, and requires a considerable time to complete it satisfactorily. Hence in a magnetic survey, in which time is of much value, it is desirable to dispense with its repetition at each station. This may be done by leaving the magnet in its box attached to the suspension thread. It is only necessary to fix the magnet in the box, when out of use, and so to prevent it from shifting in its transport from place to place.

(78) We may now briefly describe the mode of using this instrument.

The magnetometer box being put in its place on the horizontal circle, the magnet is to be freed, and the instrument levelled. The telescope is then to be turned in azimuth, until the vertical wire in the focus coincides with the zero of the magnet scale; the line of collimation of the telescope is then *q. p.* in the *magnetic meridian*. The verniers of the horizontal circle are to be then read, and their mean taken. The magnetometer box is then to be removed, and the telescope directed to the sun, or other celestial object. The vertical wire of the telescope being brought near the western limb of the luminary, the horizontal circle is to be clamped, and the verniers read. The observer should then note, with a good chronometer, the moments of contact of the western and eastern limbs of the sun with the vertical wire; the mean of these, corrected for the error of the chronometer, will be the time of passage of the centre. From this time, and from the known declination of the sun, its azimuth is to be computed.

Let A denote this azimuth; S and M, the corrected readings of the horizontal circle, when the telescope is directed to the sun, and to the magnet, respectively; then $S - M$ is the azimuth of the sun measured from the *magnetic meridian;* and the difference between this and the computed azimuth

A, is the angle contained between the two meridians, or the magnetic declination. Hence, if we denote this angle by ψ

$$\psi = A - S + M.$$

(79) It is obvious that the time to be employed in the computation of the sun's azimuth is the *apparent time* of the place of observation. Hence, in a magnetic survey, when the instrument is carried from place to place, the difference of longitudes of the stations must be known. But, further, as the rate of the chronometer cannot be depended on for any considerable time in travelling, it is essential to be able to determine its error from time to time. This may be done by noting the time, as shown by the chronometer, corresponding to an observed altitude of the sun. The true time being deduced from the sun's altitude and declination, the error of the chronometer is found. For the purpose of this observation the observer must be provided with a small sextant, or some other instrument for the measurement of altitudes.

An altitude and azimuth instrument may be employed with advantage, instead of the chronometer and sextant. In this case the azimuth of the sun is calculated from its observed altitude, and thus some of the sources of error above referred to are avoided. When this arrangement is adopted, the whole of the astronomical part of the observation should be performed with the altitude and azimuth instrument, the magnetic theodolite being used only for horizontal angles. The telescope of the theodolite is to be directed to some well-defined object in the horizon, when the magnetometer box has been removed, and the azimuth of the sun is to be referred to the same point, by means of the altitude and azimuth instrument. The transit adjustment of the magnetic theodolite may, in this case, be dispensed with. It is only necessary that its telescope should have a small motion in altitude to allow it to be directed to a distant mark a little above the horizon.

II. *Magnetic Inclination.*

(81) The magnetic inclination is observed by means of a light magnetic needle, supported on a horizontal axle passing through its centre of gravity. The force of gravity being counteracted, the needle takes the position due to the action of the terrestrial magnetic force alone. When the vertical plane in which the needle moves is parallel to the magnetic meridian, the needle will rest only when its axis is in the direction of the earth's magnetic force; the inclination of that axis to the horizon is, therefore, the magnetic inclination. The angle is measured by means of a vertical divided circle.

The axle of the needle is a cylinder of hard steel, which must be very accurately formed. This axle rests upon two agate pieces, whose upper surfaces are adjusted to the same horizontal plane, by screws bearing upon the lower edges. These surfaces are cylindrical. The agate pieces are fixed to two horizontal bars of gun-metal, which are connected with the base of the instrument; an interior moveable frame serves to lift the needle off the agates, when required.

In the earlier forms of the instrument, the vertical circle by which the inclination of the needle is measured was in the same plane with the needle itself, its interior diameter being slightly greater than the length of the needle, which played within it. In the instruments of the Dublin Magnetical Observatory, the plan of which has been generally adopted by English observers, the plane of the vertical circle is separate from that in which the needle moves, but parallel to it; and the extremities of the needle are observed by means of compound microscopes attached to the moveable arms of the divided circle. The circle is 6 inches in diameter, and is read, by verniers, to minutes; the lengths of the needles are 6 inches, 4½ inches, and 3 inches.

The vertical circle, and the supports of the needle, rest upon short pillars of gun-metal, which are fixed below to a rectangular platform. This platform, and the parts connected with it, have a motion in azimuth upon a vertical axis, which plays in a socket in the supporting stem of the instrument; and a horizontal divided circle, attached to the top of the same stem, serves to measure the azimuth of the plane in which the needle moves. The axis is rendered vertical by the aid of three adjusting screws; and a delicate level on the platform serves to test the adjustment. A detached case, formed of wood and glass, rests upon the platform, and protects the needle from the agitation of the air.

(82) The angle read off in this instrument is the angle which the axis of form of the needle makes with the line joining the zero-points of the vertical circle. This may differ from the true inclination from two causes:—1. The *axis of form* may not coincide with the *magnetic axis;* and 2. The *zero line* may not be *horizontal.* The former of these errors is corrected by making a second observation with the needle reversed on its supports. The direction of the magnetic axis remaining unchanged, the axis of form will deviate in this case, in an opposite direction to the former, and by an equal amount; so that the error is removed by taking the mean of the two observed angles. The error of the zero-line is corrected by turning the whole instrument through 180° in azimuth, and repeating the observations; the deviation of the zero-line from horizontality will disappear in the mean of the angles taken in the two opposite azimuths.

Finally, the magnetic axis of the needle will deviate from the direction of the Earth's force, whenever the axis of motion of the needle does not pass exactly through the centre of gravity, the weight of the needle conspiring with, or opposing the magnetic force, in determining the position of the needle. The error arising from this source is removed by *reversing the poles* of the needle by a pair of bar magnets, and repeating the observations; for it is obvious that the moment of the weight of the needle will in the one case conspire with the magnetic force, and in the other oppose it; and when that moment is very small (as it is in all needles nearly balanced), the mean of the two observed inclinations will be *q.p.* the inclination due to the magnetic force alone.

It will be seen from the preceding that, for a complete observation of the magnetic inclination, the position of the needle must be read off in *eight* positions—viz., with the face of the instrument *east* and *west;* with the face of the needle *direct* and *inverted;* and with the poles of the needle *direct* and *reversed.* The mean of the observed inclination in these eight positions is the inclination sought. In each of these positions the north and south ends of the magnet are both read, to eliminate the error of eccentricity; and from three to five readings are taken in each position, the magnet being lifted off its supports between the successive readings, to eliminate the error of friction.

(83) Usually the plane in which the needle moves is made to coincide with the magnetic meridian, in which case the mean of the observed angles is the magnetic inclination. But for the purpose of testing the axles of the needles, it is desirable to make, occasionally, a series of observations in various azimuths. The relation between the magnetic inclination, and the inclination of the needle to the horizon, is easily deduced.

Let the earth's magnetic force be resolved into two in the plane of the magnetic meridian, one vertical and the other horizontal. These components are $R \sin \theta$, $R \cos \theta$; R being the total force, and θ the inclination. When the needle does not move in the plane of the magnetic meridian, the latter force will be, in part, counteracted by the resistance of the supports. Let the plane in which the needle moves be inclined at the angle a to the magnetic meridian; then the effective part of the horizontal force is $R \cos \theta \cos a$. Denoting this by X, and the vertical force by Y, we have

$$Y = R \sin \theta, \quad X = R \cos \theta \cos a.$$

But, if η denote the angle which the resultant of these forces makes with the horizon,

$$\tan \eta = \frac{Y}{X};$$

and, substituting for X and Y their values,

$$\tan \theta = \tan \eta \cos a.$$

The azimuth, a, is easily determined. For it follows from this formula, that when $a = 90°$, that is, when the plane in which the needle moves is perpendicular to the magnetic meridian, $\eta = 90°$, and the needle is vertical. The vertical position of the needle, therefore, serves to determine when the plane of the instrument is perpendicular to the meridian; and the angle between this plane and the plane of observation, $90° - a$, is obtained by the help of the azimuth circle.

We may deduce the magnetic inclination from the observed inclinations of the needle in any two planes at right angles to one another, without the knowledge of the angle a. For, if η and η' denote the observed inclinations, in the planes whose azimuths are a and $90° - a$, we have

$$\cot \eta = \cot \theta \cos a, \quad \cot \eta' = \cot \theta \sin a;$$

whence squaring and adding,

$$\cot^2 \theta = \cot^2 \eta + \cot^2 \eta'.$$

A series of the values of θ having been thus obtained from observations in different azimuths, the difference between the mean, and the result obtained at the same time in the magnetic meridian, furnishes a correction for the errors of axle and limb to be applied to all future observations in the meridian. For further account of the theory of the dip-circle see Appendix.

III. *Magnetic Force.*

(84) The intensity of the Earth's magnetic force may be determined, either by observing the position of equilibrium of a needle, under the joint influence of magnetism and some other force whose law of action is known; or, by observing the time of vibration of the needle, when acted on by the magnetic force alone, or chiefly. The former of these may be called the *statical* method, and the latter the *dynamical*. We shall commence with the latter.

The moment of the force exerted by the Earth upon a freely suspended horizontal magnet is

$$m X \sin u;$$

where X denotes the horizontal component of the Earth's magnetic force, m the moment of free magnetism of the magnet, and u the angle which its axis makes with the magnetic meridian. When this angle is small, the angle itself may be substituted for its sine. But, in addition to the magnetic force, the magnet is also urged by the force of torsion of the suspension thread. The plane of detorsion being supposed to coincide with the magnetic meridian, the moment of the force of torsion is

$$h\,u,$$

h being a constant depending on the suspension thread, and varying with its length, and with the number of fibres of which it is composed. Hence, the total moment of the acting forces is $(mX+h)u$, or, if we make $h = mX \times p$,

$$mX(1+p)\,u.$$

The equation of motion of the vibrating magnet will be consequently

$$\frac{d^2u}{dt^2} + \frac{mX}{K}(1+p)\,u = 0,$$

in which K is the moment of inertia of the magnet. The integral of this equation is

$$u = U \sin \sqrt{\frac{mX(1+p)}{K}}\,.\,t,$$

the time being counted from the moment when the needle is in the magnetic meridian.

Now, when $u = U$,

$$\sqrt{\frac{mX(1+p)}{K}}\,.\,t = \frac{\pi}{2}.$$

The time, t, in this expression is half the time of vibration; wherefore denoting the latter time by T, we have

$$T = \pi\sqrt{\frac{K}{mX(1+p)}}.$$

Accordingly

$$mX(1+p) = \pi^2\frac{K}{T^2}.$$

(85) From the equation of the preceding article it follows that if the time of vibration of the needle be observed, and the constants m, p, and K, be otherwise known, the force X is determined.

Of these quantities, the ratio, p, is determined experimentally, by turning the cap of the torsion circle through any given large angle, and observing the corresponding change in the position of the magnet, in the manner already explained (76).

If the magnet be of a regular form, and uniform density, its moment of inertia K may be calculated. Thus in the case of a rectangular parallelopiped, supported by a thread whose weight may be neglected, the moment of inertia is given by the formula

$$K = \frac{a^2 + b^2}{12} \cdot \frac{W}{g},$$

a and b denoting the length and breadth of the bar, and W its weight.

When the foregoing conditions do not hold—as when the bar is supported by a stirrup of irregular form—the moment of inertia must be determined experimentally. This is done by observing the time of vibration of the bar, first, in its usual state, and secondly with its moment of inertia increased by a known amount. Let T' and T denote the times of vibration of the magnet, with and without the additional weight, and k the known moment of inertia of the latter, then we have

$$\frac{K}{T^2} = \frac{K + k}{T'^2}, \quad \text{whence } K = k \cdot \frac{T^2}{T'^2 - T^2}.$$

The added weight may be, as proposed by Professor Weber, that of two accurately turned brass cylinders, which are connected by a fine thread, and hang from the ends of the magnet. In this case their moment of inertia is given by the formula

$$k = \frac{w}{g}(r^2 + \tfrac{1}{2}l^2);$$

in which w denotes the weight of each cylinder, r its radius, and l the interval of the suspending threads, or the length of the magnet.

(86) If the same magnet, suspended by the same thread, be made to vibrate at different places, the *relative* values of the force at these places will be determined. For, if T' denote the observed time at the second station, the corresponding value of the force is given by the formula

$$m'X'(1 + p) = \pi^2 \frac{K}{T'^2},$$

m' being the magnetic moment at the second station; and dividing this equation by the former we have

$$\frac{m'X'}{mX} = \frac{T^2}{T'^2}.$$

Now, the magnetic moment of the same magnet varies with the temperature, the difference of its moments being $q.\ p.$ proportional to the difference of temperature. Therefore

$$m - m' = m'q\,(t' - t),$$

q being a constant quantity to be determined experimentally. Hence we have

$$\frac{m}{m'} = 1 + q\,(t' - t)\ ;\ \text{and}$$

$$\frac{X'}{X} = [1 + q\,(t' - t)]\,\frac{T^2}{T'^2},$$

(87) The times, T and T', in the preceding formula, are those corresponding to infinitely small arcs, while those observed correspond to arcs of finite magnitude. When the arc of vibration is small, and may be regarded as constant throughout the observation, the time corresponding to infinitely small arcs, is deduced from the observed time by means of the formula

$$T = (T)\left(1 - \frac{a^2}{16}\right),$$

the arc, a, being expressed in parts of radius.

Actually, however, the arc a diminishes from the beginning to the end of the observations; and it may be shown that the mean of the observed times is $q.\ p.$ that corresponding to the geometric mean of the extreme arcs; so that $a^2 = a'a_{,}$, a' being the initial, and $a_{,}$ the final semiarc of vibration, and

$$T = (T)\left(1 - \frac{a'a_{,}}{16}\right).$$

The observed time must also be corrected for the rate of the chronometer by multiplying by

$$\left(1 - \frac{x}{86400}\right),$$

x being the daily rate.

(88) The process here described was that originally employed for the comparison of the Earth's magnetic force at different places; the same magnet, suspended by the same thread, being vibrated at each place. It labours under two defects. In the first place we can infer by it, at most, only the *ratio* of the forces at different stations; and are unable to determine their absolute magnitudes, or to compare them with forces of another nature. And, secondly, the method fails, even in the relative determination of the magnetic forces, if the magnetic moment of the magnet employed undergoes any permanent change in the course of the observations. For these reasons it was of great importance to devise a method, in which the result shall be independent of the magnetic moment of the vibrating bar.

It will be observed that the equation of Art. (84) gives the value of mX, or the product of the Earth's magnetic force by the magnetic moment of the magnet employed, when the time of vibration has been observed, and the constants p and K are known. In order to determine the factors m and X, therefore, it is necessary to find a relation between them in which they are differently combined. This was effected by Gauss by employing the magnet so vibrated to deflect another, also suspended horizontally. The amount of this deflection serves to determine the *ratio* of the same factors, m and X; and the product and ratio being known, the factors themselves are absolutely determined.

In Gauss's method the deflecting magnet was placed so that the direction of its magnetic axis passed through the centre of the suspended magnet, and was perpendicular to the magnetic meridian. In this position it is obviously oblique to the deflected magnet, and does not produce its greatest effect. In accordance with the suggestion of Dr. Lamont, the deflecting magnet is now placed so that its magnetic axis shall be always at right angles to that of the deflected magnet. This condition is easily obtained by attaching the supporting bar to the upper plate of the divided instrument by which the deflection is measured.

(89) The magnetic theodolite, already described, answers very well for the purpose of this observation. A brass bar, divided into decimals of a foot, is attached temporarily to the upper plate of the instrument, at right angles to the line of collimation of the reading telescope; and the deflecting magnet is placed upon this, in the same horizontal plane with the suspended magnet, by the help of a sliding stirrup. A small vernier attached to the stirrup enables the observer to determine exactly the distance of the centres of the two magnets. The line of collimation of the reading telescope being brought, in the process of observation, to coincide with the magnetic axis of the suspended magnet, it is obvious that the axes of the two magnets are always at right angles.

The observations are made in the following manner. The magnet being suspended in its box, and the instrument levelled, the deflecting magnet is to be placed on the supporting bar, at a given distance from the suspended magnet, and with its north end turned towards it. The upper plate of the instrument, carrying the telescope and the deflecting magnet, is then to be moved until the vertical wire in the focus of the telescope coincides with the point of the scale of the collimator magnet corresponding to its magnetic axis. The verniers of the horizontal circle being then read, the deflecting magnet is *reversed* on its supports, so that its south end shall point to the centre of the suspended magnet. The suspended magnet is thus deflected in the *opposite* direction, and by an *equal* amount. The observations being repeated in this position, the difference of the two readings of the horizontal circle will obviously be double of the angle of deflection sought.

In order to correct for errors of centering, the deflecting magnet is now to be removed to the other side of the suspended magnet, and the observations repeated. The true deflection will be the mean of the observed deflections in the two positions.

(90) Let us now inquire in what manner the quantity sought may be inferred from the foregoing data.

The moment of the force exerted by the deflecting upon the suspended magnet, in this relative position, may be shown to be expressed by the formula

$$2mm'\left(\frac{1}{r^3} + \frac{p}{r^5} + \frac{q}{r^7} + \&c.\right);$$

in which m and m' denote the magnetic moments of the deflecting and deflected magnets, r the distance of their centres, and p, q, &c., constants depending on the distribution of free magnetism in them. At the usual distance of the magnets—not less than three times the length of the deflector—all the terms in the series beyond that containing the inverse 7th power of the distance may be neglected. The force, whose moment is thus expressed, is opposed by the action of the Earth upon the suspended magnet, tending to bring it back to the magnetic meridian; and the moment of this latter force is equal to

$$m'X \sin u,$$

u being the angle of deflection. Hence, in the case of equilibrium,

$$X \sin u = \frac{2m}{r^3}\left(1 + \frac{p}{r^2} + \frac{q}{r^4}\right).$$

We have therefore

$$\frac{m}{X} = \frac{\frac{1}{2}r^3 \sin u}{1 + \frac{p}{r^2} + \frac{q}{r^4}}.$$

The quantities, p and q, in this expression may be regarded as constant. Their values are to be obtained by observing at some one station the angles of deflection corresponding to three known distances. For we thus have three values of $\frac{m}{X}$, which equated in pairs, furnish two equations containing the two unknown quantities, p and q, alone; and by which therefore their values are completely determined.

The constants of the formula having been thus obtained, the ratio, $\frac{m}{X}$, corresponding to the observed deflection at any given distance will be known. Let the ratio so determined be denoted by Q; then

$$mX = \frac{\pi^2 K}{(1+p)T^2}, \quad \frac{m}{X} = Q; \text{ whence}$$

$$X = \frac{\pi}{T}\sqrt{\frac{K}{(1+p)Q}}.$$

(91) As the observations of vibration and deflection must be made in succession, and occupy a considerable time, it is necessary to apply a correction for the changes in the values of X and m which may occur in the course of the observation. In other words, we must reduce the observed value of mX, at the time of the experiment of vibration, to that which it had at the time of the experiment of deflection. Let ΔX denote the change of the horizontal intensity in this interval, and Δm that of the magnetic moment of the deflecting bar; then the *corrected* value of mX is

$$mX\left(1 + \frac{\Delta X}{X} + \frac{\Delta m}{m}\right);$$

in which ΔX and Δm are affected with their proper signs.

The value of $\frac{\Delta X}{X}$ is at once given by the differential instrument for the measurement of the horizontal force, to be hereafter described. The quantity $\frac{\Delta m}{m}$ is known, when we know the effect of temperature on the deflecting bar.

(92) Professor Lamont has pointed out the necessity of another correction, due to the change in the value of m produced by the Earth's inducing action. For the magnetic moment of the deflecting bar will be altered by induction, and by an amount which varies with the inclination of the bar to the direction of the inducing force. When the magnetic axis of the bar is situated in the magnetic meridian, in the process of vibration, its moment is *increased* by the full amount of the change due to the horizontal component of the Earth's force, X. On the other hand, when the same magnet is inclined to the magnetic meridian, in the process of deflection, its moment is *diminished* by the amount of the change due to the force $X \sin u$, which acts in its direction.

Let the whole change in the magnetic moment, when the magnet is in the magnetic meridian, be

$$\Delta m = \mu m.$$

Then the altered moments in the two cases are

$$m(1 + \mu), \quad m(1 - \mu \sin u).$$

The quantity μ may be found by placing the deflecting magnet vertically, with one of its poles in the horizontal plane containing the suspended magnet, the line joining that pole and the centre of the suspended magnet being perpendicular to the axis of the latter. The positions of the suspended magnet are then to be observed in four positions of the deflecting magnet. Let a_1 and a_2 be the readings of the theodolite, when the *north* end of the deflecting magnet is in that plane, and the deflecting magnet itself above and below; a_3 and a_4 the corresponding readings when the *south* end of the deflecting magnet is in the same position. Then the angle of deflection is

$$u = \tfrac{1}{4}(a_1 + a_2 - a_3 - a_4);$$

and the change of angle due to the inducing action of the Earth is

$$\Delta u = \tfrac{1}{4}(a_1 - a_2 + a_3 - a_4).$$

The relative change of the magnetic moment produced by the vertical component of the Earth's magnetic force is then

$$\mu = \text{cotang.} u \Delta u \sin 1';$$

and the corresponding effect produced by the horizontal component is obtained by multiplying by the cotangent of the inclination.

(93) In the method above explained, the element directly determined by observation is the horizontal component of the Earth's magnetic force; and the total force is thence inferred, by multiplying by the secant of the inclination. This method is inapplicable in the high magnetic latitudes. The relative error of the force, arising from a given error of inclination, varies as the tangent of that angle; and, where the inclination approaches 90°, the former error becomes so great as to render the result valueless. It is, therefore, of importance to devise a method, by which the intensity may be determined without the intervention of its horizontal component.

This end is attained by observing the position of equilibrium of a dipping-needle under the combined action of magnetism and gravity. A weight attached to the needle deflects it from the position due to the action of the earth's magnetic force; and from the new position of rest, the product of the Earth's magnetic force into the magnetic moment of the needle is determined, when the moment of the added weight is known. This mode of determining the magnetic intensity was originally suggested by Professor Christie. It has since been applied, under different modifications, by Mr. Robert Were Fox, and by the author of the present volume.

(94) Let us suppose, for generality, that the needle moves in any vertical plane, inclined to the plane of the magnetic meridian by the angle α; and let R denote the Earth's magnetic force, X and Y its horizontal and vertical components, and m the magnetic moment of the needle. Then, the effective magnetic forces are $mX \cos \alpha$, and mY; and their moment to turn the needle is

$$m(Y \cos \eta - X \cos \alpha \sin \eta);$$

in which η denotes the actual inclination of the needle to the horizon. This moment is opposed by that of the weight. Let this be applied in the manner adopted by Mr. Fox, namely, at the circumference of a light pulley, whose centre is on the axis of the cylindrical axle. Its moment is in this case independent of the position of the needle, and is equal to the weight itself, W, multiplied by the radius, r, of the pulley. Accordingly, the equation of equilibrium is

$$m(Y \cos \eta - X \sin \eta \cos \alpha) = Wr.$$

When the plane of motion of the needle coincides with the magnetic meridian, $\alpha = 0$; and substituting for X and Y their values, $R \cos \theta$ and $R \sin \theta$ (θ being the inclination), the preceding equation becomes

$$mR \sin (\theta - \eta) = Wr;$$

from which we obtain mR, the product of the earth's magnetic force into the moment of free magnetism of the needle, when W and r are known, and the angles θ and η given by observation.

(95) It is obvious that, by the preceding method, the relative values of the total force at different places may be determined, without the knowledge of the quantities, m, W, or r, provided that these quantities remain unaltered, or change only according to known laws. Now, we know that the magnetic moment, m, varies with temperature, diminishing as the temperature increases, and nearly in the same proportion. Hence, if t denote the *actual* temperature, t_0 any *standard* temperature, and m_0 the corresponding value of m, we have

$$\frac{m - m_0}{m_0} = -q(t - t_0).$$

q being a constant quantity. Accordingly

$$m = m_0 \left[1 - q(t - t_0)\right].$$

Again, the force of gravity, and therefore the weight, W, varies with the latitude; and the weight at any latitude λ is expressed in terms of the weight at the latitude of 45°, by means of the formula

$$W = W_0 (1 - e \cos 2\lambda);$$

e being a constant, whose numerical value is ·002588. When the places whose magnetic intensities are compared, differ only by a few degrees in latitude, this latter correction may be disregarded.

(96) If the magnetic moment were subject to no change but that above described, the *relative* intensities of the earth's magnetic force at different places could be completely determined. But this, as has been already observed, is not the case. The magnetic moment of a magnet diminishes slowly with time; and, it is, moreover, liable to sudden changes from mechanical concussion, or from the near approach of

other magnetic bodies. For this, and other reasons already adverted to, it is important to be able to eliminate the quantity, m, from the result. This may be effected by a supplemental observation of deflection, as in the case of the horizontal component. The product, mR, of the earth's magnetic force into the magnetic moment of the needle having been determined, as above described, by observing the position of equilibrium of the dip-needle when loaded with a weight, the ratio of the same quantities is to be found by removing the needle, and employing it to deflect another substituted in its place.

Let m and m', denote the magnetic moments of the deflecting and the deflected magnets; then the moment of the force exerted by the former to turn the latter is

$$mm'U,$$

U being a function of the distance of the centres of the two magnets, and of certain integrals depending on the distribution of free magnetism in them. The moment of the earth's magnetic force, opposed to this, is of the form

$$m'(Y \cos \eta' - X \cos \alpha' \sin \eta')$$

already assigned (94), η' being the inclination of the needle, and α' the azimuth of the plane in which it moves. Hence the equation of equilibrium is

$$Y \cos \eta' - X \cos \alpha' \sin \eta' = mU.$$

When the plane of motion of the needle coincides with the magnetic meridian, or $\alpha' = 0$, this becomes

$$R \sin (\theta - \eta') = mU;$$

which gives the *ratio* of the Earth's magnetic force to the magnetic moment of the needle, when U is known, and when the angles θ and η' are given by observation.

If now we multiply the equation of Art. (94) by this, m disappears from the result, and we have

$$R^2 \sin u \sin u' = UW r;$$

in which the angles of deflection, $\theta - \eta$, $\theta - \eta'$, are denoted for abridgment by u and u'. Thus the force is determined *absolutely* when the quantities U, W, and r, are known.

(97) But the angles u and u' are liable to error, arising from the friction of the needles on their supports; and the corresponding error of the deduced force varies inversely as the sine of the deflection. It is, therefore, requisite for accuracy that these angles should be considerable. There is no difficulty in augmenting the angle of deflection as much as we please in the first part of the process, in which the deflection is produced by a weight. But in the second the case is different; and, with the slender needles here employed, a large deflection can only be attained by placing the deflecting needle at a very short distance from the moveable one. The most convenient arrangement appears to be, to attach the former to the moveable arm of the divided circle which carries the verniers, and at right angles to the wires of the microscopes: so attached, it must always be rendered perpendicular to the deflected needle in the course of the observation, although in a different plane.

The quantity denoted by U, in this position, is a function of the distance of the centres of the two needles, and of the ratios of certain integrals which depend upon their magnetic distribution. It is easily shown that the variations of these ratios, arising from the gradual changes of magnetism of the needles, may be diregarded; so that, if the distance be invariable, the function U will be constant. This is a point of considerable importance; for it follows from it that, even if the value of U be unknown, R will be relatively determined by a process which is *independent of the changes in the magnetic moments of the needles.* Hence, if the value of the force be found at any one place, by any independent means, it will be absolutely known at all.

But the value of the constant U may be found by deflection, by means of the instrument itself, and the method therefore rendered rigorously *absolute.* In using the dip-circle for this purpose, it will be convenient to produce the equilibrium by turning the instrument in azimuth until the deflected needle is vertical; for, in this case, the deflecting magnet is horizontal, and can be placed in the usual position with respect to the deflected magnet without difficulty. For this purpose the apparatus is provided with a gun-metal bar, having a rectangular aperture, by means of which it passes over the box containing the deflected magnet, and rests on two supports fixed outside on the level of the agate planes. The deflecting magnet is to be placed on this support at different known distances, and on each side of the deflected magnet, its axis being in the plane in which the latter moves; and the apparatus is to be turned in azimuth until the deflected needle is vertical. In this case the general equation of equilibrium (96) becomes

$$-X \cos a = mU;$$

in which U is of the form

$$U = \frac{2}{r^3}\left(1 + \frac{p}{r^2} + \frac{q}{r^4}\right)$$

The quantities p and q are to be found in the usual manner, by repeating the observation at several known distances, and eliminating among the resulting equations. This being done, the deflecting magnet is to be removed from the bar, and placed in its ordinary position between the microscopes;

and the observation is to be repeated. If a_0 denote the corresponding azimuth, and U_0 the value of U,

$$-X\cos a_0 = mU_0,$$

whence

$$U_0 = U\frac{\cos a_0}{\cos a}.$$

The method here proposed appears to offer the following advantages:—

1. It is applicable with equal accuracy at all parts of the globe.

2. It dispenses with the employment of a separate instrument for the determination of the magnetic intensity, and with the separate adjustments required in placing it.

3. The constants to be determined—the magnitude of the added weight, and the radius of the pulley by which it acts—can be ascertained with more ease and certainty than those with which we have to deal in the method of vibrations, and are less liable to subsequent change.

4. The observations themselves are less varied in character than the usual ones, and may be completed in a shorter time.

CHAPTER VII.

DIRECTION AND INTENSITY OF THE TERRESTRIAL MAGNETIC FORCE AT DIFFERENT POINTS OF THE GLOBE.

I.—*Magnetic Declination.*

(98) It has been already stated that the terrestrial magnetic force is determined, both in direction and magnitude, when we know the position of the vertical plane containing the direction of the force; the angle which that direction makes with the horizon; and the number which expresses the intensity of the force itself referred to some known unit. Of these three elements the first was the earliest observed. The fact that a freely-suspended horizontal needle assumed a determinate direction was one of the highest practical importance to the navigator; and so it happened that the laws which governed this direction were studied, before the other phenomena of Terrestrial magnetism were attended to or known.

The directive property of the magnetic needle was known long before its *declination* was discovered. It is asserted that the polarity of the needle was known to the Chinese 1000 years before the Christian era; and that the property was even used by them as a means of guiding travellers by land. The first distinct intimation of the knowledge of the compass and its uses, in Europe, is to be found in the writings of Frode, an Icelandic historian, towards the end of the 11th century. But the earliest record of the observation of the declination itself is that contained in a manuscript letter of Peter Adsiger, in the library of the University of Leyden. If the authenticity of this manuscript be established, the declination of the needle was known to Adsiger, and was even measured by him, before the year 1269.

The declination of the needle was rediscovered by Columbus in 1492, more than two centuries later, in the course of his great voyage of discovery; and it was on the same occasion that he observed, apparently for the first time, that the magnitude of this angle was not invariable, but increased with the longitude.

(99) In the latter part of the 16th century, the declination of the magnetic needle was accurately determined in Paris, London, and other places; and since that time it has been carefully measured on sea and land, in every quarter of the globe which has been reached by scientific travellers. The results of these measurements were first collected by Halley. In Halley's chart of the declination, published in 1701, lines are traced at intervals of 5° through all the points of the Earth's surface at which the observed declination was the same. The *Halleyan lines*, as they have been called, excited great interest at the time, on account of their use to navigators.

It was soon found, however, that even at the same place the declination changed with the time; and that consequently the lines so constructed represented the phenomena only at the epoch of observation, or at times not remote. In the lapse of years, the position of the isogonic lines is sensibly altered. For this reason, and also because of the multiplication of observations themselves, and the improved methods of making them, charts of the lines of equal declination have been reconstructed from time to time. The principal of these are the charts of Mountain and Dobson, published in 1745 and 1756; Hansteen's map, for the epoch 1787, contained in the *Magnetismus der Erde*, published in 1819; the chart of Professor Barlow, published in 1833; and that of General Sabine, for the epoch 1840, published in the second edition of *Johnston's Physical Atlas*.

(100) Among these lines the most important are those connecting the consecutive points on the globe at which the magnetic meridian coincides with the astronomical, or the declination is nothing. Confining our attention for the present to the actual configuration of these lines, as shown in the latest of the charts above mentioned, we find that there are two principal *lines of no declination*. Of these the western traverses the Continent of America, and the Atlantic Ocean, in a direction from north-west to south-east. Commencing in the Polar Sea, in about 100° west longitude, its course has been traced through Hudson's Bay, and Lake Ontario, until it leaves the North American Continent near Cape Hatteras, in about 75° west longitude. It then traverses a portion of the Atlantic Ocean, to the eastward of the West India Islands, until it meets the Continent of South America near the mouth of the Amazon, in about 50° west longitude. Proceeding thence, in a south-easterly direction, it cuts the shores of the continent again near to Rio Janeiro, between 40° and 45° west longitude, and enters the South Atlantic, where it pursues the same direction as before. The course of this line presents but little inflexion, and is inclined to the meridian nearly at the same angle throughout.

The eastern line of no declination follows, for the most part, a similar direction It traverses European Russia from the White Sea to the Caspian, and enters the Arabian Sea in about 65° east longitude. It then pursues the same general direction in the Indian Ocean, as far as about 8° south latitude, where it makes a sudden bend, and follows the parallel of 10° south latitude, from 90° to 120° east longitude. To the eastward of this it bends again southward, intersects the north coast of Australia in about 125° east longitude, and finally emerges, and enters the great Australian bight, in about 130° east longitude.

In the space between these two lines—to the east of the former, and west of the latter—the declination is *westerly*. This space includes the eastern parts of America, the Atlantic Ocean, nearly the whole of Europe, and the whole of Africa. In the remaining division of the globe—to the west of the former line, and to the east of the latter—including the Pacific Ocean, and the greater part of Asia and America, the declination is for the most part *easterly*. There is, however, in the eastern part of Asia and the adjoining sea a *closed curve of no declination*, within which the declination is again *westerly*. This remarkable loop, inclosing part of Siberia and of the Chinese Empire, has the form of an oval, whose greater axis lies nearly in the meridian of 130° east longitude. The diameter of the oval extends from about 20° to 70° north latitude.

The point of the equator at which the westerly declination is greatest is in the Atlantic ocean, to the south of the bight of Benin, nearly in the meridian of Greenwich. There are two points of greatest easterly declination, with an intervening minimum. These three points are all in the Pacific ocean.

(101) From the form of the lines of equal declination Halley inferred that the Earth has *four magnetic poles*, two in each hemisphere, a stronger and a weaker. The positions of these poles, deduced by Professor Hansteen, are the following:—

	Lat.	Long.
Stronger, N. Pole,	70° 5′ N.	99° 0′ W.
Weaker, N. Pole,	85 21 N.	118 39 E.
Stronger, S. Pole,	69° 26′ S.	138° 35′ E.
Weaker, S. Pole,	77 17 S.	120 57 W.

(102) The lines of equal declination, although of great use to the navigator, are ill adapted to convey a distinct view of the phenomena in themselves, or to exhibit their physical relations. The most natural, as well as the most instructive mode of grouping graphically the observed results, seems to be that adopted by Captain Duperrey, in the charts published in 1836. The curves of Captain Duperrey indicate—not the deviation of the needle from the true north at each place—but its *actual direction*. The *magnetic meridians* of M. Duperrey are curves traced on the globe, to which the direction of the freely-suspended horizontal needle is everywhere a tangent. At each point, therefore, the direction of the curve is that of the magnetic meridian of the place. These meridians converge towards two points, one in the northern, and the other in the southern hemisphere. They do not, however, all meet in the same point; but the successive intersections of each pair of contiguous meridians form a closed curve, the central points of which may be denominated *magnetic poles*. The north magnetic pole, so defined, is nearly in 70° N. lat. and 98° W. long. That of the south magnetic pole is to the south of Australia, in 75° S. lat., and 138° E. long. nearly.

M. Duperrey has also traced on the globe a series of curves which are in every point normal to the preceding, or at right angles to the direction of the freely-suspended horizontal needle. These curves he denominates *magnetic parallels*. They serve, even more directly than the preceding, to point out the relations between the declination and the other magnetic elements. The magnetic parallel which deviates equally from the terrestrial equator on both sides, or that for which the sum of the latitudes = 0, may be denominated the *magnetic equator*. The mean plane of this curve is inclined to the terrestrial equator at an angle of 11°. Its ascending node is near the western coast of Africa, in about

10° E. long, measured from the meridian of Paris. Its descending node is in the Pacific ocean, in about 170° W. long.

II. *Magnetic Inclination.*

(103) The results of the observations of the magnetic inclination, made in different parts of the Earth, were first graphically represented by Wilcke, who published a chart of the lines of equal inclination in the Memoirs of the Academy of Stockholm, in the year 1768. A second, and greatly improved chart of the isoclinal lines was constructed by Hansteen for the epoch 1780, and was published in the *Magnetismus der Erde*, in 1819. The most recent map of these lines is that constructed by General Sabine for the epoch 1840, and published in the second edition of Johnston's *Physical Atlas*. These lines, in their general configuration, resemble closely the magnetic parallels already referred to. Within the tropics they are slightly inclined to the equator. The flexures increase with the latitude; and in the higher latitudes they tend to form closed curves, encompassing the points at which the inclination is 90°, or the needle assumes the vertical position. It is to these points that the name of *magnetic poles* is ordinarily given.

(104) It has been already mentioned that Halley and Hansteen inferred the existence of *four magnetic poles* from the configuration of the lines of equal declination in the higher latitudes. According to Hansteen the same conclusion is confirmed by the form of the isoclinal lines, and he concludes that there are four points on the Earth's surface at which the dip-needle assumes the vertical position. It has been pointed out, however, by Gauss that the existence of two points in the same hemisphere, for which the inclination is 90°, necessarily involves the existence of a third between them. The posi-

tion of the north magnetic pole has been exactly fixed by Sir James Ross, who reached the spot itself in his Arctic journey in 1831. It is situated in Boothia Felix in latitude 70° 5′ north, and longitude 96° 46′ west. The south magnetic pole lies to the south of Australia, and upon the Antarctic continent discovered by the same intrepid navigator. It is situated, according to Captain Duperrey, in 75° south latitude, and 138° east longitude.

(105) Much labour has been bestowed upon the determination of the position of the *line of no inclination*. Wilcke gave its position in 1768, so far as it could be determined from the then existing observations. It was redetermined upon a much larger basis of observation by Professor Hansteen and M. Morlet, its position being referred to the epoch 1780; and, finally, its position has been deduced, for the year 1825, by Captain Duperrey, from the results of the observations made by himself, from 1822 to 1825, in the voyage of the *Coquille*, together with those of other observers made nearly at the same time (1817–1830). In the former voyage the magnetic equator was crossed six times; so that certain points of the curve were fixed by direct observation. But observations of inclination taken in the neighbourhood of the equator are made to serve in determining the position of that line with nearly as much certainty as observations on the line itself. It will be shown hereafter that, in the neighbourhood of the equator, the inclination, θ, is connected with the magnetic latitude, λ, by the relation*

$$\tan \theta = 2 \tan \lambda.$$

Hence from the observed inclination we can deduce at once the distance of the place of observation from the magnetic

* This formula may be employed at all places at which the inclination does not exceed 30°.

equator; and this distance being measured in the magnetic meridian, a corresponding point of the magnetic equator is known.

The *magnetic equator* cuts the terrestrial equator to the south of the bight of Benin, in 5° 40′ east longitude. This node was determined by General Sabine. The curve thence ascends rapidly, and reaches its greatest latitude in the interior of Africa, in about 40° east longitude. It thence descends very slowly towards the equator in its progress eastward; cuts the eastern coast of Africa near Cape Guardafui; traverses the Indian Ocean in a direction nearly parallel to the terrestrial equator; crosses the Peninsula of India a little to the north of Cape Comorin; crosses the Peninsula of Siam; touches the Island of Borneo at its northernmost point, and finally reaches the equator in the middle of the Pacific Ocean, in about 173° west longitude. The eastern and western nodes of the magnetic equator are therefore very nearly antipodal. The curve thence descends to the south of the equator, to which it is nearly parallel through forty degrees of longitude, viz., from 110° to 150° west longitude; after which it descends more rapidly, and traversing the South American Continent, reaches its highest southern latitude close to the eastern shore, in about 40° west longitude. From this point it ascends rapidly, until it cuts the equator in the point from which we have set out.

It has been already said that the eastern node of the magnetic equator is in the Atlantic Ocean, in 5° 40′ east longitude. The position of the western node is less determinate; for the two equators are nearly coincident through a space of nearly eighteen degrees, from 178° east longitude to 164° west longitude. If we take the middle of this space as the western node, its position is 173° west longitude. The greatest distance of this curve from the equator, in the northern hemisphere, is in 57° east longitude nearly; its amount is 11° 40′. Its maximum of southern latitude is 15° 40′; it occurs in the interior of the South American Continent, in about 48° of west longitude. Its mean plane makes with the equator an angle of 10° 49′.

It will be observed that the course of this curve does not differ materially from the principal normal to the magnetic meridians, to which, as has been already stated, the title of *true magnetic equator* has been given by M. Duperrey; its course is, however, somewhat less regular. The irregularities of the former line, and of the magnetic curves generally, are ascribed by M. Duperrey to those which occur in the distribution of temperature, and are caused by the distribution of land and water on the Earth's surface.

III. *Magnetic Intensity.*

(106) The first observations, by which the changes of the intensity of the Earth's magnetic force depending on change of place were established, were those of Lamanon, made in the expedition of *la Perouse*, 1785-1787. These were followed by the observations of de Rossel, in the search for *la Perouse*, 1791-1794. The first published observations of the variations of the terrestrial magnetic force were those of Humboldt, made in his travels in the equinoctial regions of America in 1798-1804. By these observations the increase of the force with increase of latitude is placed beyond all doubt.

Since the publication of the observations of Humboldt, which were made in Southern and Central America, and in various parts of Europe, the attention so directed to the element of the terrestrial magnetic intensity has produced an accumulation of similar observations by later travellers. Among the most important of these, for accuracy and extent, are the observations of General Sabine, in 1818-1822, in the

Arctic regions; those of Hansteen and Due, along the coasts of Africa and America; those of Lutke, in a voyage of circumnavigation, 1826-1829; those of Hansteen, Due, and Erman, in the North of Europe and Asia, in 1827-1829; those of Fitzroy, 1831-1836, on the shores of South America, and in a voyage of circumnavigation in the southern hemisphere; those of the French scientific expeditions to the North in 1835-1838; and finally, those of Freycenet and Duperrey, in the voyages of circumnavigation of the *Uranie* and the *Coquille*.

But probably the greatest gains to magnetic science were those made by the Antarctic expedition of Sir James Clark Ross, in 1840-1843, in the *Erebus* and the *Terror*, followed by that of Captains Moore and Clarke in the same regions; by the magnetic survey of the British possessions in North America, by General Lefroy, in 1843-1844; and by the Magnetic Survey of the Indian Archipelago, by Captain Elliot, in 1846-1850, made at the expense of the East India Company.

(107) In the year 1826, Professor Hansteen grouped together the results of all the observations of magnetic intensity then known, in a chart of *isodynamic lines*. This chart was revised by the author, with the help of additional observations, and republished in 1832. In the following year, M. Duperrey presented to the French Academy a new map of the isodynamic lines, in which are included the results of his own observations. And finally, in 1837, General Sabine published in the Transactions of the British Association for the Advancement of Science, a memoir on the variation of the intensity of the magnetic force of the Earth, accompanied by a new map of the isodynamic lines, based for the most part on new observations. (See Map.)

In examining this chart, which is the most recent and the most exact that we possess, we find that the magnetic

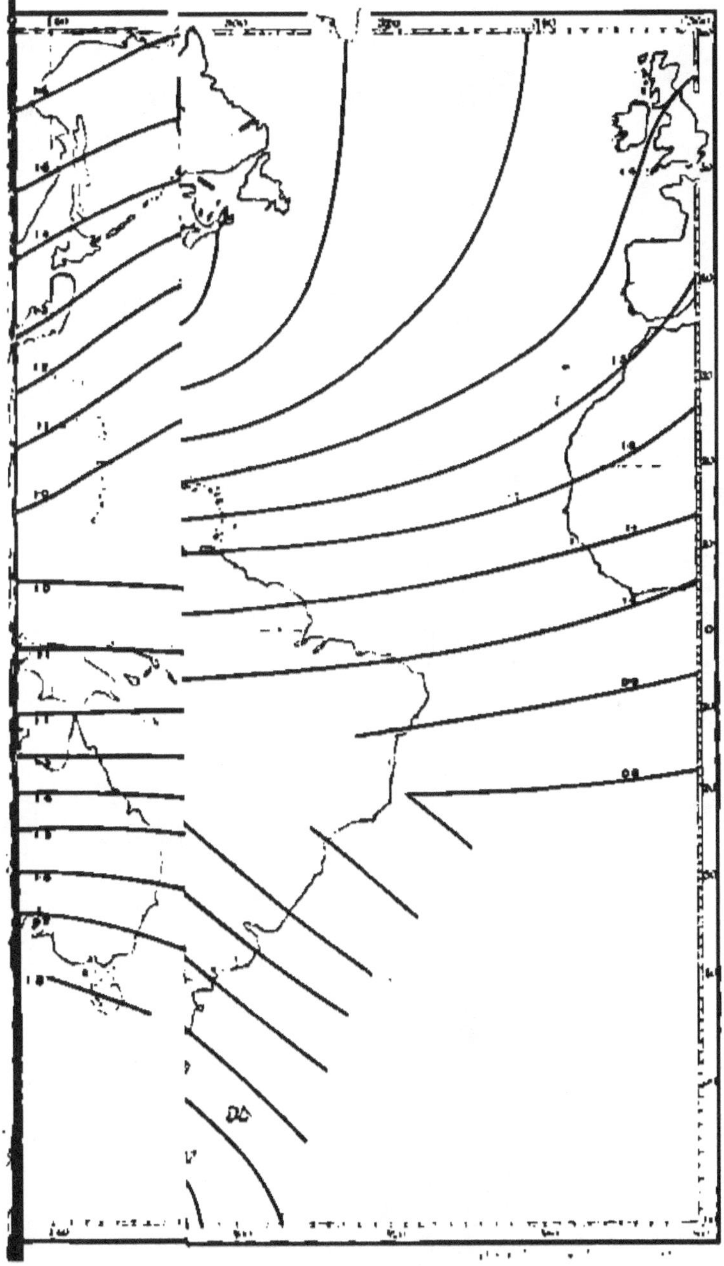

force increases, generally, in proceeding from the tropics northward and southward, and attains a maximum value at two points, or *foci*, in each hemisphere, of unequal intensity.

In the northern hemisphere the position of the stronger focus has been very exactly determined by General Lefroy. It is situated in British America, in 52° 19′ N. lat., and 92° W. long. The place of the weaker, or Siberian focus, is deduced from the observations of Erman; it is situated in 59° 44′ N. lat., and 118° E. long. The ratio of the forces at these two foci is that of 1·07 to 1. The weaker focus appears to have changed its place very considerably since the investigations of Halley, so far as its position may be inferred from the isogonic lines, while that of the stronger pole has varied little.

The two southern foci are much nearer to one another. Their positions, as deduced from the observations of Sir James Ross in his Antarctic voyage, are, the stronger in 64° S. lat., 138° E. long., and the weaker in nearly the same latitude, and in 125° W. long. The interval of longitude is accordingly less than 100°. The positions of the principal poles of force in both hemispheres are different from the points of 90° inclination, and are more distant from the terrestrial poles. The isodynamic lines, as they approach these foci, form closed curves. The observations in the southern hemisphere are not as yet sufficient to separate the curves which encompass the two foci.

(108) The line of *weakest force* on the globe has been traced with great care by General Sabine. It is an irregular line, lying for the most part to the south of the terrestrial equator. It reaches its maximum of northern latitude in the Pacific ocean, in about 165° E. long., where it attains the latitude of 14° north. Its southern limit lies in the Atlantic ocean, in about 20° W. long., where it touches the tropic of

Capricorn. It is not a line of equal intensity: on the contrary, it intersects the weaker isodynamic lines, which appear to form loops, in two points, one in the Atlantic, and the other in the Pacific ocean.

The least intensity observed by Humboldt was on a point in the magnetic equator, in latitude 7° 2′ south, and longitude 81° 8′ west from Paris. The magnetic equator was then supposed to be the locus of the points of *least intensity*, and also an *isodynamic* line; and it was accordingly inferred that the intensity thus observed was an *absolute minimum*. Humboldt accordingly referred all the other intensities observed by him to this, as the unit; and in this practice he has been followed by other observers. We now know, chiefly by the labours of General Sabine, that none of these assumptions are true; that the line of least intensity does *not* coincide with the magnetic equator, and that neither of these lines is an *isodynamic* line. Hence the unit of force thus adopted is purely arbitrary. The intensity of the force at Paris, referred to this unit, is 1·348. The comparison of the forces at London and Paris was made with great care by General Sabine, in 1827. The force in London, thus inferred, is 1.372. The forces at other places, which have been compared by observation with either Paris or London, are, by means of these numbers, reduced to the same unit. The intensity of the stronger magnetic focus has been found by General Lefroy to be 1·88; that of the weaker, as determined by Hansteen and Erman, is 1·76. The intensities of the two southern foci, as determined by Sir James Ross, are 2·06, and 1·96, respectively.

(108) Before concluding the subject of the distribution of the terrestrial magnetic force, it may be useful to refer to the hypothesis which has been employed by M. Biot for its explanation. According to this hypothesis, the direction and

intensity of the force exerted by the globe, at any point of its surface, will be the same as that emanating from a single magnet, whose axis passes through the centre of the earth in a direction perpendicular to the magnetic equator, and whose length is small in comparison with the Earth's radius.

Let EQ represent the magnetic equator, and E*m*Q a great circle on the globe, perpendicular to the plane of the equator. Let *nos* be the supposed magnet, whose centre *o* coincides with the centre of the Earth, and whose axis, *ns*, is perpendicular to EQ. Then, the length *ns* being very small in comparison with the distance *om*, the direction and magnitude of the force exerted by the magnet upon any point *m* at the Earth's surface will be given (45, 46) by the formulæ

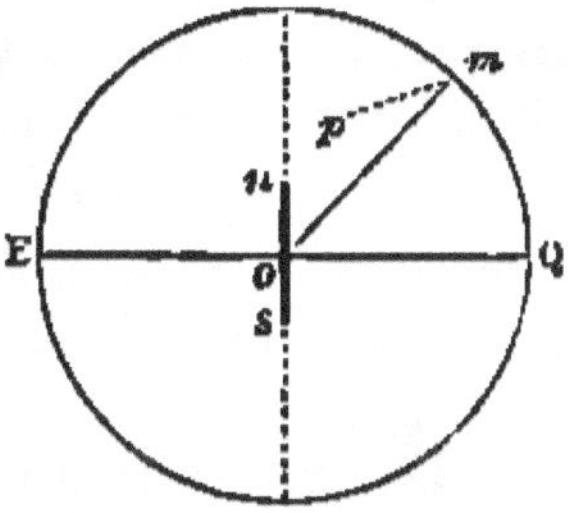

$$\text{tang } omp = \tfrac{1}{2} \text{ tang } mon, \quad R = \frac{m\mu}{a^2}\sqrt{1 + 3\cos^2 mon},$$

in which *m* is the magnetic moment of the magnet, *ns*, μ the quantity of free magnetism in the point acted on, and *a* the radius of the Earth. But if λ denote the magnetic latitude, *mo*Q, and θ the magnetic inclination, or the angle made by the direction of the force with the horizon of the place, there is $mon = 90° - \lambda$, $omp = 90° - \theta$. Wherefore

$$\tan\theta = 2\tan\lambda, \quad R = \sqrt{1 + 3\sin^2\lambda};$$

the force at the magnetic equator being taken as unity.

(110) Let us examine the consequences of these formulæ.

1. On the *magnetic equator* $\lambda = 0$, and, consequently,

$$\theta = 0, \quad R = 1.$$

I

Accordingly, the inclination will be nothing at all points of this line, and the direction of the needle horizontal. Again, the intensity of the force will be equal to unity, and less than at any other points on the Earth's surface. The magnetic equator is therefore, on this hypothesis, also the line of *minimum intensity.*

2. The points in which the axis of the magnet meets the surface of the Earth will be the *magnetic poles.* At these points, $\lambda = 90°$, and consequently

$$\theta = 90°, \qquad R = 2.$$

At the magnetic poles, therefore, the freely suspended needle takes the *vertical position,* and the force will be *double* of that at the equator.

3. The great circles passing through the line, *ns*, will be the magnetic meridians, and the declination at each point of them will be equal to the angle which they contain with the meridian of the place.

4. If planes be drawn perpendicular to *nos*, or parallel to the magnetic equator, they will intersect the globe in circles, which are analogous to the parallels of latitude, and may be called the *magnetic parallels.* For all the points of each such circle the magnetic latitude, λ, is the same. Hence θ and R are also the same, and the parallels will be *isoclinal* and *isodynamic* lines.

(111) We see from this account that the magnetic phenomena of the globe are represented, in a rude and general manner, by the hypothesis in question. In particular, it has been found that the formula,

$$\tan\theta = 2\tan\lambda,$$

is approximately true for points of the Earth's surface whose magnetic latitude does not exceed 30°; and it is probable that the law of the intensity may be depended on within the same limits. But a closer comparison of the results with those of observation shows that the discrepancies are considerable. The line of least force does not coincide with the line of no inclination; the points of greatest force on the Earth's surface are *four* instead of two; and none of these coincide with the points at which the inclination is 90°. Finally, the isoclinal and the isodynamic lines are not parallel circles, as they would be according to the hypothesis.

The theory of Gauss makes no such supposition. It regards the Earth as an indefinite assemblage of magnets, disposed in any manner; and it determines certain relations among the components of the force which hold generally. Finally, it expresses these components by general formulæ, the constants of which are to be obtained by observation.

From the observations which existed at the time of this beautiful essay, Gauss calculated the course of the magnetic curves on the Earth's surface, and delineated them in maps, which represent the condition of Terrestrial magnetism at that period, so far as the existing observations could furnish the data. But there were large blanks in these data, and large spaces on the Earth's surface wholly unvisited by observers. In particular, the Antarctic regions, at the time when Gauss wrote, were unknown and unvisited; and it is accordingly at this region of the globe that the theory is most defective. The expedition of Sir James Ross, to which we have already adverted, was undertaken mainly to remedy this defect; and the energetic head of that expedition, and his able assistants, succeeded not only in covering the inhospitable region with observations, but even (as we have seen) in determining with precision most of its critical points.

In addition to this, mainly through the exertions of General Sabine, magnetical observations have been vastly multiplied at other points of the Earth's surface; and the time has consequently arrived when a recalculation of the Gaussian constants, as they are called, may with advantage be undertaken. This laborious work is now in progress. General Sabine has completed the co-ordination of the observations; and Professor Adams has generously offered to devote his valuable time to the recalculations based upon them. The scientific world may therefore, before long, expect to see a series of charts exhibiting the actual condition of the Earth's magnetism greatly more exact than any which have been yet produced.

A brief outline of the leading points of Gauss's theory is given in the Appendix.

CHAPTER VIII.

MAGNETIC VARIATIONS. INSTRUMENTS AND METHODS OF OBSERVATION.

(112) For the complete determination of the Earth's magnetic force at any place, observation must furnish the values of three elements. Those which naturally present themselves for immediate determination are, the *intensity* of the force itself, and the two angles (the *declination* and *inclination*) which determine its direction. We may substitute for these, however, any other system of elements which are connected with them by known relations. Thus, the force being resolved into two portions in the plane of the magnetic meridian, one of them *horizontal* and the other *vertical*, these two components may be substituted for the intensity and the inclination.

The relations between the variations of these elements and those of the former are readily obtained. If R denote the force, X and Y its horizontal and vertical components, and θ the inclination, we have

$$X = R\cos\theta; \quad Y = R\sin\theta.$$

Differentiating, and dividing by the equations themselves,

$$\frac{\Delta X}{X} = \frac{\Delta R}{R} - \tan\theta \, . \, \Delta\theta; \quad \frac{\Delta Y}{Y} = \frac{\Delta R}{R} + \cot\theta . \Delta\theta.$$

Whence we have, by elimination,

$$\Delta\theta = \sin\theta\cos\theta \left(\frac{\Delta Y}{Y} - \frac{\Delta X}{X}\right);$$

$$\frac{\Delta R}{R} = \cos^2\theta \, . \, \frac{\Delta X}{X} + \sin^2\theta \, . \, \frac{\Delta Y}{Y}.$$

Thus, the variations of the two components of the force being observed, those of the total intensity and inclination are deduced. According to this arrangement, observation must furnish the changes of the declination, of the horizontal force, and of the vertical force. The instrumental means by which this is effected will be described in the following sections.

The Declinometer.

(113) The instrument designed for the measurement of the changes of the magnetic declination is a magnetic bar suspended by fibres of untwisted silk, and adjusted to the horizontal position. The actual position of the bar, and its changes of position from time to time, are read off by a telescope at a distance.

The magnetic bar of the instrument employed in the Dublin Magnetical Observatory, is a rectangular parallelopiped, 15 inches in length, $\frac{7}{8}$ths of an inch in breadth, and $\frac{1}{4}$th of an inch in thickness. In addition to the stirrup by which it is suspended, it is furnished with two sliding pieces, one of which contains an achromatic lens, and the other a finely-divided scale of glass. The scale being adjusted to the focus of the lens, the rays proceeding from each point of it are refracted parallel to one another, and to the line connecting that point with the centre of the lens; and the apparatus becomes a moving collimator, whose absolute position at any instant, as well as its changes of position from one instant to another, may be read off by a telescope at a distance. The arc-value of each division of the scale is 43″.20; and the visual angle under which it is seen in the telescope is so considerable, that it may be readily subdivided into tenths by estimation.

The magnet is surrounded by a copper ring formed of two rectangular bars, united at their extremities by circular pieces. The use of this is to check the vibrations of the bar, when accidentally disturbed, and thus to render the observation of its mean position more accurate, and more easy.

To the suspension thread is attached a small cylindrical bar, the ends of which are of smaller diameter, and support the stirrup which carries the magnet. The apertures in the stirrup, by which it hangs on the cylinder, are of the form of inverted Ys, so that the bearing points are invariable. A second pair of apertures, at the other side of the magnet, serves for the purpose of inversal; and care has been taken to render the lines connecting the bearing points of each pair of Ys parallel, so that there may be no difference in the amount of torsion of the thread in the two positions of the stirrup. The stirrup, and the other sliding pieces, are formed of gun-metal.

For the purpose of removing the torsion of the suspension thread, the apparatus is furnished with a *detorsion bar*, which (including appendages) is of the same weight as the magnet. It is a rectangular bar of gun-metal, furnished with a stirrup and collimator similar to those of the magnet. A rectangular aperture in the middle of the bar receives a small magnet.

(114) The framework of the instrument consists of two pillars of copper, which are firmly screwed to a marble base. These pillars are connected by two cross pieces of wood. In the centre of the top piece is the suspension apparatus, which is provided with a divided circle used in determining the amount of torsion of the thread. A glass tube, between this and the middle of the lower cross piece, incloses the suspension thread; and a glass cap at top covers the suspension apparatus, and completes the inclosure of the instrument.

The box which incloses the magnet, to protect it from the agitation of the air, is of wood. There are two apertures in the box, opposite to each other. The aperture in front, used for reading, is covered with a circular piece of parallel glass, attached to a rectangular frame of wood which moves in dovetails; the prismatic error of the glass (if any) is corrected by simply reversing the slider in the dovetails. The opposite aperture is for the illumination of the scale, and is also covered with glass, attached to a sliding piece of wood. The box must be rendered as air-tight as possible, to protect the magnet from the action of external currents; and a second, and smaller case, is placed within the exterior one to destroy the effect of internal currents, which are apt to be engendered within the box by changes of temperature.

(115) The observations made with this instrument are those of the *absolute declination*, and of the *variations of the declination.*

The determination of the *absolute declination* consists in the measurement of two angles, one of which is the constant angle contained between the line of collimation of the reading-telescope and the astronomical meridian; and the other, the variable angle contained between the same line of collimation and the magnetic axis of the bar. For the measurement of the former of these angles, an azimuth instrument is to be placed in front of the reading-telescope, and the theodolite telescope turned until the cross of wires in its focus is bisected by the image of the vertical wire of the reading telescope, used as a collimator. The verniors of the horizontal circle being then read, the theodolite-telescope is turned until the cross is again bisected by a distant mark, whose azimuth, Z, is known. If A denote the angle read off on the horizontal circle, the angle between the line of collimation and the astronomical meridian is

$$A + Z;$$

A and Z being affected with their proper signs.

The deviation of the line of collimation of the reading-telescope from the magnetic meridian is the difference between the actual reading of the scale, and the point corresponding to the magnetic axis, converted into angular measure. Let n denote the former reading, p the latter, and k the coefficient of reduction; then the angle sought is

$$D = k(n - p);$$

and the absolute declination is

$$A + Z + D.$$

The division of the scale, p, corresponding to the magnetic axis of the bar, is to be considered as the *zero point*, and must be determined with great exactness. It is obvious that this point will be given by the mean of two readings of the scale, with the magnet in the *erect* and *inverted* positions, provided that care has been taken to eliminate the declination changes which may occur in the interval of the two parts of the observation. The obvious method of effecting this elimination is to determine the amount of the declination change, by means of an auxiliary apparatus, and to apply it as a correction to the second result. The same thing may, however, be effected by taking a *series of readings* of the declinometer alone, with the bar alternately erect and inverted; the time chosen for observation being one in which the declination changes are small and regular, and the readings being made in as rapid succession as possible.

(110) In the Dublin Magnetical Observatory the telescope of the theodolite is employed as the reading-telescope; and the reference to the astronomical meridian is made by the help of a transit-instrument in the same room, which is also used in determining the errors of the chronometer. The centre of the theodolite is placed at the point where the magnetic axis of the suspended bar intersects the vertical plane in which the line of collimation of the transit-

telescope moves; and the base of the instrument is firmly fixed. The telescope was usually clamped in one fixed position with respect to the limb; and the angle between this position, and the line of collimation of the transit-telescope, is the angle A; the transit instrument being to the south of the theodolite, $Z = 180°$.

If, instead of the *actual* declination at any moment, we desired the *mean* declination of the day or of the month, we should take for n (instead of the actual reading) the corresponding mean result. We should thus obtain a new value of D, differing from the former by the amount of the declination change.

(117) In observing the *declination changes* the fixed telescope is alone employed. The observation consists simply in noting the points of the scale coinciding with the vertical wire, at the times

$$t - T, \quad t, \quad t + T,$$

t being the epoch for which the position of the magnet is desired, and T its time of vibration in seconds. The three readings being denoted by a, b, c, the mean point of the scale corresponding to the time t is*

$$\tfrac{1}{4}(a + 2b + c).$$

Let n denote the resulting number, deduced as above; n_0 the number for any other moment of observation, with which the present is compared; and a the angle corresponding to a single division of the scale. Then the change of angle in the position of the bar is

$$r - r_0 = a(n - n_0).$$

(118) Before the actual changes of declination can be

* See Appendix.

inferred from the changes of position of the suspended magnet, a correction must be applied for the effect of torsion of the suspension thread. It has been already shown (70) that

$$w = pu,$$

in which u is the angle which the magnetic axis of the suspended bar makes with the magnetic meridian, w the angle which the plane of detorsion contains with the same, and p a constant coefficient depending on the ratio of the magnetic force to the force of torsion, whose value is readily found by experiment. But $w = r + u$, r being the angle which the magnet makes with the plane of detorsion; hence

$$r = (p - 1)u = \frac{p-1}{p} w; \text{ and } w = \frac{p}{p-1} r.$$

Hence, if r_0 and w_0 denote the values of r and w corresponding to any given epoch, we have

$$w - w_0 = \frac{p}{p-1}(r - r_0),$$

in which the angle $w - w_0$ is the actual change of declination, and $r - r_0$ the corresponding change in the observed position of the magnet. Wherefore if we make

$$k = \frac{pa}{p-1},$$

a being the arc-value of one division of the scale,

$$w - w_0 = k(n - n_0).$$

The Bifilar Magnetometer.

(119) The variations of the horizontal component of the Earth's magnetic force may be ascertained by deflecting a horizontal magnet into a position transverse to the magnetic meridian, and observing its changes of position. For the posi-

tion of equilibrium of such a magnet depends upon the relation of the Earth's magnetic force to the deflecting force; and if the deflecting force be constant, the *changes* of position are connected with the changes of the magnetic force by a simple relation. This principle was first applied to the determination of the diurnal variations of the horizontal magnetic intensity by Professor Christie. A pair of bar magnets were placed in the magnetic meridian passing through the centre of the suspended magnet, one on either side, and with their north ends turned to the south. The suspended magnet was thereby deflected from the magnetic meridian; the magnitude of the deflection depending upon the ratio of the two equilibrating forces.

The torsion of a suspending wire may be employed with advantage, as the deflecting force, instead of the attraction and repulsion of fixed magnets. But the best mode of producing the desired deflection is to suspend the magnet by two equidistant threads, or wires, by the rotation of the upper extremities of which, round their middle point, the magnet may be forced to take up a position inclined at any required angle to the magnetic meridian. This arrangement, which is denominated the *bifilar suspension*, is due to Sir W. Snow Harris, who substituted it for that of the ordinary balance of torsion in his electrical researches. It was first applied by Gauss to the measurement of the changes of the magnetic force; and the instrument which he devised for that purpose has thence been called the *bifilar magnetometer*.

(120) The bifilar magnetometer is a magnet bar, suspended horizontally by two equidistant wires, and maintained by the rotation of their upper extremities in a position at right angles to the magnetic meridian.

It is manifest that the weight of the magnet, so suspended, tends to bring it into the position in which the two wires are in the same plane throughout. The Earth's magnetic force, on the other hand, draws the bar towards the magnetic meridian; and it will consequently rest in the position in which the moments of these opposing forces are equal. Let us in the first place consider the directive force due to the resolved part of the weight.

The line connecting the upper extremities of the wires being turned through any angle, the wires are no longer vertical. The weight is consequently raised; and its tendency to descend will engender a directive force, by which the line joining the lower extremities of the wires will be urged towards the vertical plane passing through the upper. Let half the weight be conceived to be applied to each of the former points; and let each half be resolved into two forces, one in the direction of the wire itself, and the other horizontal. The former of these is destroyed by the reaction of the fixed point; the latter is equal to

$$\tfrac{1}{2} W \tan i;$$

W being the weight of the magnet and its appendages, and i the inclination of the wires to the vertical. The effective part of this force is $\frac{1}{2} W \tan i \cos \frac{1}{2} v$, v being the angle formed by the vertical planes passing through the bearing points above and below. Hence the total moment of the directive force due to the resolved part of the weight is

$$W a \tan i \cos \tfrac{1}{2} v,$$

a being half the interval of the wires. But we have

$$\sin i = 2 \frac{a}{l} \sin \tfrac{1}{2} v,$$

l being the length of the wires. And l being always great in comparison with a, the angle i is always small, and we may substitute its sine for its tangent. Hence the total moment of the force due to the weight is

$$W\frac{a^2}{l}\sin v.$$

(121) The directive force arising from the resolved part of the weight being found, it is easy to form the equation of equilibrium. For this force is opposed by that which the Earth's magnetism exerts upon the bar, *i. e.* by the force mX, in which X denotes the horizontal component of the Earth's magnetic force, and m the moment of free magnetism of the bar. And the moment of this force to turn the bar is

$$mX\sin u,$$

u being the angle which the magnetic axis of the bar makes with the magnetic meridian. The equation of equilibrium, therefore, is

$$mX\sin u = W\frac{a^2}{l}\sin v.$$

and when the bar is brought into the position perpendicular to the magnetic meridian, in which position the Earth's magnetic force acts with the greatest mechanical advantage, we have

$$mX = W\frac{a^2}{l}\sin v.$$

(122) As all the quantities involved in the second member of the preceding equation may be known by direct measurement, we can deduce in this way the value of the product of the Earth's magnetic force into the moment of free magnetism of the bar, which is usually obtained by experiments of vibration, and so employ the instrument in measures of *absolute* force. The experimental difficulty in such a process would consist in the determination of the quantity a, which should be known to a very small fractional part of its actual value.

This difficulty has been in some degree overcome by the measuring apparatus connected with the suspension, which serves to determine the interval of the wires, at their upper extremities, to the $\frac{1}{1000}$th of an inch. But for many reasons this method is practically inferior to the ordinary process. One of the chief causes of this inferiority is, that the elasticity of the suspending wires—a force not easily valued—conspires with the directive force arising from the weight in determining the position of equilibrium; and if, to remedy this, parallel fibres of silk be adopted for the suspension, we should be involved in the uncertainty of the position of the resultant of these parallel strains, in determining the interval of the suspending threads.

(123) The chief use of the instrument is to observe the *variations* of the force. The magnet, it has been shown, is acted on by two forces, and rests in the position in which their moments are equal. But one of these forces being variable, the position of equilibrium must vary likewise; and the variations of angle are connected with the variations of force. Differentiating the equation of Art. (121) with respect to X, m, and r, and dividing by the equation itself, we have

$$\frac{\Delta X}{X} + \frac{\Delta m}{m} = \cot r \, \Delta r,$$

the angle Δr being expressed in parts of radius.

The angle Δr is observed by means of a collimator and fixed telescope, in the same manner as the changes of declination. Let n denote the actual reading of the scale of the collimator, and n_0 the reading at some other epoch; then the corresponding variation of the angle is

$$\Delta r = (n - n_0)\, a.$$

Again, if t and t_0 denote the temperatures, in degrees of

Fahrenheit, at the two epochs; and q the relative change of the magnetic moment corresponding to one degree;

$$-\frac{\Delta m}{m} = q(t - t_0).$$

And, substituting, we have

$$\frac{\Delta X}{X} = k(n - n_0) + q(t - t_0),$$

in which we have made, for abridgment, $k = a \cot v$.

(124) The scale-coefficient of the bifilar magnetometer, k, may also be determined by observing the changes of position of the suspended magnet produced by a fixed magnet, whose force conspires with, or is opposed to, the force of the Earth. For, when the distance of this latter magnet is considerable in proportion to its length, the effect of the added force is the same as that produced by a small increase (or diminution) of the Earth's magnetic force; so that if the effect produced by a *given* added force be observed, *in scale divisions* of the instrument, the scale coefficient itself will be determined.

To apply this method, let a small magnet be placed in the same horizontal plane with the bifilar magnet, and with its axis in the right line passing through the centre of the latter, and perpendicular to its axis; and let n denote the number of scale divisions corresponding to the angle of deflection. Let the deflecting magnet be then transferred into a similar position with respect to the unifilar magnet, and be placed at the *same distance* from it; and let n' be the number of scale divisions in the produced deflection. Then, the distances being considerable in proportion to the length of the deflecting magnet, the scale-coefficient of the bifilar magnet will be expressed, in terms of that of the unifilar magnet, by the formula

$$k = k' \tan 1'. \frac{n'}{n}.$$

The advantage of this method is, that it necessarily includes *all* the circumstances upon which the quantity sought depends; another important advantage is, that it may be performed without disturbing the adjustments of the instrument, and may therefore be repeated as often as is desired.*

This method is due to Mr. Broun.

(125) The magnet of the bifilar magnetometer is of the same dimensions as that of the declinometer. The collimator, by which its changes of position are observed, is inclosed in a light tube attached to the stirrup, and has a motion in azimuth; this arrangement enables the observer to choose the place of the reading-telescope according to convenience, and also facilitates the adjustment.

The suspending wire is of gold, and its diameter the $\frac{8}{1000}$th of an inch. It passes round a small grooved wheel, on the axis of which the stirrup rests by inverted *Ys*. The interval of the wires is altered at their upper extremities, by means of two screws (one right-handed and the other left-handed) cut in the same cylinder, the wires being lodged in the intervals of the threads, and their distance regulated by a micrometer head. The micrometer head is divided into 100 parts; and, as one revolution of the head corresponds to two threads of the screw, a single division is equivalent to .000519, or the $\frac{1}{2000}$th of an inch nearly.

The larger parts of this apparatus,—the box, the framework, and the support,—are similar to those of the declinometer. It is furnished with a thermometer, the bulb of which is within the box, for the purpose of ascertaining the interior temperature; and with a copper ring used in checking the vibrations. A brass weight, which is occasionally attached below the collimator, supplies the place of a detorsion bar.

* The scale coefficient of the balance magnetometer may also be found by a similar method.

(126) The following is the mode by which the magnet is brought into the position perpendicular to the magnetic meridian :—

1. The magnetic axis being brought approximately into the magnetic meridian, by turning the moveable arm of the torsion-circle, the collimator is turned by its independent motion, until some point about the middle of the scale coincides with the vertical wire of the fixed telescope. This point of the scale is noted in the usual manner.

2. The magnet being then removed, and the brass weight attached, the new point of the scale which coincides with the wire of the telescope is noted. Then, if the magnet had been placed, in the previous experiment, in its *direct* position (i. e. north end to north), the deviation of the plane of detorsion from the magnetic meridian is $u + r$, u being the angle which the axis of the magnet makes with the meridian, and r the angle of torsion, or the angle formed by the lines connecting the bearing points of the wires above and below. But these angles are connected by the equation,

$$F \sin u = G \sin r,$$

in which we have made, for abridgment, $mX = F$, $\frac{wa^2}{l} = G$.
And when the angles themselves are small, this becomes

$$Fu = Gr.$$

Accordingly the error of the plane of detorsion is

$$\left(\frac{G}{F} + 1\right) r.$$

If, on the other hand, the magnet had been *reversed* (i. e. north end to south), the error is $u - r$, or

$$\left(\frac{G}{F} - 1\right) r.$$

The moveable arm of the torsion circle is then turned

through this angle, in the opposite direction; and the plane of detorsion is in the magnetic meridian.

3. The moveable arm of the torsion circle is turned through 90°; and the plane of detorsion is perpendicular to the magnetic meridian. The collimator is then turned back, until some point about the middle of the scale coincides with the vertical wire of the fixed telescope; and the reading is noted.

4. The brass weight is now removed, and the magnet replaced. The magnetic force of the Earth will bring it back towards the magnetic meridian. Then the moveable arm of the torsion circle is turned, in the same direction as before, until the point of the scale last noted is made to coincide again with the wire of the telescope. The magnetic axis is then in the plane perpendicular to the magnetic meridian, and the adjustment is complete.

The Balance Magnetometer.

(127) In order to determine completely the laws of the changes to which the Earth's magnetic force is subject, observation must furnish the values of three distinct elements. The variations in the direction and magnitude of the horizontal component of the force are given, as we have seen, by means of the declinometer, and the bifilar magnetometer; but it remained to devise a mode of observing the third element. The means employed for this purpose in the Dublin Magnetical Observatory consisted of a magnet supported upon agate planes by a horizontal axle, and brought into the horizontal position by means of an adjustable weight. The changes of position of such a magnet will give the variations of the vertical component of the force.

Let us suppose that the vertical plane in which the needle moves is perpendicular to the magnetic meridian. In this case the horizontal component of the Earth's force is counteracted by the resistance of the supports, and the position of equilibrium of the magnet is determined by the vertical component alone. In its mean state this component is balanced by the weight, and the magnet rests in the horizontal position. But upon any variation of the magnitude of the force, the magnet will move, and take up a new position of equilibrium slightly inclined to the horizon. When the vertical force *increases*, the north end is *depressed* below the horizontal plane passing through the axis; it is raised above it, upon any diminution of the same force. The changes of force are connected with the changes of position by a relation which we proceed to investigate.

If η denote the inclination of the magnet to the horizon, the moment of the force exerted by the Earth upon it is $mY\cos\eta$, Y being the vertical component of the force, and m the magnetic moment of the magnet. But if the centre of gravity and centre of motion be not coincident, the force of gravity also exerts an effect to turn the magnet, whose moment is $wr\cos(\eta-\epsilon)$, w being the weight of the bar, r the distance of the centre of gravity from the axle, and ϵ the angle which the connecting line makes with the magnetic axis of the magnet. In the case of equilibrium, therefore,

$$mY\cos\eta = wr\cos(\eta-\epsilon).$$

When the weight is so adjusted, as to bring the magnet into the horizontal position, this becomes

$$mY = wr\cos\epsilon.$$

The change of position due to any change in the Earth's magnetic force is found by differentiating the former of these equations with respect to η and Y and m, and dividing by the equation itself. We thus obtain

$$\frac{\Delta Y}{Y} + \frac{\Delta m}{m} = [\tan\eta - \tan(\eta-\epsilon)]\,\delta\eta\,;$$

which gives, generally, the relation between the changes of inclination, and the changes of force. When $\eta = 0$, this is reduced to the simple form

$$\frac{\Delta Y}{Y} + \frac{\Delta m}{m} = \tan \epsilon \,.\, \delta\eta.$$

Accordingly the changes of the vertical force are inferred from the observed changes of angle, by multiplying by $\tan \epsilon$.

(128) Before we can infer the changes of force by the preceding formula, it is necessary to know the angle, ϵ, which the line joining the centre of gravity and centre of motion makes with the axis. In order to determine this, it would be necessary to observe the position of the magnet when inverted on its supports; and for this purpose the axle should have the form of the section of a cylinder, the axis of which coincided exactly with the knife-edge. The accuracy required in the construction of this part, however, is such as to present almost insuperable difficulties in practice; and it fortunately happens that the determination in question may be dispensed with, and the coefficient obtained, by a simpler process.

Let us suppose that the magnet is disturbed from its position of equilibrium through any small angle η; it will then, when left to itself, return to that position with an accelerated velocity, and vibrate on either side according to the law of the pendulum. The time of this vibration serves to determine the coefficient in question.

To understand this, let η_0 be the inclination of the needle corresponding to the position of equilibrium, η any other inclination deviating from the preceding, and F the moment of the force brought into play by the displacement. Then

$$0 = mY \cos \eta_0 - wr \cos (\eta_0 - \epsilon);$$

$$F = mY \cos \eta - wr \cos (\eta - \epsilon).$$

Now, let $\eta = \eta_0 + \delta\eta$, $\delta\eta$ being a small quantity. Substituting in the latter equation, and substracting the former, we have $F = -G\delta\eta$, in which

$$G = mY \sin \eta_0 - ur \sin (\eta_0 - \epsilon).$$

Hence the magnet will return to its position with a force proportional to the displacement, and will oscillate round that position according to the law of the pendulum; and the time of vibration will be given by the formula

$$T = \pi \sqrt{\frac{K}{G}},$$

K denoting the moment of inertia of the magnet.

When $\eta_0 = 0$, the value of G becomes

$$G = ur \sin \epsilon = mY \tan \epsilon,$$

since $mY = ur \cos \epsilon$. Accordingly we have

$$mY \tan \epsilon = \pi^2 \frac{K}{T^2}.$$

Now let the same magnet be suspended horizontally, and made to vibrate; and let T' denote the time of vibration in the horizontal plane. Then

$$mX = \pi^2 \frac{K}{T'^2}.$$

Dividing the former of these equations by the latter, and observing that $\frac{Y}{X} = \tan \theta$, there is

$$\tan \theta \tan \epsilon = \frac{T'^2}{T^2}.$$

Accordingly the variations of the vertical component of the magnetic force are expressed in terms of the changes of the position of the magnet, by the formula

$$\frac{\Delta Y}{Y} + \frac{\Delta m}{m} = \text{cotan}\, \theta \,.\, \frac{T'^2}{T^2} \,.\, \delta\eta.$$

The same formula holds good, whatever be the azimuth of the plane in which the needle moves.

The changes of angle, $\delta\eta$, are observed by micrometer microscopes. Let $n - n_0$ denote the number of divisions of the scale of the instrument, corresponding to the angle $\delta\eta$, and a the angle (in parts of radius) corresponding to a single division; then $\delta\eta = a(n - n_0)$. Hence, if we make for abridgment,

$$k = a \cot \theta \frac{T'^2}{T^2},$$

the changes of force will be expressed, as in the case of the horizontal component, by the formula,

$$\frac{\Delta Y}{Y} = k(n - n_0) + q(t - t_0);$$

where t denotes the temperature in degrees of Fahrenheit, at the time of observation, t_0 the standard temperature, and q the relative change of the magnetic moment of the needle corresponding to one degree.

(129) The magnet is 12 inches in length. It has a cross of wires at each end, attached by means of a small ring of copper. The axle is formed into a knife-edge, the edge of which passes as nearly as possible through the centre of gravity of the unloaded magnet. The agate planes upon which the magnet rests are attached to a solid support of copper which is firmly fixed to a marble base. The magnet is raised from the agate planes, by means of a horizontal rectangular frame, which is attached to the top of two upright pieces connected with the supporting stem. These are raised or lowered by an excentric piece passing beneath them, the excentric being made to revolve by a key. The whole is covered with an oblong box of wood, in one side of which are two small glazed apertures for the purpose of reading; the opposite side is covered with plate-glass. A

thermometer within the box shows the temperature of the interior air.

The position of the magnet at any instant is observed by means of two micrometer microscopes, one opposite each end. These microscopes are supported on short pillars of copper, attached to the base of the instrument. They are so adjusted that one complete revolution of the micrometer screw corresponds to about 5 minutes of arc; and, the micrometer head being divided into 50 parts, the arc corresponding to a single division is consequently about 0′.1.

In addition to these parts, the apparatus is provided with a brass bar of the same length as the magnet, furnished, like it, with cross wires at the extremities and knife-edge bearings, for the purpose of adjusting the fixed wires of the microscopes to the same horizontal line; and a brass rod, of the same length as the magnet, the ends of which are graduated to 10′, used in ascertaining the value of the micrometer divisions.

For the adjustment of the magnetic needle to the horizontal position, the needle is furnished with two moveable weights, one on each arm. These weights are screws moving in fixed nuts, one in a direction parallel to the magnetic axis of the magnet, and the other in a direction at right angles to it. By the movement of the former the needle is brought to the horizontal position; and by that of the latter, the centre of gravity is made to approach the centre of motion, and the sensibility of the instrument thereby increased at pleasure. The time of vibration of the needle upon its knife-edges serves to measure the sensibility, and thus to test this part of the adjustment.

(130) Unexceptionable as the principle of this instrument is in theory, the accuracy of the results has not been commensurate with that of the two others. This inferiority is

owing to the large influence which the unavoidable errors of workmanship have on the position of equilibrium of a magnet supported on a fixed axle. It has been shown that the effect of magnetizing a bar, under the most advantageous circumstances of form, and at the part of the globe where the vertical component of the magnetic force is greatest, is the same (as to its position of equilibrium) as if its centre of gravity had been transferred about the $\frac{1}{10}$th of an inch towards the north end; so that the moment of the force, exerted by the vertical component of the earth's magnetism, can never exceed this small quantity multiplied by the weight of the bar. Now, in order to render the results of this instrument comparable to those of the bifilar magnetometer, it should enable us to measure changes of the vertical force amounting to the $\frac{1}{100,000}$dth part of the whole; i. e. we have to measure effects, such as would be produced by shifting the centre of gravity through the *one-millionth of an inch.* It will be easily understood, from this statement, how great must be the effect of a minute disturbance in the parts of the instrument, or of inequalities in the bearing points of the axle; and experience has accordingly shown that it is altogether unavailable for the determination of changes of long period.

The same difficulties, arising from the same source, have been found to attach to the usual method of observing the magnetic inclination, and its changes, however refined the construction of the instrument. The sources of error seem, in fact, to be inherent in every direct process of determining the third element; and it is only by an *indirect* method that we can hope to evade them. Such is the character of the second method proposed by the author, as a substitute for the preceding.

The Induction Magnetometer.

(131) When a bar of soft iron is held in any direction not perpendicular to that of the Earth's magnetic force, it becomes a temporary magnet by the inducing action of that part of the force which acts in its direction. When the bar is vertical its lower extremity becomes a north pole, and the upper a south pole. The *small changes* of the induced magnetism may be assumed to be proportional to those of the inducing force; and, as the former may be measured by their effects, the latter become known.

To apply this simple principle to the determination of the variations of the vertical component of the Earth's magnetic force—two soft iron bars, of the same size and form, are to be placed vertically, at equal distances on either side of a small freely-suspended horizontal magnet, so that the plane containing them may pass through the centre of the magnet, and be perpendicular to its axis. Then, if the upper extremity of one of the bars, and the lower extremity of the other, be in (or near) the horizontal plane containing the suspended magnet, it is obvious that they will conspire to deflect it, the predominant pole being in one a north, and in the other a south pole.

The moment of free magnetism of the suspended magnet being denoted by m, let mU and mU' be the moments of the forces exerted upon it by the two bars. The quantities U and U' are functions of the vertical component of the earth's magnetic force; and depend also upon the quantity and distribution of magnetism in the bars, and upon their position with respect to the suspended magnet: they may likewise each contain a term dependent on the *permanent* magnetism of the bars, which is seldom wholly evanescent. These forces conspire to turn the magnet, and are resisted by the horizontal component of the earth's magnetic force, whose moment is $mX \sin u$, X denoting the horizontal component, and u the angle of deflection of the magnet from the magnetic meridian. Hence the equation of equilibrium is

$$U + U' = X \sin u.$$

Now let the two components of the earth's force undergo any small changes, ΔX and ΔY, and let $V \Delta Y$ and $V' \Delta Y$ be the changes of U and U' produced by the latter. Then, Δu denoting the corresponding change of the angle u, in parts of radius,

$$(V + V')\Delta Y = X \cos u \Delta u + \Delta X \sin u.$$

Dividing by the equation $Y = X \tan \theta$, in which θ denotes the magnetic inclination, there is

$$(V + V') \tan \theta \frac{\Delta Y}{Y} = \cos u \Delta u + \sin u \frac{\Delta X}{X};$$

or, making, for abridgment, $(V + V') \tan \theta = \frac{1}{p}$,

$$\frac{\Delta Y}{Y} = p \left(\cos u \Delta u + \sin u \frac{\Delta X}{X} \right).$$

The angle u, in this formula, being the deviation of the suspended magnet from the position which it would assume under the action of the earth alone, its changes, Δu, are the differences between the observed changes of position, measured from a fixed line, and the corresponding changes of declination.

(132) In order to correct for the effect of temperature upon the iron bars, we have only to substitute $(\Delta u - a\Delta t)$ for Δu, Δt being the actual change of temperature, and a the change of angle (in parts of radius) corresponding to a change of one degree. The coefficient, a, is determined by observing the

changes of position of the suspended magnet, when the temperature of the iron bars is raised or lowered by surrounding them with water of different temperatures, provided the Earth's magnetic force undergoes no change, either in direction or intensity, during the observations. If the observations be made at high and low temperatures alternately, and in quick succession, the changes of these elements will compensate each other in the final result, and the value of the coefficient will be given by the formula

$$a = \frac{\Sigma \Delta u}{\Sigma (t - t')}$$

The effect of an increase of temperature upon a soft iron bar is an *increase* of its induced magnetism—the reverse of its effect upon the permanent magnetism of an artificial magnet. The amount of the change is, however, very small. With the bar which has been most used in the Dublin Magnetical Observatory, an increase of 1° Fahr. produces a change of angle amounting only to $+0'{\cdot}05$; so that $a = +{\cdot}000015$, and the relative change of the force of the bar $= +{\cdot}000029$.

(133) The coefficient p will be known, if we can alter the inducing force artificially, by a small but known amount, and observe the change of angle thereby produced. This is the principle of the method devised by Dr. Lamont for the purpose; it is practised in the following manner.

A magnet is placed at a considerable distance above or below the suspended magnet, their centres being in the same vertical line; and it is so arranged as to be capable of rotation round a horizontal axis parallel to the suspended magnet in its deflected position. Let the auxiliary magnet be first placed *vertically*, in which position it exerts no *direct* action upon the suspended magnet, but only on the iron bars. Then, if R and R' denote the forces exerted by this magnet upon the two bars, $\Delta U = VR$, $\Delta U' = V'R'$; so that if ku denote the corresponding change of angle, expressed in scale-divisions of the instrument, we have

$$VR + V'R' = X \cos u \, kn.$$

Let the deflecting magnet be now turned (the position of its centre remaining unchanged), so that its axis is *horizontal*, and perpendicular to that of the suspended magnet. In this position it exerts no action upon the iron bars; but tends to turn the suspended magnet with a force whose moment we shall denote by S. The equation of equilibrium in this case is therefore

$$U + U' + S = X \sin (u + kn'),$$

kn' being the change of position of the suspended magnet due to the small added force. Hence

$$S = X \cos u \, kn';$$

and, dividing the equation of the preceding paragraph by this,

$$V\frac{R}{S} + V'\frac{R'}{S} = \frac{n}{n'}.$$

Now, the deflecting magnet being vertical, and its distance considerable as compared with its length, the force which it exerts upon the unit of free magnetism at the centre of one of the iron bars, in the direction of the joining line, and in the perpendicular direction respectively, are

$$\frac{2\mu}{e^3} \cos \phi, \quad -\frac{\mu}{e^3} \sin \phi,$$

in which μ denotes the magnetic moment of the deflecting magnet, e the length of the line connecting its centre with the centre of the iron bar, and ϕ the angle which that line makes with the vertical. And the sum of these forces, resolved in the vertical direction, is

$$\frac{\mu}{e^3}(2 \cos^2 \phi - \sin^2 \phi).$$

But we may consider the quantities e and ϕ (and therefore the force exerted by the magnet) to be the same for all points of the bar, the variations of these quantities being of the same order as those neglected in the approximation; so that

$$R = \frac{\mu}{e^3}(2 - 3\sin^2\phi), \quad R' = \frac{\mu}{e'^3}(2 - 3\sin^2\phi');$$

e' and ϕ' denoting the corresponding quantities for the second bar.

Again, if a denote the distance between the centres of the deflecting and suspended magnets, we have

$$S = \frac{\mu}{a^3}.$$

Substituting these values, and observing that $\sin^2\phi = \sin^2\phi'$, very nearly,

$$(2 - 3\sin^2\phi)\left(V\frac{a^3}{e^3} + V'\frac{a^3}{e'^3}\right) = \frac{n}{n'}.$$

Now, if b denote the horizontal distance of the axis of each bar from the centre of the suspended magnet, and h the distance of their centres above and below the plane in which the latter moves, we have

$$e^2 = (a + h)^2 + b^2, \quad e'^2 = (a - h)^2 + b^2;$$

accordingly, if we expand $a^3 e^{-3}$, $a^3 e'^{-3}$, according to the ascending powers of $\frac{h}{a}$, $\frac{b}{a}$ (stopping at the second), we find

$$V\frac{a^3}{e^3} + V'\frac{a^3}{e'^3} = (V + V')\left(1 + 6\frac{h^2}{a^2} - \frac{3}{2}\frac{b^2}{a^2}\right) + 3(V' - V)\frac{h}{a};$$

in which, since V and V' are nearly equal, the term $3(V' - V)\frac{h}{a}$ may be neglected. Also $\sin^2\phi = \frac{b^2}{e^2} = \frac{b^2}{a^2}$, q. p. And, substituting these values in the formula obtained above, it becomes

$$2(V + V')\left(1 + 6\frac{h^2}{a^2} - 3\frac{b^2}{a^2}\right) = \frac{n}{n'}.$$

But $p = (V + V')^{-1} \text{cotan}\,\theta$; wherefore, finally,

$$p = 2\,\text{cotan}\,\theta \left\{1 + 3\left(\frac{2h^2 - b^2}{d^2}\right)\right\} \cdot \frac{n'}{n}.$$

Temperature Corrections.

(134) Before concluding the account of the instruments employed in the determination of the variations of the Earth's magnetic force, it will be necessary to explain the mode of determining the corrections for changes of temperature.

The effect of temperature upon the magnetic moments of magnets is best investigated by causing them to deflect a freely-suspended magnet, and observing the deflections produced when the deflecting magnets are differently heated. For this purpose a copper trough is provided, having a cock near the bottom. In this the magnet to be tried is placed, supported on two cross ledges, and beside it a verified thermometer. The trough is then filled with water, and placed so that the axis of the magnet may be perpendicular to the suspended magnet. The apparatus being allowed to rest a sufficient time, so as to permit the magnet and the thermometer to take the common temperature of the surrounding fluid, this temperature is noted and the deflection observed. The temperature is then raised, by letting off some of the water, and supplying its place by heated water; and the experiment is repeated. In this manner a series of observations is made, at temperatures varying, in an ascending and then descending scale, from the temperature of the air at the time of the experiment to about 90° Fahr.; and, should the temperature of the air be high at the time, the scale is extended in the opposite direction, by surrounding the vessel with ice, or some freezing mixture.

(135) The equation of equilibrium of the deflected magnet is

$$mU = X \sin u,$$

in which u is the angle of deflection, and U a constant depending on the distance of the centres of the two magnets. Now let m become $m + \Delta m$ by change of temperature, and let the corresponding angle of deflection be $u + \Delta u$. Then we have $\Delta m \,.\, U = X \cos u \,.\, \Delta u$; and dividing by the original equation,

$$\frac{\Delta m}{m} = \operatorname{cotan} u \,.\, \Delta u = - q\,(t - t_0).$$

The result thus obtained should receive a correction for the change in the direction and intensity of the horizontal force which may occur in the interval of the two readings. When a series of readings is taken at high and low temperatures alternately, the corrections here referred to may be dispensed with, provided that the time chosen for the observations is one in which the magnetic variations are small and regular, and that the observations succeed one another with sufficient rapidity. If we add the resulting equations, taking the differences $t - t_0$ positively, we have

$$- q\Sigma(t - t_0) = \operatorname{cotan} u \,.\, \Sigma\Delta u.$$

In the case of the bifilar magnetometer, a further correction is required for the effect of temperature upon the suspending wires, and upon the wheel and screw which determine their interval; their dimensions being increased by an augmentation of heat, and the directive force therefore altered. The correction in the value of $\frac{\Delta F}{F}$, due to this cause, is (126)

$$\frac{\Delta G}{G} = (2e - e')\ (t - t^0);$$

in which e denotes the coefficient of the expansion of brass, and e' that of gold—the metals of which the wheel and screw, and the suspending wires, are formed. Hence the whole effect of temperature will be corrected by taking as the coefficient of $(t - t_0)$ the quantity

$$q + 2e - e',$$

instead of q. The additional terms thus introduced however are small, the numerical value of $2e - e'$ being only .000010.

(136) Some doubt has been thrown upon the certainty of this method of determining the temperature correction, upon the ground that the circumstances in which the magnet is placed in the experiment are different from those which occur in nature, the temperature of the water which surrounds it in the former case being altered rapidly, and by a large amount, while the temperature of the air changes slowly; for if the changes of the magnetic moment due to changes of temperature required *time* for their development, it is obvious that the effect would be different in the two cases. In addition to this, when the total effect of temperature is sought by examining separately its several partial effects, and combining them, the chances of error are increased, while at the same time we are involved in the uncertainty due to our analysis of the phenomenon. For these reasons it seems desirable to measure directly the complex effect of changes of temperature upon the position of the magnet suspended *in situ*. The effect in such case necessarily embraces all the circumstances of the problem, and under conditions similar to those which present themselves in nature.

With this view experiments were instituted by Captain Riddell, at the Toronto Observatory, to determine the temperature correction of the bifilar magnetometer by raising and lowering the temperature of the air of the room artificially. The currents of air induced by this process, and other causes, however, frustrated the success of this method. Under these circumstances it occurred to Mr. Broun to deduce the temperature correction from the daily observations themselves. The principle of the method which he has employed will be understood from the following.

L

It has been shown that the relative changes of either of the two components of the intensity is given by the formula $\frac{\Delta F}{F} = kn + qt$, n being the number of scale divisions of the instrument, which have passed the fixed wire of the telescope between the two epochs, and t the corresponding number of degrees of temperature. The same formula applies to daily or other means. Let this be applied to the case of the daily mean results, and let ϕ_0, ϕ_1, ϕ_2, &c., be the values of $\frac{\Delta F}{F}$ for successive days; n_0, n_1, n_2, &c., the corresponding mean scale values, and t_0, t_1, t_2, &c., the mean temperatures. Then we shall have a series of equations of the following form,

$$\phi_1 - \phi_0 = k(n_1 - n_0) + q(t_1 - t_0),$$
$$\phi_2 - \phi_0 = k(n_2 - n_0) + q(t_2 - t_0), \text{\&c.},$$

and adding,

$$\Sigma(\phi - \phi_0) = k\Sigma(n - n_0) + q\Sigma(t - t_0).$$

Now, if the change of force from day to day be assumed to be regular and uniform, and if the starting point be the *middle* of the series, we have $\Sigma(\phi - \phi_0) = 0$, and

$$\frac{q}{k} = -\frac{\Sigma(n - n_0)}{\Sigma(t - t_0)}.$$

In the practice of this method, we should select one or more series of days during which the change of mean temperature is rapid, and in opposite directions on the two sides of the starting point—in other words, the mean temperature of the middle day, t_0, should be either the greatest or the least of the series. The days selected should also be free from irregular disturbance; for it is obvious that the condition $\Sigma(\phi - \phi_0) = 0$ depends on the assumption that the change of the magnetic force from day to day is *uniform*.

(137) It remains to say a few words of the room in which the instruments above described are to be placed.

It is of the first importance that the instruments employed in the determination of the variations of the magnetic elements should be preserved, as far as possible, undisturbed after their final adjustment. For, not to speak of the interruption of the series of observations caused by such disturbance, the errors arising from the changes of position, consequent upon readjustment, are much more considerable than those to which we are liable in the determination of the changes themselves. For this reason it is inexpedient that the instruments used for the magnetic variations should be employed also in absolute determinations, even when their construction is such as to admit of such use. It is even desirable that the two classes of instruments should be kept wholly apart, in rooms separated from one another, and from other buildings.

As the differential instruments suffice to determine the changes which the magnetic elements undergo in any moderate time, the *absolute* observations may be taken at considerable intervals. For this reason, and also because one element only need be determined at a time, the room required for such observations may be of very small dimensions. A small wooden pavilion, from which iron fastenings are carefully excluded, is sufficient for the purpose.

The room for the three *differential* instruments should be of larger dimensions, and be constructed with more care. For instruments such as those above described, the room should not be less than 24 × 16 feet. With magnets of small size, the observatory may, of course, be of smaller dimensions. A room having the form of three arms of the Latin cross, 18 feet long, and 12 feet wide in the centre, will be found in most cases sufficient for the purpose. It should be constructed so as to avoid, as far as possible, currents of air, and inequalities of internal temperature; and for this reason it should be provided with a double door, and should be lighted by a single window in the middle of the roof. The three instruments may be conveniently placed in this room, in the three arms of the cross. If the scales of the magnets be read by reflexion, the reading telescopes may be placed close together, with the observer's chair in the centre, so that the three instruments may be observed in succession, without change of place. For night observation, a single lamp hung over the centre will be sufficient, its light being thrown upon the scales of the instruments by three mirrors suitably placed.

(138) It is easy to determine the corrections due to the mutual action of the magnets. For this purpose it is only necessary to *reverse* each magnet (or to turn its axis through 180°), and to observe the positions of the other two before and after the change. Half the difference of the readings, in the two positions of the first magnet, is the error caused by its action. To understand this we must recur to the expression for the moment of the force exerted by one magnet upon another, viz. :—

$$\frac{mm'}{2D^3}\{\sin(\phi + \phi') - 3\sin(\phi - \phi')\};$$

in which m and m' denote the magnetic moments of the two magnets, D the distance of their centres, and ϕ and ϕ' the angles which their magnetic axes form with the joining line. The value of this quantity is unaltered, although its sign is changed, when $180° + \phi$ is substituted for ϕ; and consequently, the disturbing effect is *equal* and *opposite* to that produced in the original position of the acting magnet.

It is scarcely necessary to advert to the advantages of this course over that which is sometimes adopted, and which consists in the *removal* of the acting magnet. The change produced is doubled, and therefore the effect of errors of observation halved; and the two parts of the observation may be made at a very short interval—an essential condition of accuracy in the elimination of the irregular changes. In the practice of this method, it is necessary to take a *series of readings*, with the acting magnet alternately in the two positions, so as to eliminate the actual magnetic changes which may be in progress during the experiment. By comparing each reading with the mean of the preceding and subsequent, and taking the mean of these partial differences, a very accurate final result may be obtained.

If the room contains any mass of moveable iron (such, for example, as the cistern of a barometer), its effect upon the magnets must be ascertained by alternate *removal* and *replacement*, and the correction added to that due to the action of the magnets upon one another. The position of the mass should afterwards remain unchanged; or if changed, the correction must be determined anew.

CHAPTER IX.

MAGNETIC VARIATIONS OF LONG PERIOD.

Secular Changes of the Magnetic Declination.

(139) The magnetic declination changes slowly at all parts of the Earth. The following Table exhibits the character and rate of this change at London, where the declination has been observed at intervals since the latter part of the sixteenth century:—

Secular Changes of Declination at London.

Year.	Declination.	Year.	Declination.
1580	11° 17′ E.	1760	19° 30′ W.
1622	6 12	1774	22 20
1634	4 5	1790	23 39
1657	0 0	1800	24 [illegible] 3
1666	0 34 W.	1806	24 8
1672	2 30	1815	24 27
1700	9 40	1820	24 11
1720	13 0	1831	24 0
1740	16 10		

Thus we see that the declination was easterly at London, from 1580 to 1657, at which latter epoch it vanished, and the magnetic meridian coincided with the astronomical. After the year 1660, the declination became westerly; and attained its maximum westerly value in London, in the year 1815, or soon after. Since that time the westerly declination has been diminishing, and the magnetic meridian been approaching the astronomical in the opposite direction.

Similar phenomena have been observed at Paris. These observations show distinctly an easterly maximum in or about the year 1580. The epoch of no declination at Paris was the year 1660. That of the westerly maximum was in the year 1814.

The observations of Gilpin, in London (1800–1805); those of Waddel (1806–1812); and those of Beaufoy (1813–1823), supply a continuous series of the values of the westerly declination in London from year to year for nearly a quarter of a century. The results are the following:—

Westerly Declination in London in the Years 1800–1823.

Year.	Declination.	Observer.	Year.	Declination.	Observer.
1800	24° 3′	Gilpin	1813	24° 20′	Beaufoy
1801	24 4	,,	1815	24 17	,,
1802	24 6	,,	1816	24 17	,,
1803	24 8	,,	1817	24 17	,,
1804	24 8	,,	1818	24 15	,,
1805	24 8	,,	1819	24 14	,,
1806	24 8	Waddel	1820	24 11	,,
1807	24 10	,,	1821	24 11	,,
1808	24 10	,,	1822	24 9	,,
1809	24 11	,,	1823	24 10	,,
1811	24 14	,,			
1812	24 16	,,			

As the epoch of the maximum of westerly declination occurs about the middle of the series, the annual change is very small.

(140) The following table, extracted from that given by General Sabine in the first volume of the Cape Observations, exhibits the nature of the secular change at that station from a very remote period.

Secular Change of the Declination at the Cape of Good Hope.

Year.	Declination.	Year.	Declination.
1605	0° 30′ E.	1753	19° 0′ W.
1609	0 12 W.	1768	19 30
1622	2 0	1780	22 16
1675	8 14	1792	24 31
1691	11 0	1816	26 31
1724	16 23	1836	28 30

From the foregoing observations it appears that the north end of the needle has moved at the Cape towards the west, from the time of the earliest observations. The rate is nearly uniform, the annual amount of the secular change being 7′.56. The magnetic meridian coincided with the astronomical in or about the year 1607.

(141) The greater accuracy now attainable with modern instruments enables us to determine the rate of the secular change from shorter series of observations. The following Table contains the mean yearly values of the magnetic declination at Dublin, for the ten years 1841–1850. The second column contains the probable values of the westerly declination in each year, calculated by the formula,

$$\psi = 26° 29'.07 - 5'.97 \times n,$$

in which 26° 29′.07 is the probable value of the westerly declination in the year 1850, deduced by the method of least squares, n the number of years reckoned from that epoch, and $-5'.97$ the yearly value of the secular change. The third column gives the excesses of the observed above the computed values.

Mean Yearly Values of the Westerly Declination at Dublin.

Year.	Observed.	Computed.	Differences.
1841	27° 23′·85	27° 22′·80	+ 1′·05
1842	27 15 ·80	27 16 ·83	− 1 ·03
1843	27 10 ·08	27 10 ·86	− 0 ·78
1844	27 4 ·93	27 4 ·89	+ 0 ·04
1845	26 58 ·80	26 58 ·92	− 0 ·12
1846	26 52 ·77	26 52 ·95	− 0 ·18
1847	26 48 ·34	26 46 ·98	+ 1 ·36
1848	26 41 ·74	26 41 ·01	+ 0 ·73
1849	26 34 ·83	26 35 ·04	− 0 ·21
1850	26 28 ·25	26 29 07	− 0 ·82

The differences in the third column indicate a *cyclical variation*, the excess of the observed above the computed declination being greatest between 1847 and 1848, and least between 1842 and 1843. Grouping the years we have

1842, 43,	difference =	− 0′·91
1844, 45, 46,	„	− 0 ·09
1847, 48,	„	+ 1 ·05
1849, 50, 41,	„	+ 0 ·01

The range of the variation is about two minutes; and the duration of the cycle, so far as it may be inferred from so short a series, about ten years.

As we have already seen (139), the secular change of declination is by no means uniform. The magnitude of the yearly change at Kew in the year 1860 was − 7′·65.

(142) At Hobarton, in the southern hemisphere the declination is *easterly;* and the mean annual increase is small. The following are the mean yearly values for the years 1843-1848.

Year.	Mean Declination.
1843, ...	9° 53′·32
1844, ...	9 54 ·93
1845, ...	9 56 ·47
1846, ...	9 58 ·42
1847, ...	9 59 ·28
1848, ...	10 0 ·61

The mean yearly increase = 1′·46.

Secular Changes of the Magnetic Inclination.

(143) The following Table gives the observed values of the magnetic inclination at London at different epochs, together with the names of the observers.

Secular Changes of the Inclination at London.

Year.	Inclination.	Observer.
1576	71° 50′	Norman.
1600	72 0	Gilbert.
1676	73 30	Bond.
1723	74 42	Graham.
1773	72 19	Heberden.
1780	72 8	Gilpin.
1790	71 33	Gilpin.
1800	70 35	Gilpin.
1818	70 34	Kater.
1821	70 3	Sabine.
1828	69 47	Sabine.
1838	69 17	Sabine.
1854	68 31	Sabine.

It thus appears that, from the time of its discovery, the inclination increased at London until about the year 1723, when it attained its maximum. Since that epoch, up to the present time, it has diminished.

A similar variation of the inclination has been observed at Paris.

(144) In the southern hemisphere the *south* end of the needle dips below the horizon; and the inclination has increased from the time of the earliest observations. The following are the observations of south inclination made at the Cape of Good Hope since the middle of the last century.

Secular Changes of the Inclination at the Cape of Good Hope.

Year.	Inclination.	Observer.
1751	43° 0′	La Caille.
1770	44 25	Ekeberg.
1780	46 46	Bailey.
1791	48 30	Vancouver.
1818	50 47	Freycenet.
1836	52 35	Fitzroy.
1840	53 08	Ross.

(145) In the years 1812–1850, a series of observations of the magnetic inclination was undertaken at the Observatory of Dublin, with improved instruments. The following Table contains the mean yearly values of the inclination thence deduced. The third column contains the probable values, calculated by the formula

$$\theta = 70^\circ\ 22'.38 - 2'.66 \times n,$$

in which 70° 22′.38 is the probable value of the inclination corresponding to the year 1850, deduced from the observed values by the method of least squares; n the number of years reckoned from that epoch; and $-2'.66$ the annual value of the secular change. The third column contains the differences of the observed and computed values.

Mean Yearly Values of the Inclination at Dublin.

Year.	Inclination observed.	Inclination computed.	Differences.
1842	70° 41′·97	70° 43′·66	− 1′·69
1843	40 ·84	41 ·00	− 0 ·16
1844	36 ·05	38 ·34	− 2 ·29
1845	34 ·02	35 ·68	− 1 ·66
1846	32 ·51	33 ·02	− 0 ·51
1847	— —	30 ·36	—
1848	28 ·55	27 ·70	+ 0 ·85
1849	26 ·77	25 ·04	+ 1 ·73
1850	24 ·36	22 ·38	+ 1 ·98

The differences of the observed and computed values show that the magnetic inclination, like the magnetic declination, is subject to a cyclical change; and that, abstracting from the secular change, the inclination was a minimum in the year 1844.

(146) The following are the mean yearly values of the inclination at Kew, where an elaborate series of observations have been made in the years 1857–1868. The means correspond to the 1st of October in each year.

Mean Yearly Values of the Inclination at Kew.

Year.	Inclination.	Year.	Inclination.
1857	68° 24′·87	1863	68° 11′·71
1858	22 ·56	1864	9 ·31
1859	21 ·41	1865	8 ·30
1860	19 ·29	1866	5 ·44
1861	17 ·42	1867	2 ·62
1862	14 ·89	1868	2 ·13

The mean yearly change is − 1′·96.

Secular Changes of the Horizontal Force.

(147) The means of observing the magnetic force in absolute measure are due to Gauss; and we consequently possess no observations of this element earlier than the date of publication of his celebrated memoir.*

The observations of the horizontal force in absolute measure, made in the Dublin Observatory, from two distinct series. In the former of these, extending through the years 1844–1846, large magnets were employed; and the method of observation was that of Gauss, in which the deflecting magnet is perpendicular to the magnetic meridian. In the second series, made in the years 1848–1850, small magnets were used at short distances, the deflecting magnet being in all cases perpendicular to the suspended magnet, according to the method of Dr. Lamont.

The process by which the horizontal component of the magnetic force is determined, from these observations, has been already explained (90, 91, 92). When the values so obtained are reduced to the zero of the bifilar magnetometer, and to the freezing temperature, they are found to differ very slightly, the probable deviation of a single observation from the mean of all being only the fraction .00034 of the whole force.

From this it may be inferred that the bifilar magnetometer had undergone no instrumental change, other than those known and allowed for; and consequently the value of the horizontal force at any time during the series of observations, is given in absolute measure by the formula,

$$X = 3.5042\,[1 + kn + q\,(t - 32°)],$$

n being the scale-reading of the magnetometer, t the tem-

* *Intensitas vis Magneticæ Terrestris ad Mensuram absolutam revocata.* Gottingen memoirs, 1833.

perature of the magnet, and k and q the changes corresponding respectively to one division of the scale, and to one degree of the thermometer.

(148) The following Table gives the mean yearly values of the horizontal force so deduced. The second column contains the corresponding values computed by the method of least squares, on the hypothesis that the increase of the horizontal force is uniform, by the formula

$$X = 3.5042 + .004344 \times n,$$

in which 3.5042 is the probable value of the force corresponding to the year 1850, n the number of years reckoned from that epoch, and + .004344 the yearly increase, which is accordingly .00124 of the whole force. The numbers in the third column are the excesses of the observed above the computed values.

Mean Yearly Values of the Horizontal Force at Dublin, in the Years 1841–1850.

Year.	X observed.	X computed.	Differences.
1841	3·4636	3·4651	– ·0015
1842	3·4695	3·4695	·0000
1843	3·4750	3·4738	+ ·0012
1844	3·4795	3·4782	+ ·0013
1845	3·4842	3·4825	+ ·0017
1846	3·4876	3·4868	+ ·0008
1847	3·4898	3·4912	– ·0014
1848	3·4937	3·4955	– ·0018
1849	3·4998	3·4999	– ·0001
1850	3·5053	3·5042	+ ·0011

The numbers in the third column show that the increase of the horizontal force from year to year is subject to a cyclical variation similar to that which has already been shown to exist in the declination and inclination. The observed force is most in excess of the computed force in 1845, and most in defect in 1848.

The absolute value of the *total* magnetic force, expressed in British units, is 10. 433. The total force diminishes from year to year, the annual amount of the change being – . 0097.

(149) The following Table contains the results of the corresponding observations made at the Kew Observatory at a somewhat later period. The epoch corresponds to the 1st October in each year.

Mean Yearly Values of the Horizontal Force at Kew, in the Years 1857–1868.

Year.	Force.	Year.	Force.
1857	3·7899	1863	3·8216
1858	3·7950	1864	3.8284
1859	3·8007	1865	3·8306
1860	3·8063	1866	3·8391
1861	3·8121	1867	3·8467
1862	3·8165	1868	3·8493

The mean annual secular increase is + 0054.

CHAPTER X.

ANNUAL INEQUALITY.

Annual Inequality of the Magnetic Declination.

(150) The difficulties which impede an exact knowledge of the annual changes of Terrestrial magnetism are very considerable. Of these the most obvious are the smallness of the phenomenon itself, and the length of its period. For its exact determination the observations must be continued through several periods, or years; while the instruments employed in the research must remain unchanged, both in construction and adjustment, throughout the whole time, or, if there be any instrumental change, its magnitude and effects must be very exactly known.

The foregoing difficulties may be surmounted by care and skill. But there are others, less obvious, which are yet more formidable. The changes of temperature, and of humidity, induce slow changes in the condition of the instruments, which affect the position of the suspended magnet. The effects of temperature upon the magnetic moments of the magnets are well known, and accurate means have been devised for their correction in the measurement of the changes of the Earth's magnetic force. But the effects of atmospheric changes upon the suspension thread of the unifilar magnetometer were less suspected, and have consequently been less guarded against; and as these changes, like those sought, observe an annual period, the two are combined, and the resulting movements of the magnet are due to their joint effect.

The obvious mode of overcoming this difficulty is analogous to that employed in the case of the bifilar magnetometer—namely, to create artificial changes of temperature, or of humidity, and to observe the effects, the actual magnetic changes being eliminated by the help of an auxiliary instrument. Unfortunately, the operation of such a disturbing cause in the case of the declinometer was not suspected until it was too late for such a process. The observations themselves, however, when combined with those made with an auxiliary instrument which was observed during part of the series, enable us to determine approximately these effects, and to eliminate them from the final results.

The calculation here referred to is given in the Appendix to the present volume.

(151) The following table gives the annual changes of position of the declination magnet, deduced from the observations of the ten years, 1841–1850. The first column contains the mean differences between the declination of each month, and that of the entire year; the second the corresponding variations corrected for the secular change; and the third, the reduced values of the same, corrected for the effects of hygrometric changes upon the torsion of the suspension thread. These are calculated by the formula

$$\Delta\psi = \Delta u + 0'.24\,\Delta h,$$

in which Δu are the mean monthly variations of position of the declination magnet, and Δh the corresponding variations of humidity, deduced from the observations of the nine years 1842–1850.

Positive numbers correspond to *easterly* deflections of the north end of the magnet.

Annual Inequality of the Magnetic Declination at Dublin.

Month.	Observed Variation.	Corrected for secular Change.	Corrected for hygrometric Change.
January,	− 0′.80	+ 1′.95	+ 0′.37
February,	− 0.07	+ 2.16	+ 1.60
March,	− 0.01	+ 1.74	+ 1.74
April,	+ 0.18	+ 1.43	+ 1.86
May,	− 0.55	+ 0.20	+ 1.33
June,	− 1.84	− 1.59	+ 0.04
July,	− 2.27	− 2.62	− 1.25
August,	− 1.97	− 2.72	− 2.17
September,	− 0.72	− 1.97	− 2.07
October,	+ 0.95	− 0.80	− 1.35
November,	+ 2.94	+ 0.69	− 0.82
December,	+ 4.17	+ 1.42	+ 0.22

It will be seen that the effect of the correction for humidity, in this instrument, is to throw the maximum and minimum of declination about a month forward, the general character of the law being otherwise little altered. The *minimum* of easterly declination occurs at the end of August, or the beginning of September; and the *maximum* in March or April. The range is 4′.03.

It will be thus seen that the minimum of easterly declination occurs about the hottest period of the year, or soon after. This is in accordance with the analogy of the diurnal change, in which the minimum of easterly declination occurs at the hottest period of the day.

(152) The law of the annual variation obtained at the Kew Observatory being at variance with that here given, it has been thought necessary to enter somewhat fully into a comparison of the corresponding results at other points of the globe.

For this purpose the stations have been separated into three groups, distinguished by their geographical positions, viz.:—1. The *north-western* group, including the European and North American stations; 2, the *north-eastern* group, embracing the stations in Asiatic Russia and China; and 3, the *southern* group, including the places of observation in the southern hemisphere. In all, *positive* numbers correspond to *easterly* deflections of the north end of the magnet.

It will be seen that the law of the annual variation is nearly the same for the several stations of the same group; and we are accordingly justified in combining them so as to perceive more distinctly the mean effects. This is done in the last column of the subjoined tables.

The following are the results* for the first group.

Annual Inequality at the North-western Stations.

Month.	Toronto	Dublin	Greenwich	Prague	Mean.
January,	+ 0'.74	+ 0'.37	+ 1.'05	+ 0'.14	+ 0'.58
February,	+ 0.13	+ 1.60	+ 0.82	+ 0.83	+ 0.85
March,	− 0.15	+ 1.74	+ 0.65	+ 0.58	+ 0.71
April,	− 0.50	+ 1.86	+ 0.84	+ 0.61	+ 0.70
May,	− 0.43	+ 1.33	+ 0.73	− 0.26	+ 0.34
June,	− 0.12	+ 0.04	+ 0.13	− 0.73	− 0.17
July,	+ 0.12	− 1.25	− 0.59	− 1.06	− 0.70
August,	0.00	− 2.17	− 0.81	− 1.17	− 1.04
September,	− 0.56	− 2.07	− 1.20	− 0.90	− 1.18
October,	− 0.02	− 1.36	− 0.51	+ 0.49	− 0.35
November,	+ 0.03	− 0.32	− 0.79	+ 0.79	− 0 07
December,	+ 0.82	+ 0.22	− 0.27	+ 0.69	+ 0.36

The *maximum* of easterly declination occurs in February or March, and the *minimum* in August or September.

* The results at Toronto have been obtained from the hourly observations made with the differential magnetometer during the years 1845,6,7, which are regarded by General Sabine as affording the best data for this determination. (*Toronto Magnetical Observations*, Vol. II. p. 8.)

The results of the second group are as follow.

Annual Inequality at the North-eastern Stations.

Month.	Peters-burgh.	Catharine-burg.	Barnaoul.	Nertschinsk.	Pekin.	Mean.
January,	+ 1'.99	+ 0'.73	+ 0'.49	+ 0'.09	+ 1'.71	+ 1'.00
February,	+ 2.64	+ 0.68	+ 1.11	+ 0.59	+ 1.94	+ 1.39
March,	+ 0.90	− 0.54	+ 1.21	+ 0.88	+ 1.15	+ 0.61
April,	− 0.80	− 0.89	+ 1.16	− 0.07	+ 0.09	− 0.10
May,	− 1.11	− 1.14	− 1.55	+ 0.20	− 1.00	− 0.92
June,	− 1.28	− 1.19	− 0.76	+ 0.24	− 1.63	− 0.91
July,	− 0.56	− 1.47	− 0.77	− 0.17	− 2.45	− 1.08
August,	+ 0.66	− 0.93	− 0.65	− 0.39	− 2.26	− 0.71
September,	− 1.27	+ 1.83	− 0.87	− 0.48	− 2.02	− 0.66
October,	− 1.22	+ 1.75	+ 0.09	− 0.26	− 0.62	− 0.05
November,	− 0.91	+ 1.28	− 0.70	− 0.16	+ 2.88	+ 0.50
December,	+ 0.78	+ 0.80	− 0.25	− 0.14	+ 2.08	+ 0.67

At the north-eastern stations therefore the *maximum* of *easterly* declination occurs in February, and the *minimum* in July—i. e., at the coldest and the hottest periods of the year. The mean curve agrees well with that of the north-western stations, the only material difference being that the maximum and minimum occur about a month earlier.

(153) The following are the corresponding results for the southern hemisphere.

Annual Inequality at the Southern Stations.

Month.	St. Helena.	Cape of Good Hope.	Hobarton.
January,	+ 0'.05	− 0'.49	− 0'.55
February,	− 0.30	− 0.72	− 0.13
March,	− 0.17	− 0.83	− 0.28
April,	+ 0.04	− 1.07	+ 0.37
May,	+ 0.02	+ 0.18	+ 0.48
June,	+ 0.23	+ 1.04	+ 0.40
July,	− 0.14	+ 0.97	+ 0.34
August,	+ 0.06	+ 1.03	+ 0.20
September,	+ 0.33	+ 0.73	+ 0.08
October,	− 0.03	+ 0.08	− 0.23
November,	− 0.12	− 0.42	− 0.46
December,	− 0.12	− 0.71	− 0.64

Thus at the southern stations the declination is *easterly* from May to September, and *westerly* in the remaining months of the year.

If now we combine the results for the northern hemisphere, and compare them with those for the southern, we find a marked correspondence, but in an *inverse direction*, the *maxima* and *minima* of the one corresponding to the *minima* and *maxima* of the other. This result, as we shall see hereafter, is in accordance with the phenomena of the diurnal change.

Mean Annual Variations.

Month.	Northern Stations.	Southern Stations.	Month.	Northern Stations.	Southern Stations.
January,	+ 0′.79	− 0′.33	July,	− 0′.89	+ 0′.39
February,	+ 1.12	− 0.38	August,	− 0.88	+ 0.43
March,	+ 0.66	− 0.43	September,	− 0.92	+ 0.38
April,	+ 0.30	− 0.22	October,	− 0.20	− 0.06
May,	− 0.29	+ 0.23	November,	+ 0.22	− 0.33
June,	− 0.54	+ 0.56	December,	+ 0.52	− 0.49

Thus the position of the freely-suspended magnet varies with the position of the sun with respect to the equator, and the simultaneous changes are in opposite directions in the northern and southern hemispheres.

Annual Inequality of the Northerly Force.

(154) The annual inequality of the northerly force in Dublin has been determined with accuracy from the results furnished by the bifilar magnetometer, the instrument having undergone no sensible instrumental change during the whole period of observation, and the effects of changes of temperature having been satisfactorily eliminated by an exact knowledge of the correction. The following table gives the

differences between the values of the force in each month, and the mean value for the entire year, the unit of force being $\frac{X}{1000}$. The numbers are the means of the results of the ten years 1841–50.

Annual Inequality of the Northerly Force in Dublin.

January, .	− 0.89	July, . .	+ 0.56
February, .	− 0.91	August, . .	+ 0.55
March, .	− 0.70	September, .	+ 0.28
April, .	− 0.40	October, . .	+ 0.14
May, .	+ 0.08	November, .	+ 0.32
June, .	+ 0.60	December, .	+ 0.38

Thus the *maximum* of the northerly force occurs in June, the *minimum* in February. The range is 1.09.

(155) The dependence of the annual inequality upon the sun's declination is, however, more distinctly seen, when we compare the variations of the two components of the whole horizontal force with one another and with the season.

Let these variations be denoted by ξ and η, of which ξ is the variation of the force in the magnetic meridian, and η that of the force at right angles to it. The magnitude of the latter will be given by the deviation of the magnet from the magnetic meridian which it produces: its amount is

$$\eta = X \sin (\psi - \psi_0) = X(\psi - \psi_0) \sin 1',$$

since $\psi - \psi_0$ is a small angle.

The following table gives the values of ξ, the unit of force being $\frac{X}{1000}$. It is corrected for secular change, the annual amount of which referred to the same unit is 1.24. The second column of the table contains the corresponding values of η, deduced from the numbers of Art. (151) by multiplying by 0.291; and the third, the corresponding values of the whole force in the horizontal plane, or $\rho = \sqrt{\eta^2 + \xi^2}$.

Annual Inequality of the whole Horizontal Force.

Month.	ξ.	η.	ρ.
January,	− 0.32	+ 0.11	0.34
February,	− 0.44	+ 0.47	0.64
March,	− 0.34	+ 0.51	0.61
April,	− 0.14	+ 0.54	0.56
May,	+ 0.24	+ 0.39	0.46
June,	+ 0.65	+ 0.01	0.65
July,	+ 0.51	− 0.36	0.62
August,	+ 0.39	− 0.63	0.74
September,	+ 0.02	− 0.60	0.60
October,	− 0.22	− 0.39	0.45
November,	− 0.15	− 0.09	0.18
December,	− 0.19	+ 0.06	0.20

On a comparison of the first and second columns it will be seen that the force in the magnetic meridian, ξ, *vanishes* in April and September, when the force at right angles to the meridian is *greatest*; while, on the other hand, the latter force vanishes in the solstitial months, when the former is near its maximum. The whole force is greatest in February and in August, and least in November or December.

(156) The law of the annual inequality of the northerly force in the southern hemisphere is the inverse of the preceding, as might have been anticipated, the maximum of the force occurring in January, and the minimum in June. This will appear from the results of the observations of the horizontal force in absolute measure, made at Hobarton in the five years 1846–1850, contained in the following table. The numbers given are the monthly means of the entire series,*

* *Hobarton Magnetic and Meteorological Observations*, Vol. II., p. xli.

together with the values obtained by applying the correction for the secular change, the annual amount of which at Hobarton is − .0006.

Annual Inequality of the Northerly Force at Hobarton.

Month.	X.	X corrected.	Month.	X.	X corrected.
January,	4.5075	4.5075	July,	4.5042	4.5045
February,	.5065	5066	August,	5032	5035
March,	5042	5043	September,	5042	5046
April,	5033	5035	October,	5032	5036
May,	5035	5037	November,	.5037	5042
June,	5028	5031	December,	5060	5056

Annual Inequality of the Magnetic Inclination.

(157) The annual inequality of the inclination at Dublin, corresponding to the four trimestral periods, is

March 31 . .	$\Delta\theta = + 0'.12.$
June 30, . .	$- 1.26.$
September 30, .	$+ 0.89.$
December 31, .	$+ 0.25.$

Thus of these periods the inclination is greatest near the time of the autumnal equinox, and least near the time of the summer solstice; and the change between these two periods is 2′.15.

A more complete determination of the annual variation of the inclination is afforded by the observations of the Kew Observatory, where that element has been regularly observed each month during twelve years. The results are given in two series, in which there appears to have been some difference in the mode of observing; but, as will be seen from the subjoined table, they agree nearly as to the law of the annual change. The inclination is greatest in October, and least in May; and the amount of the change between the two periods is 2.′58.

Annual Inequality of the Magnetic Inclination at Kew.

Month.	1857–1862.	1863–1868.	Mean.
January,	+ 0′.80	+ 0′.37	+ 0′.58
February,	+ 0.06	− 0.05	+ 0.01
March,	+ 0.71	− 0.60	+ 0.06
April,	+ 0.17	+ 0.03	+ 0.10
May,	− 1.43	− 1.31	− 1.37
June,	− 0.99	− 0.81	− 0.90
July,	− 0.39	− 0.20	− 0.30
August,	− 0.89	+ 0.02	− 0.44
September,	− 0.38	+ 0.62	+ 0.12
October,	+ 1.03	+ 1.39	+ 1.21
November,	+ 1.21	+ 0.70	+ 0.95
December,	+ 0.15	− 0.19	− 0.02

Thus, neglecting the small negative change in December, the inclination is *below* the mean in the months of May, June, July, and August; and *above* it in the remaining months of the year.

The monthly observations of the magnetic inclination at Toronto, made during the years 1845–1849, give the maximum of inclination in January, and the minimum in July. The following are the results, corrected for secular change.

Annual Inequality of the Magnetic Inclination at Toronto.

Month.	Difference.	Month.	Difference.
January,	+ 1'.40	July,	- 1'.93
February,	+ 1.06	August,	- 0.90
March,	- 0.44	September,	+ 0.13
April,	- 0.56	October,	+ 0.35
May,	- 0.38	November,	+ 0.97
June,	- 1.03	December,	+ 0.60

(158) To compare with the foregoing the corresponding variation in the southern hemisphere, we have the following results of an elaborate series of observations at Hobarton, extending over the ten years 1841–1850.* The angle measured is the inclination of the south end of the needle to the horizon.

Annual Inequality of the Magnetic Inclination at Hobarton.

Month.	Difference.	Month.	Difference.
January,	+ 0'.84	July,	- 0'.42
February,	+ 0.86	August,	- 2.10
March,	+ 1.33	September,	- 0.58
April,	+ 0.63	October,	- 0.42
May,	+ 0.46	November,	+ 0.44
June,	- 1.52	December,	+ 0.46

There is a general correspondence between these numbers and those of the northern hemisphere, the south inclination being *below* the mean from June to October inclusive, and *above* it during the remaining months of the year. But there remains still considerable discrepancy as to the epochs of maxima and minima.

* *Hobarton Magnetical and Meteorological Observations*, Vol. II., p. xliv.

CHAPTER XI.

DIURNAL INEQUALITY.

(159) ALL the magnetic elements are subject to periodical variations, dependent on the position of the sun with respect to the meridian, the period of which is accordingly the solar day.

Diurnal Inequality of the Magnetic Declination.

The diurnal change in the position of the freely-suspended horizontal needle was first observed by Graham in 1724. The magnitude of the variation in the several months was determined by Canton, in London, in 1759; by Gilpin in 1787 and 1793; and by Beaufoy in 1817–1819. The mean daily variation in London, inferred from these observations, was 10′ 44″.

In recent years the same phenomenon has been carefully observed at various places, and with more perfect instruments. We shall here describe its features as exhibited in Dublin; and afterwards examine the influence of change of place upon its magnitude and its laws.

The laws of the diurnal inequality of the magnetic declination at Dublin have been obtained by taking the means of the readings of the declinometer made at the same hour, for each month, the days of greater magnetic disturbance being omitted. From these means the diurnal inequality is deduced by the formula

$$\psi - \psi_0 = k\,(n - n_0)\,;$$

in which n denotes the mean reading corresponding to any

hour; n_0 the mean for the entire day; and k the angle corresponding to one scale division of the instrument.

It will be convenient, however, to substitute for the change of the declination, the force at right angles to the meridian by which it is produced. By these means the investigation of the laws of the magnetic changes is reduced to the determination of the variations of the three components of the terrestrial magnetic force, viz.:—the horizontal components of the force in the magnetic meridian, and perpendicular to the magnetic meridian, respectively, and the vertical component. Thus all the elements compared are homogeneous; and the numbers by which they are represented denote, not merely the relative values of each, separately, but those of all.

(160) The observations which furnish the values of $n - n_0$ in Dublin form two distinct series. In the former of these, which extended through the four years 1840–1843, the observations were taken twelve times each day—namely, at the even hours of Gottingen mean time, or very nearly, at the *odd* hours of *Dublin mean time*. In the latter series, which extended through the seven years 1844–1850, the observations were taken every third hour, from 7 A. M. to 10 P. M. inclusive.

The mean monthly values of η, for each hour of observation, having been obtained for each of these series, we may calculate an equal number of the coefficients of the periodical function

$$\begin{aligned}\eta = A_1 \cos x + A_2 \cos 2x + A_3 \cos 3x + \&c.\\ + B_1 \sin x + B_2 \sin 2x + B_3 \sin 3x + \&c.\end{aligned}$$

in which $x = n \times 15°$, n being the number of hours, and parts of an hour, reckoned from the time of the first observation. The first series of observations accordingly furnishes the values of the first twelve coefficients of the preceding equation, and the second those of the first six. Of the latter we have thus two sets of values, the arithmetical means of which may be taken as the mean values corresponding to the whole period (1840-1850). These values are given in the following Table. The last six coefficients are in all cases small, and may be neglected.

Coefficients of the Equation of the Diurnal Curve of the Easterly Force.

Months.	A_1	B_1	A_2	B_2	A_3	B_3
Jan.	+0·72	−0·06	−0·27	−0·28	+0·19	−0·14
Feb.	+0·87	+0·06	−0·36	−0·27	+0·26	−0·12
March,	+1·13	+0.20	−0·57	−0·28	+0·39	−0·07
April,	+1·22	+0.48	−0·81	−0·22	+0·40	−0·11
May,	+1·13	+0·62	−0·82	−0·03	+0·22	−0·12
June,	+1·16	+0·73	−0·82	−0·13	+0·20	−0·08
July,	+1·16	+0·62	−0·74	−0·14	+0·20	−0·06
Aug.	+1·29	+0·34	−0·80	−0·08	+0·29	−0·14
Sep.	+1·16	+0·02	−0·72	−0·09	+0·37	−0·16
Oct.	+1·01	−0·06	−0·53	−0·25	+0·36	−0·12
Nov.	+0·78	−0·14	−0·31	−0·21	+0·21	−0·11
Dec.	+0·63	−0·14	−0·25	−0·26	+0·14	−0·09
Summer,	+1·19	+0·58	−0·80	−0·10	+0·23	−0·11
Equinox,	+1·14	+0·16	−0·66	−0·21	+0·38	−0·12
Winter,	+0·75	−0·07	−0·30	−0·26	+0·20	−0·11
Year,	+1·03	+0·22	−0·59	−0·19	+0·27	−0·11

(161) A close examination of the foregoing numbers shows that the twelve months are naturally grouped in three divisions, in each of which the corresponding coefficients differ little among one another. These are—1. The *summer months*, including May, June, July, and August. 2. The

equinoctial months, viz., March, April, September, and October; and 3. The *winter months*, November, December, January, and February. The mean values of the coefficients for each of these groups, as well as those for the entire year, have been given in the preceding Table.

Transforming the periodic function in the usual manner, and taking midnight as the origin of the time, we have the following expressions for the diurnal inequality of the easterly force, corresponding to the three periods of the year, and the entire year, the unit of force being $\frac{X}{1000}$.

Summer Months.

$$\eta = 1 \cdot 32 \sin (x + 49°) + 0 \cdot 80 \sin (2x + 233°) + 0 \cdot 25 \sin (3x + 70°).$$

Equinoctial Months.

$$\eta = 1 \cdot 14 \sin (x + 67°) + 0 \cdot 69 \sin (2x + 222°) + 0 \cdot 39 \sin (3x + 62°).$$

Winter Months.

$$\eta = 0 \cdot 75 \sin (x + 80°) + 0 \cdot 30 \sin (2x + 190°) + 0 \cdot 23 \sin (3x + 74°).$$

Year.

$$\eta = 1 \cdot 05 \sin (x + 63°) + 0 \cdot 61 \sin (2x + 222°) + 0 \cdot 29 \sin (3x + 67°).$$

(162) From the foregoing equations of the diurnal inequality, we may compute the term corresponding to any time of the day. In the following Table the results corresponding to the full hours of Dublin mean time have been obtained by an equivalent graphical method, the unit of force being $\frac{X}{1000}$, as before.

Diurnal Inequality of the Easterly Force in Dublin.

Hour.	Summer Months.	Equinoctical Months.	Winter Months.	Year.
1 A. M.	+ 0·70	+ 0·68	+ 0·49	+ 0·62
2	+ 0·78	+ 0·70	+ 0·42	+ 0·63
3	+ 0·90	+ 0·70	+ 0·38	+ 0·66
4	+ 1·08	+ 0·71	+ 0·35	+ 0·71
5	+ 1·25	+ 0·72	+ 0·34	+ 0·77
6	+ 1·38	+ 0·78	+ 0·32	+ 0·83
7	+ 1·43	+ 0·85	+ 0·28	+ 0·85
8	+ 1·15	+ 0·75	+ 0·21	+ 0·70
9	+ 0·61	+ 0·48	+ 0·12	+ 0·40
10	− 0·20	− 0·21	− 0·16	− 0·19
11	− 1·21	− 1·29	− 0·72	− 1·07
Noon	− 1·93	− 1·98	− 1·16	− 1·69
1 P. M.	− 2·23	− 2·19	− 1·29	− 1·90
2	− 2·03	− 1·93	− 1·13	− 1·70
3	− 1·63	− 1·38	− 0·81	− 1·27
4	− 1·10	− 0·78	− 0·48	− 0·80
5	− 0·60	− 0·27	− 0·21	− 0·36
6	− 0·20	+ 0·09	0·00	− 0·04
7	+ 0·11	+ 0·33	+ 0·20	+ 0·21
8	+ 0·30	+ 0·55	+ 0·44	+ 0·43
9	+ 0·40	+ 0·71	+ 0·70	+ 0·60
10	+ 0·45	+ 0·76	+ 0·83	+ 0·68
11	+ 0·48	+ 0·74	+ 0·75	+ 0·66
12	+ 0·49	+ 0·70	+ 0·61	+ 0·60

(163) The general features of the phenomenon of the diurnal change, deduced from these numbers, are the following :—

I. The easterly force diminishes from 7 A. M., or 8 A. M., and the north pole of the magnet moves *westward*, until about 1 P. M., when the easterly force is a *minimum*.

II. After 1 P. M. the easterly force increases, and the north pole of the magnet returns *eastward*. This easterly movement continues until about 10 P. M., when the easterly force attains its greatest value.

III. There is a second, but much smaller oscillation during the night and early morning, the easterly force diminishing, and the north pole moving slowly westward, for a few hours before and after midnight; after which it returns to the east until 7 A. M., when the easterly force is again a maximum.

IV. In summer the westerly movement during the night disappears, the afternoon easterly movement continuing throughout the night, but at a slower rate. In winter, on the other hand, the morning easterly movement vanishes, and the magnet is almost in a state of repose from 2 A. M. to 8 A. M.

V. From the facts last mentioned it follows that the greatest range in summer is that of the westerly movement, from 7 A. M. to 1 P. M.; while, in winter, the greatest range is that of the easterly movement, between 1 P. M. and 10 P. M. The mean summer range is ·00366 × X, or 12′·6. The mean winter range is ·00212 × X, or 7′·3. The mean range for the entire year is .00275 × X, or 9′·5.

(164) The hours of *greatest* and *least* easterly force are obtained from the equation

$$\Sigma(i\,B_i \cos ir) - \Sigma(i\,A_i \sin ir) = 0.$$

In winter these hours occur somewhat earlier, and in summer somewhat later.

The hours of *mean* easterly force are in like manner deduced from the equation

$$\Sigma(A_i \cos ir) + \Sigma(B_i \sin ir) = 0.$$

In the mean of the entire year, they occur at 9ʰ 45ᵐ A. M., and at 6ʰ 10ᵐ P. M. They are somewhat later in summer, and earlier in winter. The critical hours of greatest con-

Diurnal Inequality

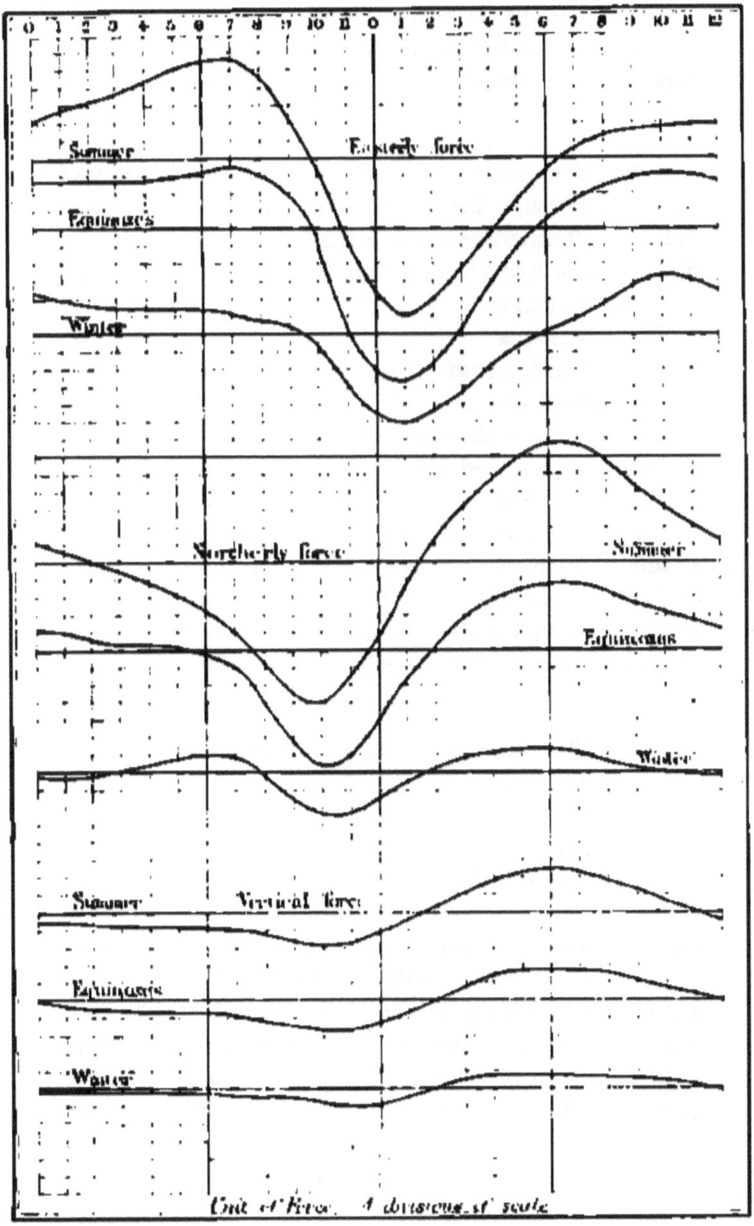

stancy throughout the year are those of the afternoon minimum and the forenoon mean, the extreme difference between these hours and the mean for the entire year being less than 30m.

(165) The greatest value of the mean rango is that of April. The range then decreases until about the middle of July, and afterwards increases, attaining a second, but smaller maximum, in August. The least value of the mean range is that of December.

Tho occurrence of the greatest ranges in April and August was first noticed by Beaufoy; and the fact was afterwards observed by Gauss. In his account of the Gottingen observations Gauss observes:—"The differences (of the declination at 8 A. M. and 1 P. M.) are not greatest at the time of the summer solstice, but appear to be smaller in June and July than in April, May, and August;" but he concludes, with Beaufoy, that the phenomenon was only an apparent one, due to the circumstance that the hours of observation were not so chosen as to exhibit the whole range near the summer solstice. From the foregoing it is apparent that the phenomenon in a real one.

(166) The characters of the diurnal inequality are similar at all the European, the American, and the Siberian stations.

At places south of the equator, however, the phenomenon is reversed, the north pole of the magnet moving to the east during the same time of the day at which its motion is westward at the northern stations, and *vice versa*. This opposition of the movements north and south of the equator was first observed by Macdonald in 1794. The phenomenon has since been more evidently shown in the results of tho observations made at the Observatory of Hobarton, in Van Dieman's Island, in latitude 42° 52′ south, during the years

1841–1847. The following table contains the mean yearly values of the easterly force at that station.

Diurnal Inequality of the Easterly Force at Hobarton.

Hour.	η	Hour.	η
1 A.M.	− 0.30	1 P.M.	+ 1.06
2	− 0.20	2	+ 1.36
3	− 0.13	3	+ 1.33
4	− 0.11	4	+ 1.03
5	− 0.19	5	+ 0.64
6	− 0.31	6	+ 0.35
7	− 0.58	7	+ 0.14
8	− 0.86	8	− 0.07
9	− 1.02	9	− 0.24
10	− 0.82	10	− 0.37
11	− 0.28	11	− 0.44
Noon.	+ 0.42	12	− 0.40

(167) The mean movements of the freely-suspended horizontal magnet in the northern hemisphere being thus reversed in the southern, it was naturally concluded that upon the equator itself they must vanish, and the needle remain stationary throughout the day. This anticipation was strengthened by the observed fact, that the magnitude of the diurnal variation diminished as the place of observation approached the equator. Further observations made at or near the equator, however, showed that the needle was not quiescent there; and physicists began to inquire what other line dividing the two hemispheres satisfied the supposed condition. This phase of opinion is exhibited conspicuously in the speculations of Arago on the subject, and in the instructions given by him to the officers of the *Bonite*, and to the commanders of other French naval expeditions.

In all this the fact was overlooked that the phenomena of the diurnal inequality depended, not simply upon the position of the place of observation on the Earth, but also upon its position with respect to the sun; and that this latter was different, even for places on the equator, at different periods of the year. At the equator, indeed, the deviations of the sun to the north and to the south are equal; and therefore it might be expected that the opposite movements of the free magnet, when the sun was north and south of the equator, should be equal, and therefore compensate each other in the mean of the entire year. According to this view the diurnal inequality should not vanish at the equator, except at the equinoxes. Its magnitude should increase with the sun's declination; and its law should be opposite when that declination was north and south, the opposite movements in the two halves of the year compensating one another in the mean of the entire year.

These conclusions were pointed out by Sir Edward Sabine as the result of the observations made at St. Helena, where, to use his words—"During one half of the year the movement of the north end of the magnet, at the hours referred to, corresponds in direction with the movement which is taking place in the northern hemisphere, whilst in the other half of the year the direction corresponds with that which is taking place in the southern hemisphere."

(168) The phenomenon is, however, more distinctly seen at places nearer to the equator. If we take the observations of declination at the two solstitial months, made at such a station, we find that, while the inequality in each of these months is by no means inconsiderable, the deviations of the needle are nearly equal in opposite directions.

This fact will be very distinctly seen in the elaborate series of observations continued during the twelve years, 1853–1864, at Trevandrum in India, in latitude 8° 30′ north, at the observatory established by the Rajah of Travancore, and under the direction of Mr. J. A. Broun. The mean results of these observations for the months of June and December are given in the following table, in which the positive numbers denote easterly deflections of the north end of the magnet.

Diurnal Inequality of the Magnetic Declination at Trevandrum, in the Solstitial Months.

Hour.	June.	Dec.	Mean.	Hour.	June.	Dec.	Mean.
12½	+ 0'.17	+ 0'.12	+ 0'.15	0½	− 1'.37	+ 0'.36	− 0'.50
13½	+ 0.30	+ 0.06	+ 0.18	1½	− 1.09	+ 0.83	− 0.13
14½	+ 0.40	− 0.08	+ 0.16	2½	− 0.70	+ 0.91	+ 0.11
15½	+ 0.43	− 0.27	+ 0.08	3½	− 0.32	+ 0.90	+ 0.29
16½	+ 0.46	− 0.50	− 0.02	4½	− 0.07	+ 0.76	+ 0.35
17½	+ 0.73	− 0.72	+ 0.01	5½	− 0.04	+ 0.42	+ 0.19
18½	+ 1.58	− 1.16	+ 0.21	6½	− 0.22	+ 0.40	+ 0.09
19½	+ 1.69	− 1.42	+ 0.14	7½	− 0.48	+ 0.39	− 0.04
20½	+ 1.07	− 0.95	+ 0.06	8½	− 0.49	+ 0.29	− 0.10
21½	+ 0.19	− 0.49	− 0.15	9½	− 0.37	+ 0.19	− 0.09
22½	− 0.59	− 0.27	− 0.43	10½	− 0.20	+ 0.12	− 0.04
23½	− 1.17	− 0.13	− 0.65	11½	− 0.00	+ 0.13	+ 0.07

It will be seen that the inequality, which is not inconsiderable in either of the solstitial months, nearly vanishes in their mean, the changes in these two months being nearly opposite.

We should thus be led to expect that the actual disappearance of the diurnal inequality would take place at the equator in the equinoctial months. This is found to be nearly the case at Trevandrum in the month of March. The change, however, is not a gradual or regular one, but the result of the balancing of opposite movements from day to day.

Similar effects, but less marked, may be traced in the results of the observations made at the observatory of the East India Company at Singapore, in latitude 1° 18′ north, under the able direction of the late Captain Elliott, R. E. The circumstance that the neutralization of the changes should take place some degrees north of the equator may be due to the difference of the solar effect upon land and water. At Trevandrum, we have seen, the inequality is greater in June than in December. At Singapore, it is the reverse, the changes in December preponderating; and we should be led to expect that the complete neutralization would occur in some intermediate latitude.

If we subtract the ordinates of the mean-yearly curve of the diurnal inequality from those for summer and winter respectively, we obtain the effect due to the sun's declination north and south. The curves so produced are of course opposed, and accord in character with the general laws of the diurnal inequality in the two hemispheres. Near the equator itself, where the mean-yearly curve vanishes, these differences of course represent the entire phenomena.

Diurnal Inequality of the Northerly Force.

(169) The diurnal inequality of the northerly force at Dublin has been investigated by a process similar to that adopted with the easterly. The monthly means of the scale readings of the bifilar magnetometer, and of its thermometer, corresponding to the several hours of observation, have been calculated for each year of observation, the days of unusual disturbance having been omitted; and from these the deviation from the mean of the day has been calculated for each hour. The results thus obtained for the four years 1840–1843, and for the seven years 1844–50, have been combined into separate means; and from these we obtain two separate values of the coefficients of the equation of the diurnal inequality. The arithmetical means of the corresponding coefficients have been taken as the resulting numbers for the entire period.

The following are the values of these coefficients for the years 1840–1850, so obtained. The means for the three divisions of the year, and for the entire year, are subjoined.

Coefficients of the Equation of the Diurnal Curve of the Northerly Force at Dublin.

Month.	A_1	B_1	A_2	B_2	A_3	B_3
January,	+ 0.00	− 0.07	− 0.20	+ 0.26	− 0.12	− 0.11
February,	+ 0.06	− 0.22	− 0.27	+ 0.26	− 0.10	− 0.12
March,	+ 0.31	− 0.57	− 0.27	+ 0.50	− 0.19	− 0.18
April,	+ 0.47	− 1.04	− 0.38	+ 0.56	− 0.14	− 0.22
May,	+ 0.31	− 1.35	− 0.32	+ 0.67	− 0.16	− 0.07
June,	+ 0.32	− 1.39	− 0.35	+ 0.54	− 0.20	+ 0.03
July,	+ 0.31	− 1.40	− 0.34	+ 0.61	− 0.22	− 0.06
August,	+ 0.32	− 1.33	− 0.24	+ 0.58	− 0.22	− 0.08
September,	+ 0.45	− 0.92	− 0.23	+ 0.54	− 0.20	− 0.16
October,	+ 0.43	− 0.45	− 0.28	+ 0.47	− 0.25	− 0.23
November,	+ 0.18	− 0.16	− 0.22	+ 0.30	− 0.15	− 0.10
December,	− 0.04	− 0.02	− 0.20	+ 0.25	− 0.10	− 0.11
Summer,	+ 0.31	− 1.37	− 0.31	+ 0.57	− 0.20	− 0.04
Equinoxes,	+ 0.42	− 0.75	− 0.29	+ 0.52	− 0.22	− 0.20
Winter,	+ 0.06	− 0.12	− 0.22	+ 0.27	− 0.12	− 0.11
Year,	+ 0.26	− 0.74	− 0.28	+ 0.45	− 0.18	− 0.12

(170) If we transform the equations of the diurnal inequality in the usual manner, by grouping together the corresponding terms, we obtain the following expressions for the diurnal inequality of the northerly force at Dublin for the three divisions of the year, as well as the mean for the entire year, expressed in thousandths of the whole. The time is reckoned from midnight.

Summer Months.

$$\xi = 1.40 \sin(x + 152^\circ) + 0.65 \sin(2x + 301^\circ) + 0.21 \sin(3x + 213^\circ).$$

Equinoctial Months.

$$\xi = 0.85 \sin(x + 136^\circ) + 0.59 \sin(2x + 330^\circ) + 0.29 \sin(3x + 183^\circ).$$

Winter Months.

$$\xi = 0.13 \sin (x + 140°) + 0.35 \sin (2x + 290°) + 0.16 \sin (3x + 181°).$$

Whole Year.

$$\xi = 0.79 \sin (x + 146°) + 0.53 \sin (2x + 299°) + 0.21 \sin (3x + 192°).$$

(171) The following are the calculated values of the force corresponding to the several hours.

Diurnal Inequality of the Northerly Force at Dublin.

Hour.	Summer Months.	Equinoctial Months.	Winter Months.	Year.
1 A.M.	+ 0.18	+ 0.26	− 0.10	+ 0.10
2	− 0.01	+ 0.15	− 0.06	+ 0.03
3	− 0.15	+ 0.04	+ 0.01	− 0.03
4	− 0.30	+ 0.04	+ 0.10	− 0.05
5	− 0.48	+ 0.06	+ 0.18	− 0.08
6	− 0.70	− 0.04	+ 0.25	− 0.16
7	− 0.96	− 0.20	+ 0.24	− 0.31
8	− 1.36	− 0.71	− 0.03	− 0.71
9	− 1.84	− 1.32	− 0.37	− 1.18
10	− 1.99	− 1.67	− 0.57	− 1.41
11	− 1.70	− 1.54	− 0.56	− 1.27
Noon	− 1.11	− 1.04	− 0.36	− 0.84
1 P.M.	− 0.38	− 0.45	− 0.14	− 0.32
2	+ 0.25	+ 0.01	+ 0.06	+ 0.11
3	+ 0.75	+ 0.42	+ 0.20	+ 0.46
4	+ 1.14	+ 0.70	+ 0.30	+ 0.73
5	+ 1.49	+ 0.86	+ 0.32	+ 0.89
6	+ 1.66	+ 0.92	+ 0.32	+ 0.97
7	+ 1.68	+ 0.90	+ 0.28	+ 0.95
8	+ 1.48	+ 0.82	+ 0.19	+ 0.83
9	+ 1.10	+ 0.67	+ 0.05	+ 0.61
10	+ 0.76	+ 0.53	0.00	+ 0.43
11	+ 0.50	+ 0.42	− 0.03	+ 0.30
12	+ 0.30	+ 0.31	− 0.05	+ 0.19

The general characters of the diurnal change, inferred from these numbers, are the following:—

I. About 6 A. M., the time varying slightly with the season, the northerly force begins to decrease rapidly; and reaches its minimum value about 10 A. M. or soon after.

II. After 10 A. M. the northerly force increases; and the increase continues until about 6 P. M., when the force is a maximum.

III. The magnitude of this change is considerably greater in summer than in winter. It is greatest in June, and least in December.

IV. In winter there is a second but much smaller variation in the magnitude of the force during the night and morning, the force diminishing until about 1 A. M., when there is a secondary minimum, and afterwards increasing until about 6 A. M., when there is a secondary maximum. This secondary oscillation disappears in the summer months, in which the force decreases continuously throughout the night and morning.

The epoch of the least force is the most constant of the critical hours. Its mean time is 10 A. M. in summer, and 10.30 A. M. in winter.

On the other hand, the epoch of greatest force varies considerably, being earliest in winter, and latest in summer. The mean time for the summer months is 6.30 P. M.; and, for the winter months, 4.25 P. M.

The range of the force is greatest in June, and least in December; and the ratio of the extremes is nearly that of 6 to 1.

(172) It will be useful and instructive to combine the two horizontal forces into one. The values of the *whole force in the horizontal plane*, so obtained, exhibit some features of the phenomenon, which are not readily perceived when

its two components are studied separately. This combination is effected by the ordinary rules for the composition of forces. Let ρ denote the intensity of the whole horizontal force, and ϕ the angle which its direction makes with the magnetic meridian, measured to the east of north; then

$$\tan\phi = \frac{\eta}{\xi}, \quad \rho = \xi \text{ secant } \phi.$$

The following are the mean yearly values of ρ and ϕ so obtained:—

Diurnal Inequality of the whole Force in the Horizontal Plane.

Hour.	ρ	ϕ	Hour.	ρ	ϕ
1 A. M.	0·63	81°	1 P. M.	1·93	260°
2	0·63	87	2	1·70	274
3	0·66	93	3	1·35	290
4	0·71	94	4	1·08	313
5	0·78	96	5	0·96	338
6	0·85	101	6	0·97	358
7	0·91	110	7	0·97	12
8	1·00	135	8	0·94	27
9	1·25	161	9	0·86	45
10	1·42	188	10	0·81	58
11	1·66	220	11	0·73	66
Noon	1·89	244	12	0·63	72

(173) The numbers of the preceding table are graphically represented in the annexed diagram, the radius-vector of the curve measuring the intensity of the force, and the angle which it makes with the magnetic meridian its azimuth. The corresponding hours are indicated on the perimeter of the curve.

It will be seen that in the early hours of the morning,—namely, from 1 A. M. to 6 A. M., inclusive,—the direction of the force changes little, being for the whole period nearly *east* (magnetic). At 6 A. M. the azimuth begins to increase;

and it becomes 180°, or the direction of the force is *south*, between 9 A. M. and 10 A. M. At 1.30 P. M. the azimuth be-

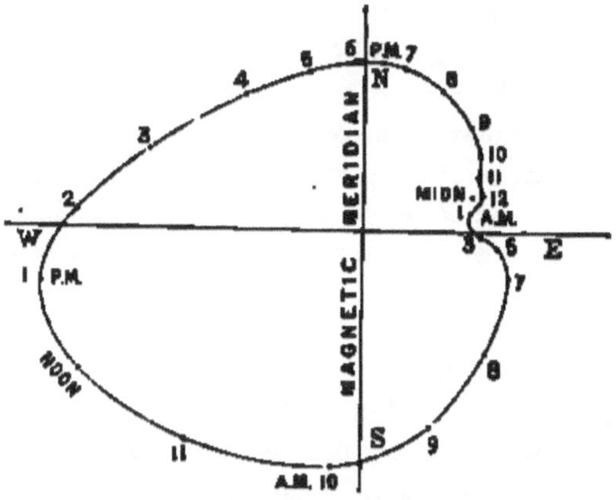

comes 270°, or the direction of the force is *west*; and at 6 P. M. it is *north*. Finally, after midnight, it reaches its stationary position in the east.

The intensity of the force is greatest at 1 P. M., and its direction is then nearly *west*. There is a secondary maximum between 6 P. M. and 7 P. M. preceded by a secondary minimum an hour or two earlier.

(174) If we form a similar construction for the separate months, we shall observe, in a very striking manner, the changes in the character of the diurnal inequality dependent upon season. The winter curves differ widely, both in form and magnitude, from those of summer; while the curves for the months nearest to the equinoxes are intermediate in both respects. It will be seen that the months resolve themselves naturally into the three groups already selected, viz., the four months nearest to the summer solstice; the four months nearest to the winter solstice; and the four months nearest to

the equinoxes. An examination of these curves reveals the following facts:—

I. The area of the summer curve greatly exceeds that of the winter curve.

II. These two curves differ notably in form, as well as in magnitude. The portion of the curve between 7 P. M. and 7 A. M. is, in winter, gathered up into a separate loop, which does not exist at all in the summer curve; and the whole curve is composed of two loops, the larger extending to the west, and corresponding to the hours of the day, while the smaller extends to the east, and corresponds to the hours of the night.

The curves for the two months nearest the equinoxes are (as might be expected) intermediate to those of summer and winter. There is a slight difference between the curve for March and April, and that for September and October, which seems to be accounted for by the circumstance that the mean epoch of the former is on the *summer side* of the vernal equinox, while that of the latter is on the *winter side* of the autumnal. From this and other facts, it appears that the usual mode of grouping the results of magnetical observations—namely, into monthly means—is not the best; and that the periods whose results are combined should commence from the sun's passage of the equator.

If we take the means of the values of the whole horizontal force at the several hours, for the several months of the year, we obtain the following results, the unit of force being $\frac{X}{10000}$, as before:—

Month	$\frac{1}{n}\Sigma(\rho)$	Month	$\frac{1}{n}\Sigma(\rho)$
January,	0·58	July,	1·41
February,	0·69	August,	1·38
March,	1·05	September,	1·14
April,	1·37	October,	0·90
May,	1·30	November,	0·54
June,	1·43	December,	0·52

The *maximum* occurs in June, and the *minimum* in December.

(175) On combining the mean values of η and ξ at the several hours of observation for the separate years, it will be very clearly seen that the whole horizontal force has undergone a notable change during the period 1841-1850. It diminished from 1841 to 1844, in which latter year it was a *minimum*. It then increased regularly until 1848, when it was a *maximum*; after which it again decreased, but more slowly. The following are the mean values of ρ for the several years.

Mean Diurnal Variation of the whole Horizontal Force at Dublin in the Years 1841–1850.

Year	$\frac{1}{n}\Sigma(\rho)$	Year	$\frac{1}{n}\Sigma(\rho)$
1841	1·05	1846	1·09
1842	0·96	1847	1·22
1843	0·91	1848	1·43
1844	0·92	1849	1·32
1845	0·97	1850	1·28

The progression is remarkably regular. The minimum occurred at the end of 1843, or the begining of 1844; the maximum took place in the latter part of 1848.

Thus the existence of a decennial period in the magnitude

of the diurnal range, first pointed out by Lamont,* is fully borne out by the Dublin observations. According to Lamont, the epoch of the minimum was 1843.5, and that of the maximum 1848.5. The observations of Cassini in 1784-1788, those of Beaufoy in 1813–1820, and those of Gauss in 1835-1841, furnished him with three additional periods of maximum range, which was thus found to have occurred in the years 1786, 1817, 1837, and 1848. From these data Lamont inferred the length of the period to be 10⅓ years.

(176) When we make a similar calculation for the twelve stations, the magnetic elements of which are given in the Appendix, we find much diversity in the forms of the polar curves which represent the direction and intensity of the horizontal force throughout the day. There are, however, some general features of the phenomena, which it will be instructive to particularise :—

I. At nearly all the stations in the northern hemisphere the direction of the force changes, throughout the day, according to the same general law. The force is directed to the *south* at 10.36 A.M., on the average; to the *west*, at 2.30 P.M.; and to the *north*, at 7.10 P.M. From the following table it will be seen that the hours at which the force is directed to these three cardinal points vary within narrow limits.

Station.	S.	W.	N.
Greenwich,	$10^h\ 30^m$ A.M.	$3^h\ 0^m$ P.M.	$7^h\ 25^m$ P.M.
Dublin,	10 25	3 15	7 35
Petersburg,	10 30	2 30	7 0
Catharinburg,	10 50	2 0	7 0
Barnaoul,	10 35	1 25	6 45
Nertchinsck,	10 45	3 30	7 15
Toronto,	10 30	1 50	7 20

* *Poggendorff Annalen*, 1851.

II. In the southern hemisphere the change of azimuth of the force takes place in an opposite direction to that in the northern. This will be seen, if we compute the directions of the resultant forces at Toronto, and at Hobarton, places which have equal latitudes north and south. Thus the point to which the horizontal magnetic force is directed follows the sun in all cases, although at unequal intervals at the different hours of the day.

III. The hour at which the force is greatest, in the northern hemisphere, ranges between noon and 2 P. M., being earliest in the British Islands, and latest in Siberia. The mean time of the maximum is 1.25 P. M.

IV. The azimuth of the maximum force is connected with the magnetic meridian of the place of observation. This will be seen by comparing the azimuths measured from the magnetic meridian with those measured from the astronomical. The extreme difference among the former, in the northern stations, is only 13°, while that of the latter is 49°. The mean azimuth (magnetic) is 262°, or W. 8° S.

V. The least intensity during the night occurs at an interval of about twelve hours from the epoch of the greatest; and the directions of the greatest and least forces are, in nearly all cases, exactly opposite.

Diurnal Inequality of the Vertical Force.

(177) The following Table contains the terms of the diurnal inequality of the vertical force at Dublin, deduced from the observations of the years 1841–1850, for the three seasons of the year, and for the entire year, the days of greater disturbance having been omitted in the calculation. They are expressed in parts of $\frac{X}{10000}$.

Diurnal Inequality of the Vertical Force at Dublin.

Hour.	Summer Months.	Equinoctial Months.	Winter Months.	Year.
1 A. M.	− 0·16	− 0·08	− 0·02	− 0·09
2	− 0·19	− 0·11	− 0·03	− 0·11
3	− 0·21	− 0·15	− 0·04	− 0·13
4	− 0·22	− 0·15	− 0·04	− 0·14
5	− 0·23	− 0·15	− 0·04	− 0·14
6	− 0·24	− 0·16	− 0·05	− 0·15
7	− 0·25	− 0·20	− 0·06	− 0·17
8	− 0·32	− 0·27	− 0·09	− 0·23
9	− 0·40	− 0·35	− 0·13	− 0·29
10	− 0·44	− 0·40	− 0·20	− 0·35
11	− 0·39	− 0·39	− 0·25	− 0·35
Noon	− 0·27	− 0·30	− 0·23	− 0·27
1 P. M.	− 0·13	− 0·17	− 0·11	− 0·14
2	+ 0·06	0·00	+ 0·02	+ 0·03
3	+ 0·26	+ 0·21	+ 0·12	+ 0·20
4	+ 0·45	+ 0·35	+ 0·19	+ 0·33
5	+ 0·56	+ 0·44	+ 0·20	+ 0·40
6	+ 0·60	+ 0·45	+ 0·21	+ 0·42
7	+ 0·55	+ 0·41	+ 0·20	+ 0·39
8	+ 0·45	+ 0·36	+ 0·18	+ 0·33
9	+ 0·32	+ 0·28	+ 0·13	+ 0·24
10	+ 0·15	+ 0·18	+ 0·06	+ 0·13
11	0·00	+ 0·08	+ 0·01	+ 0·03
12	− 0·15	0·00	− 0·03	− 0·05

The principal features of this inequality are the following:—

I. The vertical force is least between 10 A. M. and 11 A. M.; and it is greatest about 6 P. M. The amount of the range, in the mean of the year, is .00077 × X.

II. From midnight until 6 A. M. the changes are very small. There is, however, an indication of a secondary oscillation during these hours in the earlier years of the series, a secondary minimum at 2 A. M. or 3 A. M. being followed by a secondary maximum a few hours later.

III. The magnitude of the variation is, as in the case of the other components, greater in summer than in winter; and the proportion is nearly that of two to one. The law of the inequality in the equinoctial months resembles closely that for the entire year.

(178) The following equations give the resulting values of the diurnal inequality for the three periods of the year, and for the entire year, the time being reckoned from midnight:—

Summer Months.

$$\zeta = 0.52 \sin(x + 156°) + 0.26 \sin(2x + 290°) + 0.01 \sin(3x + 305°).$$

Equinoctial Months.

$$\zeta = 0.45 \sin(x + 137°) + 0.21 \sin(2x + 291°) + 0.06 \sin(3x + 108°).$$

Winter Months.

$$\zeta = 0.21 \sin(x + 140°) + 0.13 \sin(2x + 296°) + 0.06 \sin(3x + 94°).$$

Year.

$$\zeta = 0.39 \sin(x + 146°) + 0.20 \sin(2x + 295°) + 0.03 \sin(3x + 98).$$

(179) The variations of the horizontal and vertical components of the magnetic force having been obtained, the changes of the inclination are given by the formula

$$\Delta\theta \sin 1' = \cos^2\theta \frac{\zeta}{X} - \sin\theta \cos\theta \frac{\xi}{X};$$

or putting for θ its mean value in Dublin, corresponding to 1st January, 1842, and taking $\frac{X}{1000}$ as the unit of force,

$$\Delta\theta = 0.37\,\zeta - 1.07\,\xi.$$

The following table gives the mean values of $\Delta\theta$ corresponding to the several hours of observation in the years 1840–1843, for the three divisions of the year, and for the entire year, so calculated.

Diurnal Inequality of the Inclination at Dublin.

Hour.	Summer.	Equinoxes.	Winter.	Year.
- 11	- 0′.17	- 0′.24	+ 0′.27	- 0′.05
- 9	+ 0.03	- 0.03	+ 0.12	+ 0.04
- 7	+ 0.30	- 0.22	- 0.20	- 0.04
- 5	+ 0.92	+ 0.13	- 0.20	+ 0.25
- 3	+ 1.81	+ 1.22	+ 0.20	+ 1.08
- 1	+ 1.65	+ 1.43	+ 0.38	+ 1.15
+ 1	+ 0.34	+ 0.36	- 0.02	+ 0.23
+ 3	- 0.60	- 0.43	- 0.20	- 0.44
+ 5	- 1.28	- 0.66	- 0.27	- 0.74
+ 7	- 1.52	- 0.74	- 0.15	- 0.80
+ 9	- 0.98	- 0.47	+ 0.08	- 0.46
+ 11	- 0.51	- 0.38	+ 0.17	- 0.24

From the numbers of the preceding table we learn that, during the greater part of the year, the diurnal curve of inclination is a double curve, having two maxima and two minima in the twenty-four hours.

The *principal maximum* takes place about two hours before noon, its epoch being somewhat earlier in summer and later in winter. The *principal minimum* occurs between 4 P. M. and 7 P. M., being later in summer and earlier in winter. Its mean epoch for the equinoctial months is 6 P. M.

The *secondary maximum* takes place about 2 A. M., and the *secondary minimum* about 6 A. M. These epochs recede from one another in the winter months, the maximum occurring earlier, and the minimum later. In summer the secondary oscillation vanishes.

The mean daily range of the inclination at Dublin is 2′.0. It is 3′.3 in summer, and 0′.7 in winter.

(180) The changes of the total force are expressed in terms of ξ and ζ by the formula

$$\Delta R = \zeta \sin \theta + \xi \cos \theta ;$$

or, substituting the mean value of θ for Dublin,

$$\Delta R = 0.944\, \zeta + 0.330\, \xi .$$

The values of ΔR corresponding to the several hours of observation, for the three divisions of the year, and for the entire year, are given in the following table. The unit of force is $\frac{X}{1000}$ as before.

Diurnal Inequality of the Total Force at Dublin.

Hour.	Summer.	Equinoxes.	Winter.	Year.
1 A.M.	− 0.26	− 0.18	− 0.19	− 0.21
3	− 0.31	− 0.31	− 0.11	− 0.24
5	− 0.30	− 0.13	+ 0.01	− 0.14
7	− 0.41	− 0.22	+ 0.05	− 0.19
9	− 0.80	− 0.57	− 0.13	− 0.50
11	− 0.75	− 0.62	− 0.29	− 0.56
1 P.M.	− 0.15	− 0.09	− 0.03	− 0.09
3	+ 0.44	+ 0.45	+ 0.24	+ 0.38
5	+ 0.91	+ 0.60	+ 0.22	+ 0.58
7	+ 0.93	+ 0.60	+ 0.25	+ 0.59
9	+ 0.57	+ 0.36	+ 0.07	+ 0.33
11	+ 0.12	+ 0.10	− 0.08	+ 0.05

The diurnal inequality of the total force is nearly the inverse of that of the inclination, the minima of the former corresponding to the maxima of the latter, and *vice versâ*.

The *principal minimum* takes place between 10 A.M. and 11 A.M., the former hour being nearly the epoch in summer, and the latter in winter. The *principal maximum* occurs about 6 P.M. in the summer and equinoctial months; in winter it is earlier, but it is ill-defined.

The *secondary minimum* takes place about 2 A. M. The epoch of the *secondary maximum* is 6 A. M. nearly. The secondary oscillation nearly disappears in the summer months. The mean diurnal curve for the entire year closely resembles the curve for the equinoctial months, as in the case of the inclination.

The mean range of the total force is .00173 × X in summer, and .00054 × X in winter.

CHAPTER XII.

LUNAR INEQUALITY.

(181) Each of the magnetic elements is subject to a small variation, dependent upon the position of the moon with respect to the meridian. This remarkable fact was discovered by Kreil, who demonstrated the existence of a variation of the magnetic declination dependent on the lunar hour. The effect of the moon upon the other magnetical elements seems to have been first established by Mr. J. A. Broun, from a discussion of the Makerstoun observations.

For the purpose of this investigation it is only necessary to tabulate the results according to the moon's hour-angle, commencing with the observation nearest to the moon's upper meridian passage. This process having been continued until the lunation is completed, it is evident that the same solar hour will fall on each of the lunar hours in succession, so that the solar diurnal variation is eliminated from the mean results. As the lunar day exceeds the solar by $0^h.8$, or by four hours in five days, it is obvious that there will be thirteen results of the bi-hourly series in two out of five lunar days. In all such cases the first observation of the solar day has been omitted. In this manner twelve observations are omitted in each lunation, one between each pair of successive lunar hours; and the effect of this omission is to alter the mean interval from 2^h to $2^h\ 4^m$, corresponding to 30° of the lunar hour-angle.

The observations having been thus tabulated, the means corresponding to each alternate hour are to be taken for each lunation; and the corresponding results of the several lunations combined.

(182) Applying this process to the readings of the declinometer in the years 1841–1843, we obtain the following values of the lunar diurnal inequality in parts of .001 × X, *positive* numbers corresponding to *easterly* forces. The results for the periods during which the sun is north and south of the equator have been deduced separately. The numbers in the first column denote the intervals, in lunar hours, from the time of the moon's upper meridian passage.

Lunar Inequality of the Easterly Force at Dublin.

Lunar Hour.	Summer Lunations.	Winter Lunations.	Year.
– 12	– 0·19	– 0·09	– 0·14
– 10	– 0·21	– 0·08	– 0·15
– 8	– 0·06	+ 0·02	– 0·02
– 6	+ 0·09	+ 0·09	+ 0·09
– 4	+ 0·12	+ 0·13	+ 0·13
– 2	+ 0·08	– 0·01	+ 0·03
0	– 0·06	– 0·09	– 0·08
+ 2	– 0·04	– 0·07	– 0·05
+ 4	+ 0·05	– 0·02	+ 0·01
+ 6	+ 0·17	+ 0·08	+ 0·12
+ 8	+ 0·06	+ 0·07	+ 0·07
+ 10	0·00	– 0·05	– 0·03

It will be seen from the foregoing numbers that the easterly force is subject to a periodical variation, depending on the position of the moon with respect to the meridian, and having two maxima and two minima in the course of the lunar day. The phenomenon is distinctly exhibited in the results of the separate years.

The forenoon maximum occurs about four or five hours before the moon's meridian passage; the afternoon maximum about six or seven hours after it. The minima take place soon after the two meridian passages.

The mean range of the easterly force at Dublin (measured from the mean of the two minima to the intervening maximum) is 0.24. The mean daily range of the easterly force due to the sun's action being 2.60, the lunar force is to the solar as 1 to 11, nearly.

The summer and the winter lunations exhibit the same laws, there being in both cases two maxima and two minima, whose epochs coincide nearly with those for the entire year.

(180) These results agree in their main features with those obtained by Professor Kreil and Mr. Broun, from the discussion of the Prague and of the Makerstoun observations. But at Prague the lunar inequality is extremely small in winter; while, at Makerstoun, there is but one maximum and one minimum at that period of the year. At Dublin, on the other hand, the double oscillation is distinctly marked at both periods of the year, and its magnitude does not vary considerably with the season.

It is a remarkable feature of this inequality, first noticed by Sir Edward Sabine, that the hours of maxima and minima are very different in different localities. Thus at Toronto the greatest *easterly* deflections take place at the hours of the moon's upper and lower meridian passages, which are, very nearly, the hours of the greatest *westerly* deflections at Dublin; and at Hobarton, and St. Helena, the hours of maxima and minima differ from both, and from one another. This diversity in the features of a phenomenon, which are in other respects so accordant, suggests the conclusion that lunar action is its *remote*, and not its *immediate* cause. In this, as well as in other respects, the phenomena are analogous to those of the tides, the hours of whose arrival at different points of the Earth's surface follow the moon's passages by very unequal intervals.

(184) The following table exhibits the lunar inequality of the northerly force at Dublin, deduced from the observations of the same years, 1841-1843. It will be seen that the northerly force is subject to a variation, whose period is a lunar day, altogether analogous to that of the easterly.

Lunar Inequality of the Northerly Force at Dublin.

Lunar Hours.	Summer Lunations.	Winter Lunations.	Year.
− 12	− 0.06	+ 0.01	− 0.03
− 10	− 0.01	+ 0.02	+ 0.01
− 8	+ 0.08	+ 0.07	+ 0.07
− 6	+ 0.04	+ 0.05	+ 0.04
− 4	− 0.02	0.00	− 0.01
− 2	− 0.08	+ 0.04	+ 0.01
0	− 0.01	+ 0.02	+ 0.01
+ 2	0.00	+ 0.05	+ 0.08
+ 4	+ 0.08	− 0.03	+ 0.03
+ 6	− 0.01	− 0.03	− 0.02
+ 8	− 0.10	− 0.12	− 0.11
+ 10	− 0.08	− 0.07	− 0.08

Thus the northerly force, like the easterly, has two maxima and two minima in the lunar day. The maxima occur at Dublin about three hours after the moon's meridian passages; and the minima about three-and-a-half hours before them. There is little difference in these epochs between the summer and the winter lunations.

The two maxima are nearly equal; but the afternoon minimum is greater than the forenoon one. The amount of the range, measured from the mean of the two minima to the intervening maximum, is .00014 × X.

When we combine the values of η and ξ graphically, as has been already done in the case of the solar inequality, we obtain a curve with two loops, one lying within the other. The smaller or interior loop corresponds to the hours from

-4^h to $+6^h$; the larger or exterior loop to the remaining hours of the lunar day. The points of the curve corresponding to the lunar hours -4^h and $+6^h$ being close to the nodes, the direction and magnitude of the whole horizontal force are nearly the same at these hours. The progression in each loop is *direct* (or in the direction of the movement of the hands of a watch), as in the solar variation.

(185) The next table contains the corresponding values of the lunar inequality of the vertical force at Dublin, deduced from the observations of the year 1843. The numbers plainly indicate the existence of two maxima and two minima in the course of the lunar day, as in the case of the two other elements.

Lunar Inequality of the Vertical Force at Dublin.

Lunar Hours.	ζ	Lunar Hours.	ζ
− 12	+ 0·05	0	+ 0·02
− 10	0·00	+ 2	+ 0·02
− 8	0·00	+ 4	− 0·01
− 6	− 0·02	+ 6	− 0·06
− 4	− 0·07	+ 8	− 0·01
− 2	+ 0·10	+ 10	+ 0·01

If, disregarding the magnitude of the separate values which are somewhat uncertain, we take the middle of the positive and negative periods for the epochs of maxima and minima, the former will be seen to coincide nearly with the times of the moon's meridian passages, and the latter to occur about six hours after.

(186) As the period of the lunar inequality differs from that of the solar, they will combine in every variety of phase, the lunar variation at one time conspiring with the solar, and

at another opposing it, as in the analogous case of the tides. The resultant oscillation will thus vary with the moon's age; and its range will have two maxima and two minima in the course of the month.

Confining our attention to the easterly force,—it has been shown above that its two minima, in the lunar diurnal inequality, occur about one hour after the moon's meridian passages, above and below. Now these periods will coincide with the hour of the solar minimum, which is one hour after the sun's upper meridian passage, when the interval of retardation of the moon is 0 and 12 hours, respectively—i. e. on the day of conjunction, and on the fifteenth day of the moon's age. And the interval of time between the maximum and minimum being nearly the same in the two oscillations, the maxima of both will nearly coincide on the same days. Accordingly, the range of the easterly force should be greatest on the two days just mentioned; while it should be least between the seventh and eighth, and between the twenty-second and twenty-third days.

To examine this, the daily range of the declination, from 7 A. M. to 1 P. M., has been calculated for each day of the ten years 1841-1850, and the numbers arranged according to the moon's age, beginning with the day of conjunction. Taking the means of the corresponding numbers for the twelve lunations of each year, and combining the values for the separate years so obtained again into single means, we obtain the numbers of the following table, reduced into parts of the force:—

Range of the Easterly Force at Dublin.

Day.	Range.	Day.	Range.
0	3·00	15	3·04
1	2·99	16	3·07
2	3·12	17	2·95
3	3·17	18	3·00
4	3·04	19	3·09
5	2·95	20	2·95
6	2·82	21	2·78
7	2·80	22	2·70
8	2·80	23	2·69
9	2·68	24	2·73
10	2·69	25	2·68
11	2·73	26	2·87
12	2·77	27	2·88
13	2·94	28	2·98
14	2·94	29	3·00

These numbers exhibit very distinctly the two maxima, and the two minima, above referred to. The maxima are found to occur on the second or third, and on the sixteenth day of the moon's age; the minima on the ninth or tenth, and on the twenty-third day. The whole range of the variation is 0·44, which is, as was to be expected, very nearly the double of the range of the lunar diurnal inequality.

The mean magnitude of the entire range is 2·89. It is above the mean from the 28th to the 5th day of the lunation, and from the 13th to the 20th; it is below the mean in the other two quarters.

CHAPTER XIII.

MAGNETIC DISTURBANCES.

(187) THE distinctive character of a magnetic disturbance is a rapid movement of the suspended magnets, causing them to deviate considerably from their normal positions, and in opposite directions alternately. The duration and the magnitude of these oscillations are as yet outside the domain of law, and probably depend upon so many co-operating causes that, like the gusts and lulls of the wind in an atmospheric storm, they will long baffle all attempts to refer them to their actuating forces, or even to reduce them to order.

The first important discovery in connexion with magnetic disturbances was the recognition of their simultaneity at very distant places. This remarkable fact was first made known by a comparison of the observations of the changes of declination, made in 1818 by Arago, at Paris, and by Kupffer, at Kasan, places differing from one another by more than forty-seven degrees of longitude.

For the fuller investigation of this interesting phenomenon, an elaborate system of simultaneous observations of the declination was organised by Humboldt, in 1827, at several stations in Germany and in Russia, the observations being taken hourly at stated times in the year. This organization was greatly extended and improved by Gauss, in the year 1834. The magnetic stations were largely increased in number, the observations having been continued through 24 hours of the same absolute time at twenty-three places in Europe; and the synchronism of the disturbances having been found to extend to the minutest changes, the observations were taken at the short intervals of five minutes. A comparison of the results of these observations showed that the minutest changes at any one place of observation had their counterparts at every other, the curves by which they were graphically represented corresponding in all respects, except in the magnitude of the inflexions.*

(188) In the great magnetic co-operation, established by the British Government and by the East India Company, in 1840, the system was still further extended, and the three magnetical elements were observed. The comparison of the results so obtained has shown that, while the greater disturbances were synchronous at all points of the globe, yet the parallelism of the inflexions no longer subsisted at very remote places. Thus the forces which produce these abnormal effects operate at the same absolute time at all parts of the earth, while the manner of their operation varies with the locality.

During the occurrence of one of these *magnetic storms* (as they have been called), all the magnetic elements are not always affected at the same precise time. A considerable disturbance of one element is, however, generally accompanied by similar changes of the other two, although it may be at different moments of time, and in different degrees. For this reason, what are called "days of disturbance," may be defined from the behaviour of a single element.

(189) But notwithstanding the irregularity in the magnitudes and actual epochs of these changes, they exhibit a

* The stations at which this system was carried out were Altona, Augsburg, Berlin, Bonn, Brunswick, Breda, Breslau, Cassel, Copenhagen, Kracow, Dublin, Freyberg, Gottingen, Greenwich, Halle, Kasan, Leipsic, Marburg, Milan, Munich, Naples, St. Petersburg, and Upsala.

tendency to recur at certain hours of the day, and at certain seasons of the year, which shows itself in their mean values. This remarkable and important fact was discovered by Kreil. To prove it, we have only to take the differences (without regard to sign) between the actual readings of the declinometer, and the monthly means corresponding to the same hour. The means of these differences will measure the *tendency to disturbance*, and will exhibit any periodicity which exists in it.

The following Table presents the results of such calculation for the whole period of the bi-hourly observations at Dublin, reduced into parts of the force.

Mean Departures of the Easterly Force from its normal Values at Dublin, at the alternate hours.

Hour.	Mean Disturbance.	Hour.	Mean Disturbance.
1 A. M.	0·75	1 P. M.	0·52
3	0·59	3	0·54
5	0·62	5	0·54
7	0·59	7	0·57
9	0·55	9	0·73
11	0·51	11	0·73

The prominent fact established by these numbers is the great prevalence of disturbances during the four hours of the night, from 9 P. M. to 1 A. M. If the numbers be projected in a curve, of which the abscissa denotes the *time*, and the ordinate the *mean disturbance*, it will be seen that the latter begins *suddenly* to increase at 7 P. M., and reaches nearly its highest value at 9 P. M. From that hour, until 1 A. M., it continues nearly of the same magnitude; and it then decreases as rapidly as it had before increased, and regains its mean value about 3 A.M. During the remaining sixteen hours, from 3 A.M. to 7 P.M., the ordinate of the disturbance curve is below its mean value. The absolute minimum occurs about noon; but the change throughout the day-hours is small.

(190) If we combine the twelve results for each month into a single mean, we are enabled to perceive the influence of *season* upon the mean disturbance. The following Table gives the mean departures of the easterly force from its normal values for each of the twelve months, deduced from the observations of the ten years, 1841–1850:—

Annual Variation of the Mean Disturbance at Dublin.

Month.	Mean Disturbance.	Month.	Mean Disturbance.
January,	0·48	July,	0·57
February,	0·57	August,	0·56
March,	0·58	September,	0·67
April,	0·57	October,	0·66
May,	0·52	November,	0·59
June,	0·48	December,	0·45

From these numbers it will be seen that the *mean disturbance* observes an *annual*, as well as a daily period. The progression of the numbers is remarkably regular. The variation is a double one, with two maxima and two minima. The *maxima* occur in the equinoctial months, March and September; the latter being the best defined. The *minima* are in the solstitial months, June and December. The mean value of the disturbance of the easterly force for the entire year, as deduced from the observations of the ten years, is $.00056 \times X$.

(191) If we combine the results into yearly means, we obtain the following numbers:—

Secular Variation of the Mean Disturbance at Dublin.

Year.	Mean Disturbance.	Year.	Mean Disturbance.
1841	0·71	1846	0·57
1842	0·57	1847	0·64
1843	0·46	1848	0·68
1844	0·49	1849	0·57
1845	0·45	1850	0·59

The traces of a periodical change are here very evident. The maximum occurs in 1847 or 1848; the least values in the years 1843, 1844, 1845.

Thus the *decennial period*, which had been already proved to exist in the diurnal range of the declination, holds also in the mean disturbance. This fact was pointed out by Sir Edward Sabine, in his discussion of the observations at Toronto and Hobarton; and he identified this period with that which Schwabe had previously shown to exist in the frequency of the solar spots. The observations of M. Schwabe extended through the long space of thirty-four years; and therefore included three complete decennial periods. The ten-year period in these observations is very remarkable. The maxima of frequency of the solar spots were found to occur in the years 1828, 1837, 1848, and 1860; and the minima in the years 1833, 1843, and 1855.

(192) In what has preceded we have considered only the *magnitude* of the changes produced by disturbance, without regard to sign. But magnetic disturbances exert a systematic effect upon the *direction*, as well as on the magnitude of the magnetic elements. For the investigation of the laws of these, it will be convenient to separate the days of distur-

bance from the rest; and to discuss the results according to the methods which have been already applied to ordinary days, taking the differences of the results at the several hours and the *regular* monthly mean. In this calculation it will be advisable to take a somewhat lower limit than before for the days of disturbance, so as to include a number of days sufficiently large to furnish a probable mean result. We have accordingly defined *a day of disturbance* to be one in which the mean departure of the readings of the declinometer from their normal values for the month is *once and a half* the average. The mean disturbance of the easterly force, calculated in the manner described, is 0·60, the unit of force being .001 × X, as before. Consequently a day of disturbance is assumed to be one in which the mean departure of the easterly force from its normal values is 0·90, or upwards. The following table shows the number of such days in each of the ten years, 1841–1850.

Number of Days of Disturbance in each Year.

Year.	Disturbed Days.	Year.	Disturbed Days.
1841	57	1846	43
1842	26	1847	42
1843	17	1848	47
1844	26	1849	34
1845	20	1850	23

These numbers show, in a conspicuous manner, the great disparity which exists in different years as regards the frequency of disturbance. The years appear in this respect to arrange themselves *in groups*, rather than in the orderly progression of a period. Thus the three years, 1846–1848, form a group of frequent disturbance; while the four preceding years, 1842–1845, are of the opposite character.

(193) The next table gives the number of disturbed days in the *several months* of the ten years. The average number in each month is 33.5 :—

Number of Days of Disturbance in each Month.

Month.	Disturbed Days.	Month.	Disturbed Days.
January,	18	July,	21
February,	28	August,	25
March,	24	September,	36
April,	20	October,	33
May,	21	November,	28
June,	13	December,	16

From the foregoing numbers it will be seen that the *frequency of disturbance* observes an *annual period*, having two maxima and two minima in the year. The maxima occur in February or March, and in September or October, the autumnal maximum being the greater. The minima occur in the two solstitial months, June and December. These, as well as the foregoing results, accord with those already obtained from the examination of the *mean disturbance*.

(194) We now proceed to the calculation indicated in (192). The following table exhibits the *diurnal inequality* of the easterly and northerly forces on days of disturbance, deduced from the bi-hourly observations. The results are given separately for the three divisions of the year.

Diurnal Inequality on Days of Disturbance.

Hour.	Summer Months.		Equinoctial Months.		Winter Months.		Year.	
	w.	e.	w.	e.	w.	e.	w.	e.
1 A.M.	+ 1·03	− 0·84	+ 0·68	− 0·64	+ 1·44	− 0·92	+ 1·05	− 0·60
3	+ 0·94	− 1·27	+ 0·89	− 0·83	+ 0·23	− 0·55	+ 0·68	− 0·88
5	+ 0·52	− 1·13	− 0·24	− 0·98	+ 0·06	− 0·55	+ 0·11	− 0·89
7	+ 0·34	− 2·05	− 0·29	− 1·10	− 0·68	− 0·27	− 0·21	− 1·14
9	− 0·29	− 3·02	− 0·73	− 2·23	− 0·78	− 1·01	− 0·60	− 2·08
11	− 1·85	− 2·43	− 1·89	− 2·01	− 1·86	− 1·10	− 1·87	− 1·85
1 P.M.	− 2·63	− 0·28	− 2·59	− 0·14	− 2·38	− 0·29	− 2·58	− 0·23
3	− 2·01	+ 1·34	− 1·58	+ 0·95	− 1·76	+ 0·20	− 1·78	+ 0·83
5	− 0·60	+ 1·99	− 0·14	+ 0·94	− 0·57	+ 0·08	− 0·43	+ 1·00
7	+ 0·41	+ 1·45	+ 1·08	+ 0·84	+ 0·76	− 0·75	+ 0·75	+ 0·25
9	+ 1·06	+ 0·21	+ 1·63	− 0·47	+ 1·79	− 1·50	+ 1·49	− 0·59
11	+ 1·31	− 0·95	+ 2·02	− 1·40	+ 1·24	− 1·62	+ 1·52	1·32

When the numbers of this table are projected in curves, along with those of the regular diurnal inequality, it will be seen that the disturbance-curve of the easterly force intersects the normal curve twice. The epoch of the descending node occurs between the hours 3 A. M. and 4 A. M.; and that of the ascending node between the hours 5 P. M. and 6 P. M. Thus the disturbance-curve is above the normal curve from 6 P.M. to 4 A. M., nearly; and below it during the remainder of the day. Consequently, the effect of disturbance on the easterly force is *positive* during the former period, which includes the greater part of the night; and *negative* during the latter, or day hours. The *maximum* occurs about 10 P. M., and the *minimum* about 8 A. M.

The mean difference for the entire day is negative; and consequently the westerly changes preponderate over the easterly. The difference, however, is small.

The curves of disturbance of the easterly force differ from

Mean Diurnal Inequality on Normal Days and on Days of Disturbance

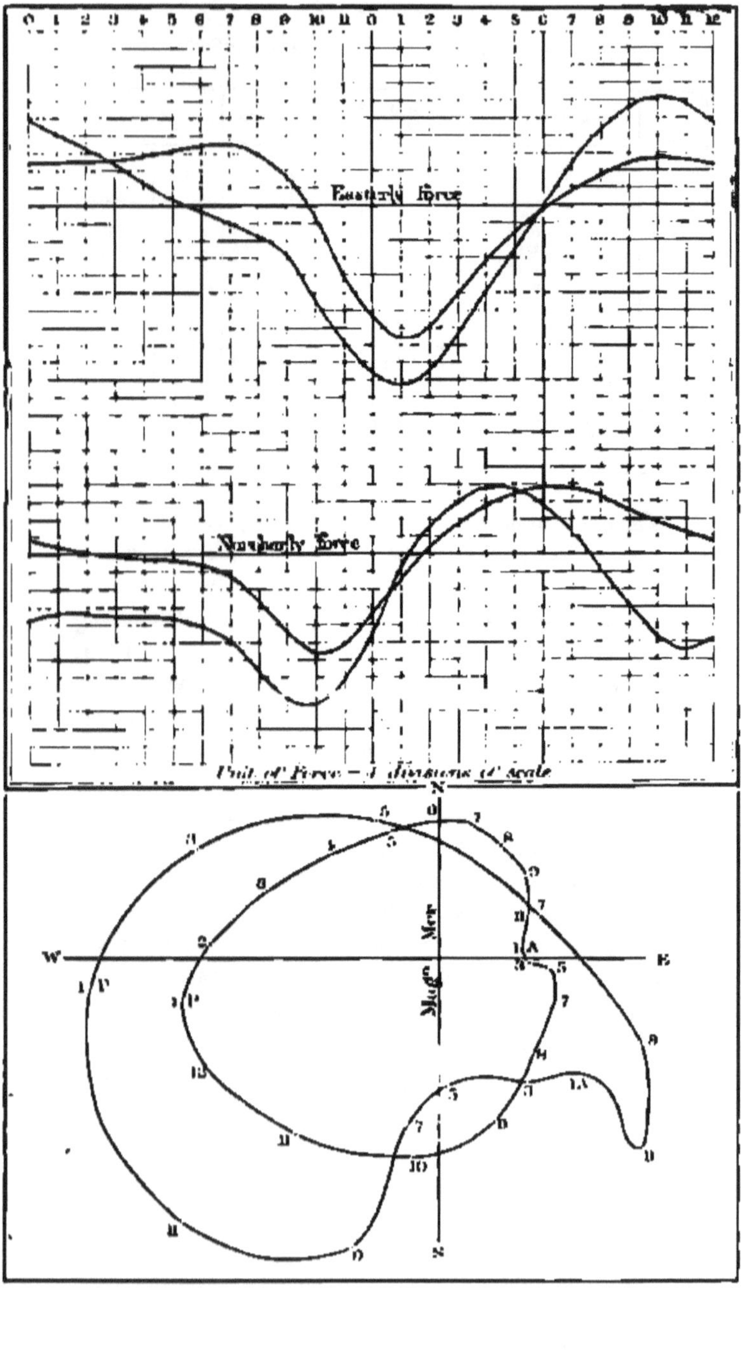

one another at the different periods of the year much less than the normal curves; and the range is nearly the same throughout the year.

The curve of disturbance of the *northerly* force lies below the normal curve at all hours of the day, with the exception of a few hours following noon. In the summer months these hours range from 1 P.M. to 7 P.M.; in the equinoctial months the period is more contracted; and in winter it vanishes altogether, and the curve of disturbance is below the normal curve throughout the entire day. The interval is greatest about two or three hours before noon; and again about one or two hours before midnight.

The mean daily value of the northerly force on days of disturbance is *negative*; and consequently the *mean effect* of disturbances is to diminish that force.

The curve of disturbance of the northerly force shows a marked *annual inequality*. The range of the ordinate is widely different at the different periods of the year, being greatest in summer and least in winter, as in the case of the regular diurnal inequality.

(195) When the two components of the horizontal force are graphically combined, in the manner already applied to the regular variations of the same elements, the disturbance curve presents the following characters:—

I. The curve is much larger than the normal curve, and is external to it at every hour, excepting the hours from 5 A.M. to 7 A.M. inclusive, and the hour 6 P.M. Hence the *whole horizontal force* is in general increased on days of disturbance; the increase is greatest about 11 P.M., when there is a marked maximum in the curve.

II. The azimuth of the force on days of disturbance is greater than the corresponding azimuth in the normal curve, excepting during the six hours from 11 A. M. to 5 P.M., inclusive. The difference is greatest about 11 P. M.

III. The chief diversity in the law of the diurnal force at the different seasons of the year is due to the great development of the northerly force in the summer, as compared with the winter months, the range of the easterly force varying little.

(196) Subtracting the normal values of the two component forces, η and ξ, from their values on days of disturbance (194), we obtain measures of the hourly effects of the disturbing force in the two directions. The following table gives the mean yearly values of $\Delta\eta$ and $\Delta\xi$ thus found, together with the corresponding values of ρ and ϕ :—

Diurnal Inequality of the Horizontal Disturbing Force in Magnitude and Direction.

Hour.	$\Delta\eta$	$\Delta\xi$	ρ	ϕ
1 A. M.	+ 0·54	− 0·76	0·93	145°
3	+ 0·17	− 0·77	0·79	168
5	− 0·55	− 0·88	1·03	212
7	− 0·96	− 0·86	1·29	228
9	− 0·99	− 1·02	1·42	224
11	− 0·81	− 0·70	1·07	229
1 P. M.	− 0·72	− 0·01	0·72	269
3	− 0·55	+ 0·34	0·65	302
5	− 0·10	+ 0·20	0·23	333
7	+ 0·51	− 0·52	0·72	136
9	+ 0·83	− 1·07	1·35	142
11	+ 0·63	− 1·54	1·75	152

From the numbers of the third column we learn that the disturbing force is a *maximum* at 11 P. M. and at 8 A. M., and a *minimum* at 5 P. M. Comparing the values of the azimuths, ϕ, with those of corresponding hours in the regular diurnal inequality, we find that the *disturbing force is perpendicular to the ordinary diurnal force at the two hours of maximum* above mentioned. The directions of the two forces are nearly coincident from 11 A. M. to 5 P. M. inclusive.

(197) The effects of disturbance upon the vertical force have been obtained by comparing the results of all the observations with those obtained when the days of greater disturbance are omitted. The following table gives the results for the three periods of the year, and for the entire year. They are of course much smaller than those which would be obtained by the process above applied, although proportional in magnitude.

Effect of Disturbances on the Vertical Force at the several Hours of the Day.

Hour.	Summer Months.	Equinoctical Months.	Winter Months.	Year.
1 A. M.	−·044	−·112	−·048	−·068
3	−·077	−·056	−·014	−·049
5	−·103	−·073	−·025	−·067
7	−·087	−·066	−·020	−·038
9	−·058	−·028	−·015	−·034
11	−·021	−·009	+·006	−·008
1 P. M.	+·035	+·031	−·001	+·022
3	+·038	+·049	+·041	+·043
5	+·050	+·089	+·047	+·062
7	+·037	+·033	+·079	+·050
9	−·025	−·028	+·008	−·015
11	−·216	−·065	−·020	−·100

The effect of disturbances upon the vertical force resembles closely their effect upon the northerly component.

It is *positive*, or the vertical force is increased by disturbances, during the eight or nine hours following noon, and *negative* during the remainder of the day. In the summer and equinoctial months, the epochs of no effect occur between 11 A. M. and noon, and between 8 P. M. and 9 P. M.; in winter both epochs are about an hour later. The *maximum* occurs about 6 P. M., and the *minimum* about midnight.

As in the case of the northerly force, there is a minor oscillation in the values of ζ during the night, a *secondary maximum* occurring about 3 A. M., followed by a *secondary minimum* about two hours later.

The effect of disturbances on the daily mean is *negative*, or the vertical force is diminished, in the summer and equinoctial months. In winter the positive and negative effects nearly balance one another in the mean of the day.

From the foregoing numbers it is easy to calculate the effects of disturbances upon the inclination and total force. Their mean effect is to *increase* the inclination, and to *diminish* the total force, except for a few hours following noon. The maximum effect upon the inclination takes place about 10 P. M.; it is earlier in winter and later in summer. The maximum effect upon the total force takes place, in the mean of the year, about 11 P. M.; it is, on the contrary, earlier in summer and later in winter.

(108) The three components of the magnetic force are all *diminished* on days of disturbance, in the mean of the entire day. The mean values of the three components, on such days, are

$$\Delta\eta = -0{\cdot}14\,; \quad \Delta\xi = -0{\cdot}56\,; \quad \Delta\zeta = -0{\cdot}10.$$

From these results it follows that the azimuth of the disturbing force, measured from the magnetic meridian in the direction NESW., is 104°; and that the force is directed *upwards*, forming an angle of 10° with the horizon.

(199) The principal results at which we have thus arrived, in relation to the diurnal changes, may be summed up as follows:—

1. The *oscillatory movement* of magnetic disturbances observes a daily period. It is greatest about one hour before midnight, and least a little before noon.

2. The effect of disturbances on the mean values is, in general, to increase the ordinate of the diurnal curve (whether positive or negative) of each of the three components of the force. The negative ordinates are in all cases more augmented than the positive, so that the *mean effect of disturbances*, for the entire day, is *negative*.

3. The deviation of the diurnal curves of disturbance from the normal curves is greatest about 11 P. M., for all the components. The deviation at this hour is *positive* for the easterly force, and *negative* for the other two components.

4. The whole disturbing force in the horizontal plane rotates in the same direction as the sun. Its direction is perpendicular to the ordinary diurnal force at the two hours of maximum. It is nearly coincident with it from 11 A. M. to 5 P. M., inclusive.

5. When the whole values of η and ξ are combined, it is found that the *whole horizontal force* is much greater on days of disturbance than on normal days, at all hours excepting 6 P. M. and 7 P. M.

6. There is a remarkable *maximum* in the value of the same resultant on days of disturbance at 11 P. M., followed by an equally remarkable *subsidence of the force* about 6 A. M. This change is most conspicuous in the winter months.

7. The diurnal force on days of disturbance is subject to an *annual inequality*, the force being greatest in summer, least in winter, and of intermediate value in the equinoctial months. The variation occurs chiefly in the values of the northerly component.

(200) We have hitherto considered the mean effects of disturbances at a single station. To a great extent, however, these may be taken as typical. The effects of magnetic disturbances upon the variations of long period (the *annual* and the *secular*) are similar at all parts of the globe at which magnetical observations have been made; and even in the *diurnal* change, the augmentation of the three components of the force by the effect of disturbances takes place alike at all.

But when we come to examine the proportionate effects of such changes, and the epochs of their maxima and minima, we find great diversity. Thus, at point Barrow, in latitude 72° N., the effect of disturbances is to augment greatly the forenoon maximum of the easterly force; while at Toronto, and at all the European stations, they increase the maximum at 10 P.M.

The effects of disturbances upon the diurnal changes are much greater as the place nears the poles; and are very different in different meridians, thus indicating the presence of local centres of action. In many cases the magnitude of the effects is such as to mask the regular law. This was first noticed in the observations of declination made by Foster and Ross in 1825 at Port Bowen, (lat. 73° N., long. 90° W.). The easterly minimum varied between 10 A. M. and 1 P. M.; and the maximum between 9 P. M. and 2 A. M.

The observations of the same element in 1852-4, by Captain Maguire, at Point Barrow, are still more instructive. The effect of disturbances in the mean of the entire series of observations, which extended over seventeen months, is to double the easterly maximum at 8 A. M., and to render the hour of the afternoon minimum wholly uncertain. These irregularities to a great extent disappear when the greater disturbances have been omitted in the calculations.

The observations of Sir Leopold M'Clintock, in 1858-9, at Port Kennedy, have enabled Sir Edward Sabine to throw further light upon the laws of the diurnal variations. The declination at Port Kennedy is N. 136° W.; while that of Point Barrow is N. 41° E. The north poles of the needles at the two stations, which are at opposite sides of the earth's magnetic pole, thus point in opposite directions. Now, when disturbances are removed, the observations gave the greatest deflections at 8 A. M. and 2 P. M., as in other places. But they showed further that the positions were referred in both to the *magnetic meridian* of the place, and not to the *astronomical*, the deviations of the magnet at 2 P.M., for example, being in both places *to the left* of an observer looking towards the magnetic pole at each place, and therefore *geographically* in opposite directions.

But probably the most remarkable contribution to our knowledge of the phenomena of magnetic disturbances is that contained in the observations of General Lefroy in 1843-4, in the British possessions in North America.* These observations were taken at Fort Chipewyan, at Lake Athabasca (lat. 59° N. long. 114° W.), and at Fort Simpson (lat. 62° N. long. 121° W.). The observations were made hourly during six months, with all the appliances of a complete magnetical observatory. They reveal the fact that, in addition to the maximum of mean disturbance of the declination which prevails in Canada and the United States at 10 P. M., there is another and *much* greater maximum at 5 A. M., in which the easterly movement greatly preponderates over the westerly. The maximum disturbance of the northerly force occurs an hour or two earlier.

* *Magnetical and Meteorological Observations at Lake Athabasca and Fort Simpson.*

APPENDIX.

I.

GENERAL THEORY OF THE DIPPING NEEDLE.

In the account of the dipping-needle given in (81–83), it is supposed that the needle is supported on an axle passing through its centre of gravity, in which case, we have seen, its position of equilibrium is that due to the earth's magnetic force alone. But as this condition can seldom be perfectly attained in the construction of the needle, it is necessary either to find a correction for the effect of the weight or to arrange the observations in such a manner as to eliminate that effect. In general the needle is nearly balanced; and it is ordinarily assumed that the effect of its weight is eliminated from the result, by taking the mean of the observed inclinations in four positions; namely, with the poles of the needle direct and reversed, and (in each case) with the face of the needle east and west. It is necessary to know within what limits this elimination may be regarded as practically complete; and, when that is not the case, to ascertain the nature of the correction required. For this purpose we must examine the theory of the needle somewhat more generally.

Let w denote the weight of the needle, r the distance of its centre of gravity from the axle, and γ the angle which he connecting line makes with the magnetic axis of the needle. Then, if the centre of gravity be *above* the magnetic axis, the moment of the weight to turn the needle is $wr\cos(\eta-\gamma)$, η being the inclination of the magnetic axis to the horizon. In the position of rest, this moment is equal to that of the earth's magnetic force, or to $mR\sin(\eta-\theta)$, in which R denotes the magnetic force of the earth, and m the magnetic moment of the needle. Hence

$$wr\cos(\eta-\gamma)=mR\sin(\eta-\theta).$$

Now, let the needle be inverted on its supports, in which case the centre of gravity will be *below* the magnetic axis. Then η' denoting the new inclination, we have

$$wr\cos(\eta'+\gamma)=mR\sin(\eta'-\theta).$$

And dividing the former equation by the latter,

$$\frac{\cos(\eta-\gamma)}{\cos(\eta'+\gamma)}=\frac{\sin(\eta-\theta)}{\sin(\eta'-\theta)}.$$

Let unity be added and subtracted on both sides; and let one of the resulting equations be divided by the other. We thus obtain, after an easy reduction,

$$\tan(\theta-S)=\tan D\cot S\cot(D+\gamma);$$

in which we have put, for abridgment,

$$\eta+\eta'=2S,\quad \eta-\eta'=2D.$$

By means of this equation the angle θ is given in terms of S, D, and γ, in a formula suited to logarithmic computation.

When the needle is nearly balanced, D and $\theta-S$ are both small, and we may substitute the angles themselves for their tangents; and we have

$$\theta-S=D\cot\gamma\cot S.$$

Wherefore if the angle γ be once determined, the inclination may in all cases be deduced from the two observed angles, η and η'.

The angle γ is eliminated by inverting the poles of the needle. Let S', D', and γ', denote the values of S, D, and γ, after the inversion of the poles. Then $\gamma + \gamma' = 180°$; and

$$\text{cotan}\,\gamma + \text{cotan}\,\gamma' = 0.$$

Or, substituting the values of these quantities deduced from the preceding formula,

$$\frac{(\theta - S)\tan S}{D} + \frac{(\theta - S')\tan S'}{D'} = 0.$$

whence, putting for abridgement, $\dfrac{D}{D'}\dfrac{\tan S'}{\tan S} = k$,

$$\theta = \frac{S + kS'}{1 + k}.$$

Substituting this expression for θ in the formula of the preceding paragraph, we have

$$\text{cotang}\,\gamma = \frac{k(S' - S)\tan S}{(1 + k)D};$$

and this quantity being once known, the inclination may be inferred from the two observed angles, without further inversion of the poles.

It is often of use to throw the needle entirely out of balance by an added weight, so as to bring other parts of the axle into play. In order to determine the inclination from the observed positions of such a needle, we must return to the original equation. Expanding and dividing, this becomes

$$\frac{1 + \tan\gamma \tan\eta}{1 - \tan\gamma \tan\eta'} = \frac{\tan\eta - \tan\theta}{\tan\eta' - \tan\theta};$$

from which we have

$$-\tan\gamma = \frac{\cot\eta - \cot\eta'}{\tan\theta(\cot\eta + \cot\eta') - 2}.$$

Now let the poles of the needle be inverted, and let ζ and ζ' be the corresponding inclinations. Then we have, in like manner,

$$-\tan\gamma = \frac{\cot\zeta - \cot\zeta'}{\tan\theta\,(\cot\zeta + \cot\zeta') - 2};$$

and equating these expressions,

$$\tan\theta = \frac{\cot\eta - \cot\eta' - (\cot\zeta - \cot\zeta')}{\cot\eta\cot\zeta' - \cot\eta'\cot\zeta}.$$

This is Mayer's formula. It is independent of the condition that the magnetic moments of the needle should be equal before and after the reversal of the poles. It is, however, inapplicable to the case of needles nearly balanced.

II.

GENERAL THEORY OF TERRESTRIAL MAGNETISM.

The following is a brief abstract of Gauss's *Memoir*.

If $d\mu$ denote the quantity of free magnetic fluid in any element of the Earth, and ρ its distance from the point (xyz), and if we make

$$V = -\int \frac{d\mu}{\rho},$$

the components of the Earth's magnetic force, ψ, at the point (xyz) are

$$\xi = \frac{dV}{dx}, \quad \eta = \frac{dV}{dy}, \quad \zeta = \frac{dV}{dz}.$$

The complete differential of V is

$$dV = \frac{dV}{dx}\,dx + \frac{dV}{dy}\,dy + \frac{dV}{dz}\,dz = \xi dx + \eta dy + \zeta dz,$$

$$\text{or } dV = \psi \cos\theta\, ds,$$

θ being the angle which the direction of the force makes with ds. Hence it follows that, if ϕ denote the force resolved in the direction ds,

$$dV = \phi ds; \text{ and } V - V_0 = \int \phi ds.$$

The force in any direction therefore is

$$\phi = \frac{dV}{ds}.$$

This is also evident from the equation $\xi = \frac{dV}{dx}$, since the direction of x is arbitrary.

On the surface of the Earth, V is a function of the longitude, λ, and of the north polar distance, u. But in the meridian, $ds = R du$, R denoting the radius of Earth; and in the parallel to the equator, $ds = R \sin u \, d\lambda$.

Hence, if X denote the component of the force in the meridian, and Y that perpendicular to it, we have

$$X = -\frac{dV}{R du}, \quad Y = -\frac{dV}{R \sin u \, d\lambda}.$$

Generally, V is function of u, λ, and r, and we have

$$X = -\frac{dV}{r du}, \quad Y = -\frac{dV}{r \sin u \, d\lambda}, \quad Z = -\frac{dV}{dr},$$

r being the distance of the point (xyz) from Earth's centre.

V is a function of the three coordinates u, λ, and r. It may be expanded in a series proceeding according to the inverse powers of r, so that

$$V = R\left(P_0 \frac{R}{r} + P_1 \frac{R^2}{r^2} + P_2 \frac{R^3}{r^3} + \&c.\right)$$

in which the coefficients P_0, P_1, P_2, &c., are functions of u and λ alone.

In order to determine the form of these coefficients, let (u_0, λ_0, r_0) be the polar coordinates of $d\mu$, so that ρ is the distance of the points (u, λ, r) and (u_0, λ_0, r_0), then we have

$$\rho^2 = r^2 - 2rr_0[\cos u \cos u_0 + \sin u \sin u_0 \cos(\lambda - \lambda_0)] + r_0^2.$$

Let $\frac{1}{\rho}$ be developed in a series proceeding according to the inverse powers of r, so that

$$\frac{1}{\rho} = \frac{1}{r}\left(T_0 + T_1 \frac{r_0}{r} + T_2 \left(\frac{r_0}{r}\right)^2 + \&c.\right)$$

Then we have

$$P_0 \frac{R^2}{r} + P_1 \frac{R^3}{r^2} + P_2 \frac{R^4}{r^3} + \&c. = \frac{1}{r}\int T_0 d\mu + \frac{1}{r^2}\int T_1 r_0 d\mu + \frac{1}{r^3}\int T_2 r_0^2 d\mu \ \&c.;$$

so that

$$P_0 R^0 = -\int T_0 d\mu\ ;$$
$$P_1 R^1 = -\int T_1 \nu_0 d\mu\ ;$$
$$P_2 R^2 = -\int T_2 \nu_0^2 d\mu, \ \&c.$$

$T_0 = 1$, and since $\int d\mu = 0$, we have $P_0 = 0$.

The form of the functions, P_1, P_2, P_3 is thus determined. The function V fulfils the condition

$$\frac{d^2 V}{dx^2} + \frac{d^2 V}{dy^2} + \frac{d^2 V}{dz^2} = 0.$$

which, transformed to polar coordinates, is

$$r\frac{d^2(rV)}{dr^2} + \frac{d^2 V}{du^2} + \cot u \frac{dV}{du} + \frac{1}{\sin^2 u}\frac{d^2 V}{d\lambda^2} = 0.$$

There will evidently be corresponding partial differential equations for each of the coefficients P_1, P_2, P_3, &c.

Let P denote the nth coefficient; then the equation which it must satisfy is

$$n(n+1)P + \frac{d^2 P}{du^2} + \cot u \,.\, \frac{dP}{du} + \frac{1}{\sin^2 u}\frac{d^2 P}{d\lambda^2} = 0.$$

From this equation we obtain the general form of the coefficient P. If we represent by (n, m) the following function of u only

$$\left(\cos^{n-m} u - \frac{n-m \,.\, n-m-1}{2 \,.\, 2n-1}\cos^{n-m-2} u \right.$$
$$\left. + \frac{n-m \,.\, n-m-1 \,.\, n-m-2 \,.\, n-m-3}{2 \,.\, 4 \,.\, 2n-1 \,.\, 2n-3} \times \cos^{n-m-4} . u - \&c.\right)\sin.^m u\ ;$$

then

$$P_1 = a(1, 0) + (b \cos\lambda + c \sin\lambda)(1, 1)$$
$$P_2 = d(2,0) + (e\cos\lambda + f\sin\lambda)(2, 1) + (g\cos 2\lambda + h\sin 2\lambda)(2, 2)$$
$$P_3 = i(3, 0) + (j\cos\lambda + k\sin\lambda)(3, 1) + (l\cos 2\lambda + m\sin 2\lambda)(3, 2)$$
$$+ (n\cos 3\lambda + o\sin 3\lambda)(3, 3).$$
$$P^4 = p(4, 0) + (q\cos\lambda + r\sin\lambda)(4, 1) + s\cos 2\lambda + t\sin 2\lambda)(4, 2)$$
$$+ (u\cos 3\lambda + v\sin 3\lambda)(4, 3) + (w\cos 4\lambda + x\sin 4\lambda)(4, 4).$$

P_1 has 3 indeterminate coefficients; P_2 has 5; P_3 has 7; and

P_4 has 9. Hence, if we include terms P to the 4th order, we shall have 24 coefficients to be determined.

Every given value of X, Y, or Z furnishes an equation between the coefficients; and for each place at which the three elements are known, we have three such equations. Hence, in order to obtain the general expressions of X, Y, Z, to the fourth order inclusive, it would be sufficient (theoretically) to know the *three* elements at *eight points* on the earth's surface. This supposes that the elements are perfectly determined. In order to get a reliable result from actual observations, the number of determinations should be much greater than the number of unknown coefficients.

Substituting for V its expansion

$$V = R\left(P_1\frac{R^2}{r^2} + P_2\frac{R^3}{r^3} + \&c.\right)$$

in the expressions of the three forces X, Y, Z, above given, we obtain

$$X = -\frac{R^3}{r^3}\left(\frac{dP_1}{du} + \frac{R}{r}\frac{dP_2}{du} + \frac{R^2}{r^2}\frac{dP_3}{du} + \&c.\right)$$

$$Y = -\frac{1}{\sin u}\cdot\frac{R^3}{r^3}\left(\frac{dP_1}{d\lambda} + \frac{R}{r}\frac{dP_2}{d\lambda} + \frac{R^2}{r^2}\frac{dP_3}{d\lambda} + \&c.\right)$$

$$Z = \frac{R^3}{r^3}\left(2P_1 + \frac{R}{r}3P_2 + \frac{R^2}{r^2}4P_3 + \&c.\right)$$

When the point (xyz) is on the earth's surface, $R = r$, and we have

$$X = -\left(\frac{dP_1}{du} + \frac{dP_2}{du} + \frac{dP_3}{du} + \&c.\right)$$

$$Y = -\frac{1}{\sin u}\left(\frac{dP_1}{d\lambda} + \frac{dP_2}{d\lambda} + \frac{dP_3}{d\lambda} + \&c.\right)$$

$$Z = 2P_1 + 3P_2 + 4\ P_3 + \&c.$$

The general value V on the earth's surface is

$$V = R(P_1 + P_2 + P_3 + \&c.)$$

III.

EFFECTS OF THE VARIATIONS OF THE HUMIDITY OF THE AIR UPON THE POSITION OF A MAGNET SUSPENDED BY SILKEN FIBRES.

THESE effects have been obtained in the Dublin Observatory by a comparison of the results of two instruments observed simultaneously. It is in the highest degree probable that the effects of changes of humidity are different upon different suspension threads; and if there should occur any twist in these threads (as is nearly unavoidable), and if it should so happen that such twists were in opposite directions in two threads (as appears to have been the case in the Dublin instruments), the effects of humidity upon them would be opposite, and the corresponding results would differ by their sum. The *ratio* of the effects produced by the same change of moisture upon the two instruments being otherwise known, the actual effects upon each will be determined.

In the second volume of the Dublin Magnetical Observations, a correction of the monthly means of the results of observation has been deduced, based upon a similar principle. The correction so deduced rested upon the assumption, that the instrumental changes referred to were measured by the changes of the *temperature* of the air within the Observatory. But it seems most probable that these effects are the results of the variations of *humidity;* and consequently, that the correction deduced on the former hypothesis is exact only so far as the two changes are proportional. For this reason, as well as on account of the importance of the result itself, the investigation is here resumed on the latter supposition.

The readings of the two declinometers at 10 A. M., in the years 1848 and 1849, together with the simultaneous readings of the dry and wet thermometers, were noted from day to day when the changes of humidity were considerable. The means of those results gave the following changes of reading of the two instruments, corresponding to an increase of 1° in the depression of temperature due to evaporation:—

$$\Delta n = -0.22, \quad \Delta n' = +0.17.$$

And the corresponding changes of angle are

$$k = -0'.15; \quad k' = +0'.14.$$

It thus appears that the effects of changes of humidity upon the two instruments were nearly equal, and in opposite directions, an increase of humidity deflecting the magnet of the large declinometer to the *eastward*, and that of the small declinometer in the contrary direction.

These results, however, do not furnish the whole effects of humidity upon the suspension threads, which seem to require a considerable time for their development. For this latter purpose we must have recourse to the monthly changes of position of the two magnets. Accordingly, let Δu and $\Delta u'$ be the observed changes of position of the two magnets, measured to the eastward; $\Delta \psi$ the actual change of declination: and Δh the corresponding change in the humidity of the air, the point of saturation being 100. We may put

$$\Delta u = \Delta\psi + k\Delta h; \quad \Delta u' = \Delta\psi + k'\Delta h;$$

whence $$\Delta u - \Delta u' = (k - k')\Delta h.$$

Now, if we compare the observed changes of angular position of the two magnets with those of humidity for the three summer months (June, July, and August); and for the three winter months (December, January, and February), of the years 1848 and 1849, we have the following results :—

Summer Months.

$$\Delta h = -4.2, \quad \Delta u - \Delta u' = -2'.24, \quad k - k' = +0'.53.$$

Winter Months.

$$\Delta h = +3.8, \quad \Delta u - \Delta u' = +1'.62, \quad k - k' = +0.43.$$

Hence the mean value of $k - k' = +0.48$. And since $k = -k'$ $k = +0'.24$; and the actual values of $\Delta\psi$ will be given by the formula

$$\Delta\psi = \Delta u - 0'.24\ \Delta h.$$

The following Table gives the monthly values of $\Delta\psi$ thus calculated. The values of Δu are the mean values for the years 1841-1850; those of Δh commence a year later.

Annual Variation of the Magnetic Declination, corrected for Changes of Humidity.

Month.	Δu	Δh	$\Delta\psi$
January,	+1'·95	+0·6	+0'·37
February,	+2·18	+2·4	+1·60
March,	+1·74	0·0	+1·74
April,	+1·43	−1·8	+1·86
May,	+0·20	−4·7	+1.33
June,	−1·59	−0·8	+0.04
July,	−2·52	−5·3	−1·25
August,	−2·72	−2·3	−2·17
September,	−1·97	+0·4	−2·07
October,	−0·80	+2·3	−1·35
November,	+0·69	+4·2	−0·32
December,	+1·42	+5·0	+0·22

IV.

DIURNAL INEQUALITY OF THE HORIZONTAL COMPONENTS OF THE MAGNETIC FORCE.

In this supplement the author has put together the mean values of the diurnal changes of declination and of the northerly force, at the colonial, and at most of the foreign stations, at which observations of the two elements have been continued for several years.

The following table contains the elements (Geographical and Magnetical) of the several stations.—

Station.	Lat.	Long.	Decl.	X.	Years.	Hour.
Munich, . . .	+ 48° 9′	+ 11°30′	− 16°11′	4·21	1843–45	+ 7m
Prague, . . .	+ 50 5	+ 14 25	− 15 11	4·03	1840–49	+ 18
Petersburg. . .	+ 59 56	+ 30 18	− 5 41	3·60	1850–55	+ 21
Catherinburg. .	+ 56 49	+ 60 35	+ 7 23	3·99	1850–55	+ 22
Barnaoul, . .	+ 53 20	+ 83 57	+ 8 48	4·45	1853–55	− 6
Nertchinsk. . .	+ 51 19	+ 119 30	− 5 54	4·80	1851–55	+ 18
Toronto, . . .	+ 43 40	− 79 22	− 1 23	3·53	1843–47	+ 3
Hobarton, . .	− 42 52	+ 147 27	+ 9 56	4·50	1841–47	+ 10
St. Helena, . .	− 15 56	− 5 40	− 23 27	5·38	1843–47	− 2
Cape of Good Hope	− 33 56	+ 18 29	− 29 7	4·51	1841–45	+ 34
Singapore, . .	+ 1 19	+ 103 57	+ 1 40	3·11	1843–45	

The positive signs denote *north* latitude, *east* longitude, and *east* declination.

In the last column are given the number of minutes to be added to, or subtracted from, the hours of the table, so as to give the exact local time.

Diurnal Inequality of the Magnetic Declination.

Positive Numbers correspond to Easterly Deflections of the North end of Magnet.

Hour.	Toronto.	Munich.	Prague.	Petersburgh.	Catherinburg.	Barnaoul.	Nertchinsk.	St. Helena.	Cape of Good Hope.	Hobarton.	Singapore.
1 A.M.	+ 0′·54	+ 1′·18		+ 1′·40	+ 1′·14	+ 0′·70	+ 0′·92	+ 0′·13	+ 0′·51	− 1′·02	+ 0′·03
2	+ 0·52	+ 1·15	+ 1·28	+ 1·40	+ 1·00	+ 0·81	+ 1·03	+ 0·09	+ 0·45	− 0·70	+ 0·05
3	+ 0·71			+ 1·49	+ 0·97	+ 0·70	+ 1·10	+ 0·06	+ 0·41	− 0·46	+ 0·03
4	+ 1·12	+ 1·02	+ 1·64	+ 1·60	+ 1·11	+ 0·81	+ 1·14	+ 0·04	+ 0·34	− 0·39	0·00
5	+ 1·93			+ 1·76	+ 1·39	+ 0·93	+ 1·25	+ 0·12	+ 0·19	− 0·67	− 0·02
6	+ 2·98	+ 1·67	+ 2·23	+ 1·90	+ 1·91	+ 1·19	+ 1·49	+ 0·44	+ 0·05	− 1·07	+ 0·10
7	+ 3·99	+ 1·99		+ 2·22	+ 2·37	+ 1·71	+ 1·96	+ 0·08	− 0·57	− 1·98	− 0·12
8	+ 4·44	+ 2·41	+ 2·73	+ 2·38	+ 2·82	+ 2·09	+ 2·28	− 0·83	− 1·67	− 2·95	− 0·05
9	+ 3·63	+ 1·41		+ 1·78	+ 2·49	+ 2·13	+ 1·71	− 1·13	− 2·72	− 3·52	− 0·88
10	+ 1·24	− 0·39	− 0·74	+ 0·06	+ 1·12	+ 1·39	+ 0·45	− 0·75	− 2·47	− 2·82	− 0·82
11	− 1·89	− 2·55		− 2·25	− 0·91	− 0·05	− 1·11	+ 0·18	− 1·41	− 0·97	− 0·47
Noon.	− 4·02	− 4·32	− 5·27	− 4·22	− 2·97	− 1·78	− 2·34	+ 0·76	− 0·01	+ 1·45	− 0·05
1 P.M.	− 5·07	− 4·90	− 5·90	− 5·41	− 4·75	− 2·93	− 3·36	+ 0·89	+ 0·90	+ 3·64	+ 0·34
2	− 4·87	− 4·27	− 5·21	− 5·19	− 5·01	− 3·66	− 3·32	+ 0·40	+ 1·39	+ 4·66	+ 0·54
3	− 3·83	− 2·90		− 3·96	− 3·90	− 2·91	− 2·07	+ 0·04	+ 1·17	+ 4·56	+ 0·60
4	− 2·48	− 1·47	− 1·92	− 2·47	− 2·71	− 1·96	− 1·80	− 0·38	+ 0·63	+ 3·54	+ 0·59
5	− 1·29	− 0·55		− 1·12	− 1·42	− 1·80	− 0·80	− 0·55	+ 0·20	+ 2·20	+ 0·41
6	− 0·48	+ 0·24	+ 0·13	− 0·10	− 0·56	− 0·57	− 0·20	− 0·38	+ 0·17	+ 1·20	+ 0·23
7	− 0·12			+ 0·46	+ 0·16	− 0·13	+ 0·07	− 0·07	+ 0·36	+ 0·48	+ 0·11
8	+ 0·18	+ 1·09	+ 1·42	+ 1·13	+ 0·44	+ 0·03	+ 0·22	+ 0·07	+ 0·45	− 0·21	− 0·02
9	+ 0·52			+ 1·50	+ 0·83	+ 0·39	+ 0·28	+ 0·19	+ 0·49	− 0·81	− 0·10
10	+ 0·70	+ 1·55	+ 1·55	+ 2·03	+ 1·02	+ 0·53	+ 0·50	+ 0·26	+ 0·48	− 1·28	− 0·14
11	+ 0·71			+ 2·16	+ 1·21	+ 0·66	+ 0·62	+ 0·28	+ 0·47	− 1·52	− 0·12
12	+ 0·68	+ 1·38	+ 1·80	+ 1·73	+ 1·25	+ 0·68	+ 0·77	+ 0·24	+ 0·48	− 1·38	− 0·03

Diurnal Inequality of the Northerly Force.

Hours.	Toronto.	Munich.	Prague.	Petersburgh.	Catherinburgh.	Barnaoul.	Nertchinsk.	S. Helena.	Cape of Good Hope.	Hobarton.	Singapore.
1 A.M.	+0·01	+0·22		+0·05	+0·13	+0·25	+0·20	−0·45	−0·09	+0·16	−0·33
2	+0·04	+0·16	+0·39	−0·08	+0·05	+0·13	+0·15	−0·41	−0·05	+0·16	−0·31
3	+0·02			−0·06	+0·04	+0·03	+0·08	−0·38	−0·03	+0·14	−0·29
4	+0·10	+0·20	+0·36	−0·11	+0·03	−0·04	+0·03	−0·35	−0·01	+0·14	−0·27
5	+0·14			−0·16	+0·08	−0·09	+0·02	−0·33	+0·02	+0·16	−0·25
6	+0·19	+0·13	+0·20	−0·26	+0·10	−0·15	+0·02	−0·30	+0·14	+0·16	−0·18
7	+0·08	−0·01		−0·35	+0·04	−0·22	−0·06	−0·15	+0·31	+0·05	+0·01
8	−0·22	−0·29	−0·44	−0·44	−0·07	−0·38	−0·18	+0·13	+0·42	−0·13	+0·33
9	−0·58	−0·57		−0·72	−0·25	−0·57	−0·35	+0·47	+0·35	−0·45	+0·64
10	−0·87	−0·70	−1·04	−0·91	−0·33	−0·72	−0·48	+0·80	+0·21	−0·75	+0·87
11	−0·94	−0·62		−0·90	−0·40	−0·71	−0·53	+1·02	+0·11	−0·88	+0·01
Noon	−0·70	−0·35	−0·67	−0·71	−0·35	−0·53	−0·46	+1·10	+0·05	−0·82	+0·76
1 P.M.	−0·29	−0·09	−0·38	−0·20	−0·27	−0·28	−0·29	+0·91	0·00	−0·51	+0·51
2	+0·13	−0·02	−0·19	+0·11	−0·15	0·00	−0·10	+0·62	−0·01	−0·13	+0·24
3	+0·47	+0·02		+0·36	−0·04	+0·23	0·00	+0·37	0·00	+0·18	+0·03
4	+0·61	−0·01	−0·03	+0·46	+0·02	+0·42	+0·18	+0·13	−0·01	+0·33	−0·11
5	+0·58	−0·01		+0·45	+0·05	+0·42	+0·28	−0·08	−0·03	+0·40	−0·19
6	+0·44	+0·09	+0·22	+0·51	+0·08	+0·38	+0·23	−0·27	−0·11	+0·32	−0·26
7	+0·30			+0·73	+0·11	+0·34	+0·24	−0·39	−0·20	+0·30	−0·31
8	+0·17	+0·23	+0·45	+0·73	+0·19	+0·32	+0·23	−0·47	−0·26	+0·29	−0·34
9	+0·13			+0·57	+0·23	+0·32	+0·23	−0·51	−0·26	+0·22	−0·37
10	+0·10	+0·31	+0·48	+0·45	+0·26	+0·33	+0·22	−0·53	−0·24	+0·22	−0·37
11	+0·06			+0·91	+0·25	+0·30	+0·22	−0·52	−0·19	+0·18	−0·38
12	+0·01	+0·27	+0·31	+0·14	+0·19	+0·28	+0·18	−0·48	−0·14	+0·17	−0·36

V.

ON THE DIRECT MAGNETIC INFLUENCE OF A DISTANT LUMINARY UPON THE DIURNAL VARIATIONS OF THE MAGNETIC FORCE AT THE EARTH'S SURFACE.*

It has been usual to ascribe the ordinary diurnal variations of the terrestrial magnetic force to solar heat, either operating directly upon the magnetism of the earth, or generating thermo-electric currents in its crust. The credit of these hypotheses has been somewhat weakened by the discovery of a variation which is certainly independent of any such cause, namely, the lunar variation of the three magnetic elements; while at the same time new laws of the solar diurnal change have been established, which are deemed to be incompatible with the supposition of a thermic agency. There has been, accordingly, a tendency of late to recur to the hypothesis that the sun and moon are themselves endued with magnetism, whether inherent or induced; and it is therefore of some importance to determine the effects which such bodies would produce at the earth's surface, and to compare them with those actually observed.

I have endeavoured, in what follows, to solve this question, on the assumption that the supposed magnetism of these luminaries is inherent. The result will show the insufficiency of the hypothesis to explain the phenomena; and will therefore bring us one step nearer to their explanation, by the removal of one of their supposed causes.

Let x, y, z be the coordinates of any point of a fixed magnet, referred to three rectangular axes passing through

* From the *Philosophical Magazine*, for March, 1858.

its middle point; a, b, c those of a distant magnetic element m; and e their mutual distance. Then, if μ denote the quantity of free magnetism contained in the element ds of the magnet at the point (x, y, z), the force exerted by μ on m is

$$\frac{m\mu ds}{e^2};$$

and its resolved portions in the directions of the three axes of coordinates are

$$\frac{m(a-x)\mu ds}{e^3},\quad \frac{m(b-y)\mu ds}{e^3},\quad \frac{m(c-z)\mu ds}{e^3}.$$

Let the magnitudes of the lines connecting the points (a, b, c) and (x, y, z), respectively, with the origin be denoted by u and s, and let the angle contained by their directions be ω. Then

$$e^2 = u^2 - 2us\cos\omega + s^2;$$

and if s be so small in comparison with u that the squares and higher powers of $\frac{s}{u}$ may be neglected,

$$e^{-3} = u^{-3}\left(1 + \frac{3s}{u}\cos\omega\right).$$

Again, if α, β, γ denote the angles contained by the axis of the magnet with the three axes of coordinates,

$$x = s\cos\alpha,\quad y = s\cos\beta,\quad z = s\cos\gamma.$$

Substituting these values in the expressions for the components of the force above given, integrating, and observing that $\int\mu ds = 0$, we have, for the components of the total force exerted by the magnet on the magnetic element,

$$\frac{Mm}{u^3}\left(3\frac{a}{u}\cos\omega - \cos\alpha\right),$$

$$\frac{Mm}{u^3}\left(3\frac{b}{u}\cos\omega - \cos\beta\right),$$

$$\frac{Mm}{u^3}\left(3\frac{c}{u}\cos\omega - \cos\gamma\right);$$

in which we have put, for abridgment, $M = \int \mu ds$. The angle ω is connected with α, β, γ by the relation

$$u \cos \omega = a \cos \alpha + b \cos \beta + c \cos \gamma.$$

Now let the point (a, b, c) be on the earth's surface, and let us suppose, for simplicity, that the acting magnet is in the plane of the equator. Let that plane be taken as the plane of (x, y), and the line connecting the centre of the magnet and that of the earth as the axis of x. Then, if the distance of the acting magnet be considerable, relatively to the earth's radius, b and c are small in comparison with a, and we may neglect the small quantities of the second order, $\frac{b^2}{a^2}, \frac{c^2}{a^2}, \frac{bc}{a^2}$. Wherefore, substituting for $\cos \omega$ its value, the components of the acting force become

$$\frac{Mm}{a^3}\left(2 \cos \alpha + \frac{3b}{a}\cos\beta + \frac{3c}{a}\cos\gamma\right),$$

$$\frac{Mm}{a^3}\left(-\cos\beta + \frac{3b}{a}\cos\alpha\right),$$

$$\frac{Mm}{a^3}\left(-\cos\gamma + \frac{3c}{a}\cos\alpha\right).$$

But if D denote the distance of the centre of the magnet from the centre of the earth, r the earth's radius, λ the latitude of the point (a, b, c) on its surface, and θ the angle contained by the meridian passing through it with that containing the acting magnet,

$$a = D - r \cos\lambda \cos\theta, \quad b = r \cos\lambda \sin\theta, \quad c = r \sin\lambda.$$

Hence the maximum values of $\frac{b}{a}, \frac{c}{a}$ are equal to $\frac{r}{a}$; and if we disregard the terms containing them in comparison with the rest, the preceding values are reduced to

$$2\frac{Mm}{D^3}\cos\alpha, \quad -\frac{Mm}{D^3}\cos\beta, \quad -\frac{Mm}{D^3}\cos\gamma$$

Now, in place of a single magnet, let there be an indefinite number distributed in any manner throughout the entire magnetic body; and let us make for abridgment,

$$\Sigma (M \cos \alpha) = P, \quad \Sigma (M \cos \beta) = Q, \quad \Sigma (M \cos \gamma) = R.$$

Then, if the radius of this body be small in comparison with its distance, we may neglect the variations of D, and we shall have for the three components of the acting forces,

$$X = \frac{2mP}{D^3}, \quad Y = \frac{-mQ}{D^3}, \quad Z = \frac{-mR}{D^3}.$$

In order to determine the effect of these forces upon a freely suspended horizontal magnet at the earth's surface, we must resolve X and Y in the direction of the tangent, and of the radius, of the parallel of latitude. The resolved forces are, respectively,

$$X \sin \theta + Y \cos \theta, \quad X \cos \theta - Y \sin \theta.$$

Again, resolving the forces Z and $X \cos \theta - Y \sin \theta$ in the direction of the tangent to the meridian, and in the direction of the radius of the earth, we have finally the three components, viz.,

$X \sin \theta + Y \cos \theta$, horizontal, and directed eastward;

$Z \cos \lambda + (X \cos \theta - Y \sin \theta) \sin \lambda$, horizontal, and directed northward;

$-Z \sin \lambda + (X \cos \theta - Y \sin \theta) \cos \lambda$, vertical, towards centre.

Of these, the latter has no effect upon the horizontal magnet; the moment of the two former to turn it is

$$(X \sin \theta + Y \cos \theta) \cos \delta - \{Z \cos \lambda + (X \cos \theta - Y \sin \theta) \sin \lambda\} \sin \delta;$$

δ denoting the magnetic declination; or, substituting for X, Y, Z their values,

$$\frac{m}{D^3} \Big\{ \cos \delta (2P \sin \theta - Q \cos \theta) - \sin \delta (2P \cos \theta + Q \sin \theta) \sin \lambda$$
$$- R \cos \lambda \sin \delta \Big\}.$$

But the moment of the earth's magnetism, opposed to this, is

$$U \Delta \delta \sin 1',$$

in which U denotes the horizontal component of the earth's magnetic force. Wherefore

$$\Delta \delta = \frac{1}{D^3 U \sin 1'} \Big\{ \sin \theta \, (2P \cos \delta - Q \sin \lambda \sin \delta) - \cos \theta \, (2P \sin \lambda \sin \delta + Q \cos \delta) + R \cos \lambda \sin \delta \Big\}$$

At the equator, this is reduced to

$$\Delta \delta = \frac{1}{D^3 U \sin 1'} \Big\{ \cos \delta \, (2P \sin \theta - Q \cos \theta) + R \sin \delta \Big\}.$$

To determine the effect of the magnetic body upon the horizontal component of the earth's magnetic force, we must resolve the horizontal parts of the disturbing forces, viz., $X \sin \theta + Y \cos \theta$, and $Z \cos \lambda + (X \cos \theta - Y \sin \theta) \sin \lambda$, in the direction of the magnetic meridian. We have thus

$$\Delta U = (X \sin \theta + Y \cos \theta) \sin \delta + \{ Z \cos \lambda + (X \cos \theta - Y \sin \theta) \sin \lambda \} \cos \delta$$

$$= \frac{1}{D^3} \Big\{ \sin \theta \, (2P \sin \delta + Q \sin \lambda \cos \delta) + \cos \theta \, (2P \sin \lambda \cos \delta - Q \sin \delta) - R \cos \lambda \cos \delta \Big\}.$$

And at the equator,

$$\Delta U = \frac{1}{D^3} \Big\{ \sin \delta \, (2P \sin \theta - Q \cos \theta) - R \cos \delta \Big\}.$$

Lastly, if V denote the vertical component of the earth's force, we have

$$\Delta V = -Z \sin\lambda + (X\cos\theta - Y\sin\theta)\cos\lambda$$
$$= \frac{1}{D^3}\left\{(2P\cos\theta + Q\sin\theta)\cos\lambda + R\sin\lambda\right\};$$

a result which, as might have been anticipated, is independent of the magnetic declination. At the equator,

$$\Delta V = \frac{1}{D^3}(2P\cos\theta + Q\sin\theta).$$

From the foregoing we learn:—

1. That the effect of a distant magnetic body on each of the three elements of the earth's magnetic force consists of two parts, one of which is *constant* throughout the day, while the other varies with the *hour-angle of the luminary*.

2. Each of these parts varies inversely as the cube of the distance of the magnetic body.

3. The variable part will give rise to a *diurnal inequality*, having one maximum and one minimum in the day, and subject to the condition

$$\Delta_\theta + \Delta_{\pi+\theta} = 0.$$

The third of these laws does not hold, with respect either to the solar-diurnal or to the lunar-diurnal variation. Thus, in the solar-diurnal variation of the declination, the changes of position of the magnet throughout the night are comparatively small, and do not correspond, with change of sign only (as required by the foregoing law), to those which take place at the *homonymous* hours of the day. The phenomena of the lunar-diurnal variation are even more opposed to the foregoing law, the variation having two maxima and two minima of nearly equal magnitude in the twenty-four lunar hours, and its values at homonymous hours having for the most part the same sign. Hence the phenomena of the diurnal variation are *not* caused by the *direct magnetic action* of the sun and moon.

The magnitude of the phenomenon is equally inconsistent with its explanation by direct action. Mr. Stoney has shown* that the maximum effect upon the declination magnet which would be produced by the moon—supposing it to be equally magnetic with the earth, bulk for bulk—is less than one-tenth of a second.

* *Phil. Mag.*, October, 1861.

THE END.

www.ingramcontent.com/pod-product-compliance
Lightning Source LLC
Chambersburg PA
CBHW031420020726
47499CB00005B/1520
9783742831057